THE
CIPHER

Praise for THE CIPHER

"*The Cipher* is a stone-cold landmark of the genre. Written by a sphinx, a gift, the rarest of talents. And like the works of M.R. James, Shirley Jackson, Poe, and Stephen King, horror isn't the same, in all its current height and depth, without it. Be prepared: this book will change you."
—JOSH MALERMAN, NYT-best-selling author of *Bird Box* and *Malorie*

"Audacious, acerbic, grotesque, ravishing, stifling, sensual, iconic—there will never be another novel like this one."
—DANIEL KRAUS, NYT-bestselling author

"Those of us who have been around awhile remember the impact Kathe Koja's *The Cipher* made on the scene when it first appeared in 1991. It was like a perfect onyx jewel wrested from Hell: gorgeous, hideous, and terrifying. We'd never seen anything like it before. Its return to print is something to be celebrated by anyone who loves brilliant horror fiction. *The Cipher* is a stone-cold classic."
—NATHAN BALLINGRUD, award-winning author of Wounds and North American Lake Monsters

"When I first read *The Cipher* in 1991, I hardly knew what to make of it. But I knew one thing for sure: horror fiction had never seen anything like Kathe Koja's obsessive and impressionistic prose and ruthlessly dire worldview before . . . Koja's fearless depiction of bickering twenty-something art failures stumbling upon an actual nothing and then watching with detached fascination as their squalid lives disintegrate around it was the darkest kind of revelation for me. I haven't stopped thinking about *The Cipher* in the thirty years since, and my numerous reads of it always yield fresh new horrors from its reflective deeps."
—WILL ERRICKSON, *Too Much Horror Fiction*

"This entry into the body-horror canon carries with it the kind of fatalism horror readers prize—it's going to end badly, for sure, but just how badly?"
—BOOKLIST

"Unforgettable . . . So visceral and so right."
—LOCUS MAGAZINE

"Koja has created credible characters who are desperate for both entertainment and salvation . . . this powerful first novel is as thought-provoking as it is horrifying."
—PUBLISHERS WEEKLY

"Kathe Koja, an author who *Library Journal* once described as a collaboration between Clive Barker and William S. Burroughs, possesses a writing style unmatched by anyone else in the business. *The Cipher* is her first novel, but it shines like the work of a true master. Never have I experienced something so visceral and ugly and beautiful all in one package. It is a piece of art that manages to simultaneously disgust and delight its audience."
—MAX BOOTH III, LITREACTOR

"Kathe Koja is a poet . . . the kind that prefers to read in seedy bars instead of universities, but a poet."
—NEW YORK REVIEW OF SCIENCE FICTION

"An ethereal rollercoaster ride from start to finish."
—DETROIT FREE PRESS

"Combines intensely poetic language and lavish grotesqueries."
—BOING BOING

"A smart read that changes as it moves along. It really makes you think and it is utterly terrifying. The things that Kathe Koja explores in this book are still relevant in horror today . . . Mindblowing."
—CEDAR HOLLOW HORROR REVIEWS

"An original, exciting and disturbing horror novel, truly deserving of its reputation."
NOCTURNAL REVELRIES

ALSO BY KATHE KOJA

The Cipher
Bad Brains
Skin
Strange Angels
Kink
Extremities: Stories
Under the Poppy
The Mercury Waltz
The Bastards' Paradise
Christopher Wild
Velocities: Stories

THE CIPHER

KATHE KOJA

Meerkat Press
Atlanta

Author Photo by Rick Lieder
Cover design by Keith Rosson
Book design by Tricia Reeks

Shikatsube No Magao, from *Utamaro: Songs of the Garden*, translated by Yasuko Betchaku and Joan B. Mirviss. Copyright © 1984 Metropolitan Museum of Art. Published by Viking Press.

ISBN-13 978-1-946154-33-0 (Paperback)

Library of Congress Control Number: 2020939366

This is a work of fiction. Names, characters, businesses, places, events and incidents are either the products of the author's imagination or used in a fictitious manner. Any resemblance to actual persons, living or dead, or actual events is purely coincidental.

Printed in the United States of America

Published in the United States of America by
Meerkat Press, LLC, Atlanta, Georgia
www.meerkatpress.com

For Rick, who was there.

With thanks to Tricia Reeks, for being ready to have fun, and to Christopher Schelling, for everything.

Could my wish be fulfilled,
I would want to be the balm
For a sore,
Dissolved
By your saliva.
  —Shikatsube No Magao

Conscious or unconscious, it doesn't matter in the real world.
  —Rick Lieder

CONTENTS

ONE

Nakota, who saw it first: long spider legs drawn up beneath her ugly skirt, wise mouth pursed into nothing like a smile. Sitting in my dreary third-floor flat, on a dreary thrift-shop chair, the window light behind her dull and gray as dirty fur and she alive, giving off her dark continuous sparks. Around us the remains of this day's argument, squashed beer cans, stolen bar ashtray sloped full. "You know it," she said, "the black-hole thing, right? In space? Big dark butthole," and she laughed, showing those tiny teeth, fox teeth, not white and not ivory yellow either like most people's, almost bluish as if with some undreamed-of decay beneath them. Nakota would rot differently from other people; she would be the first to admit it.

She lit a cigarette. She was the only one of my friends who still smoked, without defiance or a guilty flourish, smoked like she breathed but not as often. Black cigarettes, and sweetened mineral water. "So. You gonna touch it today?"

"No."

Another unsmile. "Wiener." I shrugged. "Not really." "Nicholas Wiener."

So I didn't answer her. Back to the kitchen. Get your own mineral water. The beer was almost too cold, it hurt going down. When I came back to the living room, what passed for it—big windows, small floor space, couch, bed and bad chair—she smiled at me, the real thing this time. Sometimes I thought I was the only one who ever saw that she was beautiful, who ever had. God knows there wasn't much, but I had eyes for it all.

"Let's go look at it," she said.

The one argument there was no resisting. Quietly, we had learned to do it quietly, down the stairs, turn right on the first landing (second floor to you), past the new graffiti that advised LEESA IS A HORE (no phone number, naturally; thanks a lot assholes) and the unhealthy patina of aging slurs, down the hall to what seemed, might be, some sort of storage room. Detergent bottles, tools, when you opened the door, jumble of crap on the floor, and beyond that a place, a space, the dust around it pale and easily dispersed.

Behold the Funhole.

"Shit," Nakota said, as she always did, her prayer of wonder. She knelt, bending low and supporting herself on straight-stiff arms, closer than I ever did, staring at it. Into it. It was as if she could kneel there all day, painful position but you knew she didn't feel it, looking and looking. I took my spot, a little behind her, to the left, my own prayer silence: what to say before the unspeakable?

Black. Not darkness, not the absence of light but living black. Maybe a foot in diameter, maybe a little more. Pure black and the sense of pulsation, especially when you looked at it too closely, the sense of something not living but alive, not even some*thing* but some—process. Rabbithole, some strange motherfucking wonderland, you bet. Get somebody named Alice, tie a string to her . . . We'd discussed it all, would discuss it again, probably tonight, and Nakota would sit as she always did, straight-backed as a priestess, me getting ripped and ripping into poetry, writing shit that was worse than unreadable in the morning, when I would wake—more properly afternoon, and she long gone, off to her job, unsmiling barmaid at Club 22 and me late again for the video store. She might not come again for days, or a day, one day maybe never. I knew: friends, yeah, but it was the Funhole she wanted. You can know something and never think about it, if you're any good at it. Me, now, I've been avoiding so much for so long that the real trick becomes thinking straight.

Beside me, her whisper: "*Look* at it."

I sometimes thought it had a smell, that negative place; we'd made the expected nervous fart jokes, the name itself—well, you can guess. But there was some kind of smell, not bad, not even remotely identifiable, but there, oh my yes. I would know that smell forever, know it in the dark (ho-ho) from a city block away. I couldn't forget something that weird.

For the millionth time: "Wouldn't it be *wild* to go *down* there?"

And me, on cue and by rote, "Yeah. But we're not."

Its edges were downhill and smooth. They asked for touch. Not me, said the little red hen, the little chicken, uh-uh. Smell rising around me, it did that sometimes, Nakota insisted she could almost catch the scent at its strongest (which meant nothing, she was a nose-drop addict, she couldn't smell her own shit which she claimed didn't stink anyway) rising humid as a steam cloud but who knew from what fluid, what wetness, its humidity had birth? A moist center? Things, inside? That was Nakota's guess, but I knew, absolutely knew that it was the Funhole itself, the black fact of it, sending up that tangible liquidy smell.

How long, tonight? An hour? Twenty minutes? No telling till we got back to my flat, checked the clock; it was time to do that. Rising, more reluctant, her hair in the dusty half-dark as black as the Funhole, short chop swinging around those fierce cheekbones, elbows bending as she sat straight and then stood; my knees cracked, we both jumped, then smiled on a breath, got out.

Up the stairs, down my hall. "You coming in?"

Stopping before we reached my door, her headshake. "No."

"Got your smokes?"

She patted her skirt pocket, she liked those stupid ugly resale-shop skirts, fake fifties poodle skirts with poodles that she restitched into gargoyles, fanged lizards worthy of the most hideous touristy fake kimonos. That, and T-shirts of bands so obscure even I'd never heard of them. God. Half the time she looked like a bag of rags someone'd left out for the Salvation Army. Or the garbage man.

"How 'bout your nose drops?" You know, you should shut up, I advised myself, but not fast enough to miss her scorn: "My mother's dead, thanks, I look after myself now." Then a grave glance, the closest she came to kindly. "I'll see you," she said, squeezed my elbow—her signature good-bye—and left, that graceful trudge, puke-colored skirt swinging around thin hips. What, me disappointed?

I used to know those hips, yeah, felt the pointy midge of those bones, bony back, small small tits, I once compared them to SuperBalls and she laughed through her fury; she couldn't help it, she always did like my jokes. The last time we'd made love, measure it in years, it had been at my drunken insistence and bad, oh, was it bad? It was so bad that halfway into it, and her, I knew in sudden bright horror that she was actually being *nice* to me. This was so disorienting that I crawled off her, away, into the bathroom where I sat hunched among the towels heaped wet and dirty on the wet and dirty floor, close by the toilet, shaking my head. She appeared, naked and thin as a ruler, stood in the diffused light of the bedroom and observed that she had never actually made a man sick before. I think it was her smile, all teeth, that made me finally barf.

But: that cold grin, Nakota, I wanted her still, always, in the dreamy way you want to dive the Marianas trench, or walk in space: you know you never will, so it's okay to moon over it. Like mooning over the Funhole, only not quite. Long ago she had made it plain that those days were over, her deliberate graft of a scab over the ridiculous wound of my love, or something equally stupid but just as painful; a romantic, me, in my own sick wistful way. I can take a hint, but I can't live with it.

Inside I cranked shut the windows I'd opened for her cigarette stink, leaving the one by the couchbed open; I'd always liked night air, especially when I was a kid and was told it was bad for me. Shut that window! You'll get pneumonia! Very cool outside tonight, maybe even kissing forty; stupid Nakota, no jacket. You'll get pneumonia.

Hunger headache, in the mirror my sallow face pale. Okay, what's to eat. I hated to shop, it all turned into shit eventually anyway, so as a result there was usually very little to eat and none of it very good. Or fresh, but I was inured to mold, I could eat anything and keep it down. Beer kills the germs, I told people. Tonight it was cracker-and-peanut-butter sandwiches, the. peanut butter cheap and thick, the consistency, I told myself as the crackers broke and crumbled, of actual shit. Though of course I had never eaten any, not that I remembered, and that's the sort of thing you would remember, isn't it? What would happen if you stuck food down the Funhole?

"God, stop it," mumbling aloud around a mouthful of sludge like some derelict in the park, shut up, shut up, drink some beer, read the paper. Ann Landers, my boyfriend wants to secrete stuff in my root cellar, I'm only eleven so what the hell? CITY FUNDS NEW SEWAGE PLANT. Imagine that. Two new movies opening, one about sex and one not. Won't see either, I get enough movies at work. Video Hut, Assistant Manager speaking, may I help you? The screens going every open hour of the day, pushing this movie, that movie, trailer after trailer until we can all, even the dumbest of us, recite them word for word. Once in despair I tried to melt my Video Hut name badge in the microwave: stylized red popcorn box, kernels round as breasts popping voluptuously free above my misspelled name, the whole lurid thing nearly three inches wide. Wouldn't melt, either. I don't know what it did to the microwave.

I took a beer to bed with me, along with a new old copy of *Wise Blood*. Flannery O'Connor, God I love her. She died before I was born. I have everything she's ever written. That night, knees up under the fraying red quilt, I didn't read so much as flip, skipping around to my favorite parts, I could recite them but at least they were worth recitation. I was feeling okay from the beer, halfway reading and halfway thinking of Nakota, flabby little halfway erection, cool night air turning cold on my cheek. Was the air from the Funhole cool, too, if you put your face by it? Directly above it, say? nice and close? Would there be a sensation of vacuum? suction, gentle pull like a lover's tug to bed?

"*Stop* it," alarmed, pulling myself upright, scared, yeah, wouldn't anyone be? No. Nakota wouldn't. She'd go like a zombie, sleepwalking down into the lip, so soft, opened like a kiss, black kiss to suck you down, suck you off, *yeah* stupid tentpole dick and where are *you* going, you fucking dummy? I was shaking, I put everything down, got up fast and turned on the stereo, loud, rude-boy reggae. I did not like this, I did not like any of this at all, do they call it a siren song because it cuts through everything else?

Beer. Beer cures everything, maybe even this.

Standing at the refrigerator, oblivious of its stored-cooler scent, can burning cold into my hand, I do not want to go in there, in the dark, I don't even want to think about seeing the, seeing it, drink, drink and fall asleep, and I did.

. Woke up with a headache that moved immediately to my stomach in a slow barrel roll of nausea as soon as I sat up, but there were no voices in my head but my own and I was glad, glad as I cursed my way into the shower, glad as I drove breakfastless to work beneath trees bare as telephone poles and signs for things I never did or would. In my pocket, hasty hidden crush like pornography, the bad poem (poems?) I had written in my fear; I would not read them, I was ashamed to throw them away.

At a red light I dared to pull one out, unroll it: the first thing I saw was the word "nacht," and next to it something scribbled out so ferociously the paper was bent outward. Or inward. Depending on your bent.

Long spin of the workday, coworkers joking in humors I never felt, dreaming over my register, watching customers thread the aisles like rats in a maze: good rat, here's your titty video. I had started there, Video Hut, some months before, and by virtue of being the employee least likely to say no became assistant manager. Shitty pay but I bet you knew that; really, my needs were even smaller than my check. Making no living as a card-carrying poet had accustomed me to a philosophy that made minimalism seem lavish, I had lived like a cockroach for so long that a full tank, a full refrigerator were no longer even desirable: I mean, what would I do with it all?

So: my squalor: third-floor flat, one small room and two smaller, couchbed and shitty furniture, real good stereo and even better prints— Klee and Bacon and Bosch predominant, the best ones clipped from back issues of *Smithsonian* that I got free from the throwaway pile at the library—and my favorite, a black-and-white photograph of Nakota, wrapped in rags like cerements, rising from the tomb of my bathtub, in my other, seedier place, though God knows this one was pretty seedy. At least I never cared when it got wrecked during a party.

It was at one of my parties that we found the Funhole, not, I think now, by accident but by secret true design; I understand why they call it looking for trouble. Did I say wrecked? Especially that night: detritus smeared all over, puddles of spilled beer and toppled ashtrays and some crusted cheeselike stain on the shower curtain that even I, drunk as I was (and I was), couldn't bear to look at. Nobody was left but me and Nakota, and some girl whose name I still don't know, she openmouthed, as dead-looking as any live person can be, her skin a special color and her wingback hair stiff with gel and still sprightly, as if, ignoring its comatose platform, it was ready for more fun.

"Any more beer left?" I could hardly talk, but I was skimming, yeah, I felt *good*. Nakota, snorting some weird concoction she got from this guy in Southfield, nostrils rimmed in alarming pink, shook her head to let me know she disapproved of my addiction while coddling hers.

I don't know, now, how we got into the second-floor hall, but I recall the still, dank basement-air, the way it smelled; I have a thing for smells, you must have noticed. Nakota was the one who opened the door: I definitely remember that, and her hand as she pulled me inside. Terrier instinct for the Big Bad, that's what I think now, but then? who knows, maybe I thought I was going to get laid or something. Lucky me.

Dark inside, and so drunk I almost fell—can you imagine?—right across it, right *into* it maybe; she grabbed my sleeve, ripped it to the cuff. Her voice, her *growl*: "*Look*," pointing me, "look at that."

Just as it is, no bigger or smaller, and we stood there so long I began to believe I was hallucinating, not only the Funhole but everything around me; it was that strange. The coarse dark of the room itself, the mashed cleanser boxes and the coiled piles of rags, Nakota's breathing like a runaway train, and that, it, before me, defying disbelief. You always think you'd like it if the Twilight Zone came true. You can forget that shit.

"*Shit*," said Nakota.

I don't remember getting back to my flat, don't remember anything though I would love to now. Waking to the urgent need to piss and vomit, with luck not simultaneously, noticing in passing that the passed-out hair-girl was gone and Nakota, sitting up, awake, yeah, probably hadn't even been to sleep yet. She gave me a nod as I stumbled past her, another on my slower, more painful way back.

"Let's go," she said, for the first time, "look at it."

She named it, of course, it was the kind of thing she was best at. Named it and claimed it, although I wasn't about to fight her for mineral rights. Frankly I was scared of it, not as much then as I am now, but scared as any reasonably normal person would be.

"Who knows what the hell it is?" arguing over instant coffee (me) and sluggish mineral water (her). The flat reeked of smoke; we'd been fighting, slow and tense, for hours already. Never questioning it, even then, never a shred of doubt, just the birth of the eternal disagreement. Because how could we, how could anyone deny that calm black fact, stationed there on the floor in a crummy unused storage room in a crummier building on a street no developer would ever claim? No romance about this, not at least to me: is romance possible, with a cast, a slant, this painfully oblique?

Speculation, sure. Where'd it come from, where—Nakota's first, still most passionate concern—did it lead to? "If you went *down* there," her eyes all shine.

"If *you* went down there."

"Oh *yeah*."

"That's what I'm afraid of." Wouldn't you be?

Had someone somehow put it there? She scoffed, and I had to agree; it was of no one's making, not a thing like that. Did it just grow there? She, enamored, proffered that theory and had it embellished past baroque before I could even say yes or no: what strange seed, she came back to that idea over and over, what could have the beginnings necessary for the making of something like that?

"It's alive." Her ominous smile.

"It is not," knowing we were both wrong but not able to say how. "It's not even an it, Nakota, it's a, it's—"

"A what? A place? A condition?" What a sneer, exquisite as a skeleton's bony glare, cigarette hanging out of her thin mouth, black against her sallow skin. "You don't know any more than I do."

She was right about that, though we did our best to find out. Strange that I never went without her, never checked it out on my own. Was I afraid? Sure, but not for the reasons you'd think. From the first she was first, me hanging a little behind, her idea to wield the flashlight (no good), her idea to throw something down it (an asphalt rock plucked from the parking lot, not too big and not too small; it made no sound, no sound at all, can you imagine how spooky that is?). An empty glass: nothing, though the glass was warm when it came back, the heavy string that held it warm too. A camera, my single idea, but we never did, couldn't figure out how to make it work, and we couldn't afford one that would shoot by itself. A piece of paper, her idea (that should have been mine, some poet I am) but nothing still.

Talking it over, and over and over, theories abundant, her eyes slitted and hands not so much expressive as martial, me with my hesitancy and my beer, building fences for her to jump.

Just like now, today, the phone with its irritable little buzz: "Video Hut, howmayIhelpyou."

"Hey Nicholas." Over the phone she sounded colder than normal, but for her that *was* normal, just her phone voice, she would have made a great Inquisitor. "I'm coming over tonight."

"Yeah?" She wasn't coming to savor my presence, which gave me the right to fuck with her, a little and in a joshing way. "I was planning on going out tonight. Maybe tomorrow."

"I'll be there after work."

She was, too, still in her barmaid outfit, which looked better than her regular clothes; at least everything was the same color, a decent black. She had something in a medium-sized paper bag; she held it like it was heavy. Seeing it made me nervous, I didn't know why, but with Nakota you never knew anyway, you never got any warning. "What's that?" I said.

"You'll see. Ready?" She was. In fact almost jittery, which made me more nervous still. But I'm stupid. I go along with stuff.

"Let's go," I said.

Careful and quiet as always; still it was a wonder no one ever saw us, or that we never saw anyone. Maybe everybody in the building was in on our little secret. It wasn't the kind of thing you'd talk about, none of us ever talked to each other anyway, I couldn't identify half of my neighbors by sight. I only knew the ones who were close by or obnoxious. Just like life itself.

When we got into the room Nakota did a weird thing: she looked for a lock, swore when there was none. Carefully she set the bag down. "What're you going to do?" I said, standing a little farther back than usual. "Tie me up and throw me in?"

She looked almost sorry she hadn't thought of that herself. "Good thinking, but no. It is an experiment, though," and she reached for the bag, pulled it down and away. "Something we haven't tried before."

A big pickle jar, gallon jar, filled with bugs.

All kinds of bugs: flies and roaches and beetles and mosquitoes, even a couple of dragonflies. It was beautiful, kind of, and kind of nauseating too. "Why aren't they eating each other?" I asked, and realized I was whispering.

Nakota whispered too. "I sprayed some shit in there," and, declining to elaborate, pushed the jar, nearer and nearer the Funhole, till it sat at the lip itself, far closer than we had ever dared to go.

"Now what?"

"Now we wait awhile." Her voice was shaking, she was so excited. "See what happens."

We waited quite a while, there in the dark, my back against the unlocked door, Nakota for once at my side. Her scent was higher, her breath never slowed; she tried to smoke but I told her no, not in that airless firetrap, firm whisper, as firm as I ever got with her anyway, and she gave in. The insects jumbled, up and down, fighting the barrier they couldn't see, then, "Look," her sharp whisper but I was looking already, staring, watching as the bugs, one by one, began to drop, dying, to the floor of the jar, to whir in minute contortions, to, oh Jesus, to *change*: an extra pair of wings, a spare head, *two* spare heads, colors beyond the real, Nakota was breathing like a steam engine, I heard that hoarseness in my ear, smelled her hot stale-cigarette breath, saw a roach grow legs like a spider's, saw a dragonfly split down the middle and turn into something else that was no kind of insect at all.

Finally they were all dead, stayed dead for a long time, or maybe it only felt long. I got courage enough to reach for the jar but Nakota cut me off: what instinct told her that?

"Wait," she said, hand on my arm, voice very very dry.

And they boiled up, glass-bound airborne convulsion of wings and legs and shiny bodies and dead colors, mashed together like food in a blender, round and round so fast that the jar rocked on the floor, tiny polka till it finally spun still and stayed. My mouth was open. It took effort to shut it.

Nakota said, "Now."

I did not want to touch that jar.

It was hot, I snatched my hand away, more cautiously used the front of my T-shirt to twist off the lid. "Aw *shit*," and just looking made me miserable, I had to turn my head away. Nakota took the jar carefully into her lap and, to my disgust, began picking through its contents.

"Nakota—"

"Shut up," mildly, then, "Look at this."

"No." I sat back down, head canted back against the door, eyes closed as she went through her nauseating autopsy, listening to her small murmurs of surprise. Finally I heard the lid screw on, felt her hand on my shoulder.

"Nicholas. Look. It's not that bad."

"I don't want to." But of course I did.

It really wasn't that bad, if you had a strong stomach. She had hand-picked the best pieces, the strangest I should say: tiniest heads on double-jointed necks, a little splay of wings, four to the bunch, the half-intact body of the cockroach with the long spiderlegs. Her trophies, plucked from the underworld, displayed on a dusty floor. She was smiling, she touched my arm.

"Aren't they beautiful?"

"No," I said, and they weren't, not to me. I had no desire to touch them but I did: to please her, yeah. Stupid reason, I know. Chances are she couldn't have cared less. Balancing the least objectionable, the four-leaf-clover wings, admiring despite myself their crazed patterning, so delicate, etched and slanted glyphs in a language I could never hope to master. All at once I had a horrifying urge to eat those wings, stick them in my mouth, crunch their altered sweetness and I thrust them away, literally, pushed my arms out at Nakota; the wings fell gently to the floor.

"Take it easy," angrily, rescuing them in one cradling hand. After a moment she said, "I need a bag or something."

All the way upstairs I fought the image, mutant bodies whirling in blind hurricane, carne back with an empty plastic bread bag that said "Nature's Wheat." She filled it with her prizes, all the care of a researcher with difficult data, knotted the bag with meticulous ease.

"So." I wouldn't look at it, nodding to indicate the horrible mess in the jar. "What're you going to do with that?"

She shrugged. "Throw it away, I guess."

"In the Dumpster?"

"Why not?"

Why not? I insisted on wrapping it back in its paper bag, I wanted to make her carry it but I knew she wouldn't. Careful down the stairs, holding it as far away from me as I could.

"I have never," I said, "understood the word 'gruesome' before."

"It's not that bad."

Lots of trash in the Dumpster. Worried, I perched on the shaky ledge of a rusty black Toyota, rearranging junk, slick snotty-feeling trash bags, the better to stuff you into oblivion my dear. I made a joke about disposing the bodies, turned and saw no one. Bitch. Took her bugs and went home. The Toyota creaked, I jumped down, went upstairs. No chance of eating, uh-uh, and when I slept it was to dreams of pain, infestation of tiny vengeance and no matter how frantically I waved my arms, they found a way in anyway.

Early, and hot, and inexplicably crowded, me jammed ass to belly with, my luck, not Nakota: an opening, the Incubus Gallery, some friends of hers had a show. Metalworker, and everything looked like crucified clowns.

"They make money off this shit?"

"You used to sell your poems," Nakota hissed back, nasty, but technically she was wrong: they were printed, my poems, my terrible American haiku, but no one ever actually paid me for them. Would I be working at Video Hut if there was any other way? Still I suppose I deserved to fail: with the black towering inspiration like the Funhole before me, what was I making of it?

All through the opening, as we drank cheap bad wine out of little plastic cups that smelled like mold, Nakota kept one hand in her jacket pocket: you could see her fingers moving in there, gently, as she talked. She had them with her, she whispered, the bugs in a new heavy plastic envelope; her eyes were shiny, she was wearing a T-shirt that read, in dripping shock-show letters, "Ant Farm." "Joke," she said, smugly patting her tits.

"Stop playing with yourself," I told her, "it's not worth it."

When the wine was gone I made her leave; she didn't want to but she did want to show me the bugs. We drove to a coffee shop down the street from Club 22, she had to be to work later, sat in an orange laminate booth and drank coffee worse than the wine, her spindly legs jittering, insect dance; I tried not to think that.

"Runes," she said.

"Runes my ass. What do you mean, runes?"

"I'm serious. I think they're some kind of language."

I had had somewhat the same idea, but hearing her say it pissed me off, made me somehow nervous too; Nakota's notions had taken me places that I had never dreamed of going, but the places were rarely good ones. "You've been reading too much Weekly World News," I said, looking down into my cup. "'Giant Baby Born to Dead Man,' all that shit."

Like handling filigree, fresh plastic parting to show me her remnant pets, and "Come on, not here," and she ignored me, and again I looked. This time I saw the beauty, if there is beauty in death, little weird corpses I didn't want to touch.

"Can't you see them? Look," her stubby chewed nail a breath above one wing, slow limn of its traceries. "Look at that."

"Greek to me," I said, as coldly as I could, sitting deliberately back, the booth my temporary limit. "Maybe it helps to be crazy," but it was really no use, and a small part of me even enjoyed seeing that shine to her again, a glow like the makeup I knew she never wore, her hands gentle as a mother's as she put them back, musing tilt as she lifted the coffee cup in those newly nurturing hands.

"I thought, what about a mouse," she said.

At first I didn't understand, then when I did felt sick. "Oh come *on*," pushing my own cup away, "aren't the bugs bad enough? How gross do you want to get, anyway?"

"Who're you, the Humane Society? It would just be a fucking *mouse*, Nicholas."

She was serious. The mad scientist. And a part of me wondered, too, with an ugly curiosity, just what might happen to one of our furry friends dangled down that gaping blackness, what it might look like if it survived the trip; watch that first step, it's an asskicker. My wonder drove me out of the booth, to sit grimly in the car while she finished—and she took her fucking time about it, you may be sure—and I said nothing until we sat idling outside Club 22, rhythmic slow cough of the exhaust, desultory rain on the windshield and reggae very softly on the radio.

"Come on, Nakota," and I touched her, something I rarely did any-more, my fingers as gentle on her wrist as hers had been on the insects. "You don't really want to do that, do you? Do you?"

Swiveling on the seat, hair swinging with the motion, mouth small and meaner than I had ever seen it: "You're so stupid, Nicholas. You'll always be stupid, and you know why? Do you want to know why you'll always be stupid? It's because you're afraid to be anything but." She didn't bang the door—she had never been a door slammer—but I drove away as if she had.

No call, nothing, for two, three days. Fine. I could live the rest of my life without seeing what happens to a mouse when it kisses death, especially weird death; but her words hurt me, irritated me like a splinter growing up to be a sore. Afraid. Don't be a stupid macho bastard, I told myself, and meant it, but it wasn't so much the accusation of fear as the implication that she was somehow—it sounds ridiculous—intellectually braver than I, that she had the guts to push a thing past its limits, to turn it upside down and shake it with all her might, when I was frightened to handle it at all. Maybe it really was as petty-simple as who's the better man; I'd like to think I'm smarter than that, but who knows. At least my own stupidity can't surprise me much anymore.

It was stupid to miss her, but I did that too, and felt not bad at all but even justified: she was a pain in the ass like none other, bossy and reckless and careless of my objections and especially my feelings, but she was my partner in this, she had been there from the start, she *knew*. Most of all, she was Nakota, and that was changeless as the Funhole itself.

Guess who called who.

"I can come over right now," she said, and, I thought to her credit, there was no triumph in her voice. When she arrived, I knew why: box in her hand, tiny scramblings inside, the sound of scared little feet.

My face did something that even felt ugly, but surprised? No. Not really. She knew it, too. Set the box down on the kitchen table, moved across the room to sit, smoking, on the edge of the closed couchbed.

"Come on, admit it," she said. "You want to know too."

"Yeah, just like I want to know how I'll look when I'm dead, but I'm not in a hurry for that either. For God's *sake*, Nakota! What's next, a baby?"

"A shitty little pet-store rat is hardly a human being," but there was something there I didn't like at all, maybe the too obvious disgust at my words, the shifty overplay. Maybe she knew it too, heard a greed even she didn't want to know she had. Whatever, she turned away, profile hidden by the clean swing of her hair, and an illogic memory came to me: she in my arms in some ice-cold bedroom, red print sleeping bag pulled half around us, me near sleep and chewing with my lips a piece of her hair as it lay across my face. I put my hand up, hiding or warding, I didn't want to see her just then. When I looked up she was looking right at me.

"You don't have to go with me," she said.

Do you even have to ask?

Crouching beside her, hating my own excitement, her fingers blunt and steady as she knotted a handmade fishing-line harness around the mouse's chest and back, and I said something, nervous stupid whisper about nice job and she looked at me, very seriously, and said, "I always think things through." The mouse, nose going a mile a minute, squirming in a terror that reached crescendo as Nakota's firm dangle brought it over the maw of the Funhole: to the mouse it must have looked like Armageddon, deeper than death, and its back arched in a spasm so fierce that I thought the harness would snap and the mouse fall to an unexplored death, but Nakota's work was good and the fishing line held.

"Now," she said.

I looked, then, not at the mouse descending, but at her, so close to the edge, the slow untremored movement of her hand, the calm track of her eyes as she watched the process she had started move relentlessly to fruition, but there was a cool frustration there too, unsatisfied, and would be until she made that trek herself; not as long as I'm alive. As the mouse went deeper I snatched a glance, its whiteness a living shock against the Funhole, its claws seeking purchase on what could not be climbed, and I thought, Something bad will happen now, worse than the bugs.

But nothing did. The mouse went deeper still, deep until we could barely see its color, and Nakota said, without turning her head, "Maybe you were—"

and a blast of fur and fluid hit her right in the face, she cried out, made as if to scrape crookedly at her fouled eyes and I saw her knee move, heedless, horrifyingly close and I grabbed her and hauled her sideways as a puff of sweet air came out of the Funhole, heaven's air might smell so good. Shaking, so hard I could barely sit up, but my grip on Nakota was strong enough to hurt.

"Ow," she said, and I let her go, to wipe twohanded at herself, T-shirt up like a towel, and I stared at her breasts as if I had never seen them before. The T-shirt came away gummy. She reached fingers like feelers into her hair, gave her head a gentle shake which dislodged something, some piece, and "Fucking A," she said, and incredibly she laughed, holding up a tail, part of a tail, that had turned to bright primary mosaic and was firm as a rock; she waved it to demonstrate, shook her head again and found a foot. The toes had split and splayed, the claws gone bigger than the foot itself, enormously distended and humped and hideous and she laughed again, really delighted, and I saw a shred of something slick and red stuck to the side of her mouth, etched laugh line of horrible mirth, and I scrambled past her, pushing her nearly as hard as I had held her, out out out of my way.

When she at last emerged I was sitting on the landing, as far away from the door as I could get without actually deserting her. Nothing could have forced me back, maybe not even a scream, her scream, who knows. Anyway, anything that would make Nakota scream would probably scare me into catatonia. I still felt sick, all over. "Get what you came for?" I asked her as she stopped before me, not clean but cleansed. This kind of adventure was not only her climate, it was maybe the only climate in which she was meant to live. She had her little specimen, or what fragments she had been able to collect, clutched loosely in her right hand; with her left she reached to raise me up. She looked like she could do it, too, strength without effort, toothpick arms infused like Atlas.

"I want to wash up," she said. "This shirt is fucked too."

The water ran a long time. I sat on the couchbed, drinking beer, my glance a nervous walk from her mouse pieces and back, there and back, wanting not to want to touch them. They were so incredibly *weird*, though. You almost had to touch them, if only to assure yourself that they were really there. Hard rock tail, its shimmer under my dim-bulb lamps, the monstrous foot, and part, maybe, of a head, what had once been a head. Lying there on the fake wood of the coffee table, artifacts of a place whose climate and architecture were enough to warp the fabric of the visitor, tourist or not, go on, idiot, pick up the damned head already! So I did.

Squeamish, but then the sheer steamroller exhilaration of the bizarre came over me; I felt as I had when I, we, first discovered the Funhole: my God, this is so *strange*. Gently I fingered the strained skull, its half-flayed muzzle, the eye socket now elongated upward, shaped to a sloping triangle, stretched like old rubber and like old rubber crumbling too, its limits delicate, frost pictures drawn by the terrible dark.

Nakota, humid shower smell and murmuring over my shoulder:

"It's so beautiful, Nicholas, isn't it," her last words not inviting agreement but laying down a challenge, and for once I rose to it, reached behind to fondle her hip as I fondled the head, feeling both to be equally strange, equally desirable. Her wet hair dribbling down, fluid on her almost skeletal collarbones, one drop above her breast a slow prismed tremble of light as some freakish angle caught it, jeweled it as I half turned to rise, put my tongue on that wayward drop, imagining as I did that it was the source of the scent given off tonight by the Funhole, black nectar and I bit at her nipple, the half head still safe in my thoughtful grasp. Now her murmur was approval, I was pleasing her at last, pulling her with one hand, nipple still between my teeth and I bit harder, releasing only to lay her down and kneel between her damp and narrow thighs. To guide myself inside I set down the head, and consumed by her wetness I forgot it, or rather disremembered for my thoughts then were unlike the fleshy dreams that usually partnered sex: instead they were explicit, sharp and detailed as the best hallucinations: myself fucking the Funhole, thrusting with all my might, its subtle pull become a vacuum so stark and demanding that I felt myself coming, far more quickly than I wanted, for either me or Nakota. Looking down I saw her, eyes closed, mouth working, the gruesome little half head pressed and lolling at her nipple, and in that sight was my orgasm, stretched and distorted like the head itself.

Slow panting sighs as I lay down, the sweat on my chest cooling as I pressed against her. Eyes still shut, a graven smile beginning as she raised the head, aiming that twisted muzzle not at her lips but mine.

"Kiss me," she said.

And I did.

The next morning my lips still held that bitter kiss; I could not, did not want to believe that I had actually touched the misshapen mouse mouth with my own. Scrubbing the skin from my mouth with the flattened bristles of my toothbrush, rubbing and rubbing till I had a clown's smile of abrasion, thinking of the mouse head at Nakota's tiny nipple, strange nursling; she would never wake disgusted at what she'd done the night before.

Gone, of course, when I woke up; how she managed those noiseless exits baffled me, I was a pretty light sleeper but her movements hadn't roused me, nor the sound of the closing door. To hope for any kind of note was out of the question. The only indication she had been there at all was the damp coiled towel on the tiny bathroom floor.

More than usually surly at work, a surprise because I should have been happy, shouldn't I, more than happy, Nakota and I were lovers again, weren't we? Were we? Not really. Not me. It was the Funhole we'd been screwing, not each other; even the memory as it made me shudder made me hard. Styrofoam cup poised at my mouth, the heat of the coffee soothing my sore skin, I closed my eyes and tried not to think of Nakota's next experiment, or my possible part in it. What did they use to say? "Just say no"?

Why did I waste my time waffling, of course I would say yes to it, I had an incurable problem saying no to Nakota. Why? Simply a lover's reluctance to piss off the beloved, especially one as nuclear-irritable as Nakota? Or maybe my own reluctance to stop this process, my own near-genetic laziness that found her as easy a tool as any and handier than most? The question exhausted me; I refused to try to understand. Skid and drift, that was me and the way I lived my life, foolish, hopeless, irredeemable, a broom-closet hellhole my epiphany, my one true love a woman who had never come close to loving me, even on my best days, her best days, this woman my lover now again in what was at most a terminal waste of time. Ah God, the happy hells I can create, you too, all of us. Even Nakota. We are all our worst best friends. Don't agree? Go fuck yourself.

My disgust bred the same in others, increased as the day waned, as if it were a worsening virus and me Typhoid Nicholas and pretty damned glad about it too. Fat women in "Damn I'm Good" T-shirts and men with bald heads and tit videos and teenagers with shitty attitudes, all of them leaning across the counter, slapping their plastic cards and nails drumming, impatient with my lack of speed. I could have gone slower, was tempted to, realized it would just keep them there that much longer. So I rushed, pissed and uncaring, grabbing their money and slamming the register drawer with a rote fillip as patienceless as their stares, responding to their rudeness with my own point-blank fuck-you glare.

When my shift was over, without even counting out my drawer I left, into a growing rain, complement to my mood but making it worse. Rain leaked down the inside of my window; I tried to crank it all the way closed but the last sullen half inch defeated me. The whole car smelled like a wet dog.

So did my flat: I'd left the night's window open a crack, or maybe Nakota had. Sure, blame it on her. I sat at the kitchen table, on the one chair that didn't teeter, scooping salsa from the jar with saltines, reading the paper, trying to ignore my mail, trying to ignore the almost certain knowledge that the phone would ring, she would call with a bright new atrocity. And what would I say? Why ask when you know?

She didn't call.

Working, I told myself, but I knew Thursday wasn't one of her nights. Where then? Lots of places, the Incubus Gallery, maybe another shitty opening, maybe anything with her. Maybe sitting hunched up over her mouse head, trying to tease out its secrets, to decipher from its. deformities the specifics of its journey, telling over the new abnormalities like a rosary for a special new religion; high priestess, she was made for it. The cult of the Funhole. Step right up, we can't offer you salvation or forgive your sins but we can give you one hell of a ride, just check out Mr. Mouse here, or his pioneering compatriots, the Flying Bug Brothers. Let me especially draw your attention to the one with two heads.

When I slept it was a surfacing, uneasy sleep, no question of rest. Dreams instead, plenty of them, dreams of frustration that rose, froze into fear, mild at first then so rich with terror that I woke, over and over again, my mouth dry enough to be painful, afraid to get up and get a drink of water. Worse yet, my dick was inexplicably hard. I refused to acknowledge it, I didn't want to begin to think why. It took forever to get back to sleep.

Leaving for work, running late and damn, the phone, her? It was. "How about tonight?" blunt, no niceness in her, my sweet Nakota, and me smiling, her tame asshole, yup uh-huh.

"Come over," I said, rubbing keys in random hand, wanting to ask where she was calling from and knowing better than to try. "You know what time I get home."

"I might get there a little early."

"Don't, Nakota," not knowing what she had in mind, sure she wouldn't spend the minutes in passive waiting at my bower door.

"Don't tell me what to do," and she hung up on me, oh good I told myself, heart running hard, now you've pissed her off. Nothing less predictable than a pissed-off Nakota, and you, dickhead, you had to load the gun, didn't you. I stood there in my own anger until, looking without seeing, the dull numerics of the clock on the counter turned over: 8:28, *shit.*

Down the stairs, halfway and I forgot my fucking badge, up the stairs again and down, looking once and furiously at the storage-room door, nondescript portal to all that was confusion in my life, but then again without confusion—jamming ignition key, some jolly bastard on the radio—without *confusion*, why where would I be?

Imagination can be hell. I spent the whole day jittering, thinking what if this, what if that, mistakes all around that I could barely notice. I kept seeing Nakota's hand, cool and firm on the storage-room door, walking into some black Xanadu I could never fathom, much less cure. Vanishing like a rock in a gravel pit, a tar pit, sucked in and down and down, loving every second of course but then that did me no good at all, did it now? Did it?

"You charged me twice." Mean little mouth, skinny little Mediterranean mustache. Scent of Tabu, in all the world my least favorite perfume. "You charged me *twice,*" more feelingly, the pure injustice apparently tearing her a new asshole.

I didn't say I was sorry. Reringing the transaction I pondered, I wanted to stick her headfirst down the Funhole, I'll charge you twice all right. Legs twitching like a mantis, blue muu-muu pant suit going down, down, down, I'll show you taboo.

Slewing home, water spraying in the omnipresent rain, skirting red lights and I never noticed the side of my hair, the side of my face getting wet from the damned driver's-side window, broken crank and all but I had bigger fish: is she there, what's she doing, what *isn't* she doing. Is she *there*? "There" maybe meaning still reachable, and if not, then what? Drop her a line, right? You can laugh at the damnedest things, or I can anyway.

I went not to my door but the Funhole's. Wet footprints, a curl of mud on the scuffed wood of the hallway, look Ma, I'm a detective: it's Nakota, in the Funhole, with a wrench. Or a dagger. Or a fucking nuclear device. Or a baby's head floating limply in ajar, my hand all at once sorry on the doorknob, a deep cellular reluctance to see what might be there to be seen.

I went in.

Nakota, wet like a shower, mangy hair and mangy clothes, some ratty sport coat hung over her bony broken-hanger shoulders and swiveling from her squat to face the opening door with a face wary as an animal's; seeing me, she had the balls to smile. Not a nice one, either, but did I really need to tell you that?

"You're late," was all she said, turning at once in graceful dismissal back to her business. Her coat smelled disconcertingly like dog farts, in particular the juicy ones my dog Jenny used to cut, or maybe it was the Funhole. Or maybe I was going crazy, olfactory hallucinations one of the rarer signs, but what the hell, I lived no ordinary life, now did I? I realized my hands were shaking; touching one to the other, even my own skin could feel the depth of its cold.

"You're early," I said.

"I'm trying something new," she said, barely bothering to look at me. Not even the murk of the room could mar the thoughtful glimmer of her gaze, so pretty, Nakota, especially when contemplating things no one else can stand to think about. A memory, a parking lot of a bar called the Pelican, muggy Florida midnight and she, front and center in the dwindling circle, watching with eyes ashine the drunken chain-saw fighters, the frail scent of blood, the stink of gasoline. "They do it every other week," she told me, matter-of-fact hand on the hood of my blue Dodge Charger, watching me puke on my tires. "Not the same guys, of course." Of course.

"What are you trying?" I asked now, head canted back, just a little, a careful angle so I didn't actually have to see it until I heard what it entailed. "Why couldn't you wait for me?"

She ignored the second question. "I tried to get a cat," she said, "but I couldn't. Actually," an almost, what, embarrassed smile, "I think I probably could have, but, shit. I like cats," and she laughed a little, and I noticed how close she knelt to the darkness, how nonchalant. "Anyway this is better, in a way," and she hauled up, for an instant, her descending prize: in a plastic baggie, a human hand.

My throat closed up, dry thumping fist begun in my aching chest and I pushed backward with a horror so simple I could have described it in a word: No. No.

"No," I said, in an almost conversational voice, and she gave me a headshake of mild disgust: "Take it easy," she said, dropping the hand a little lower, "it's not like I cut it *off* anybody, or anything. I got it from Useless."

In my terror the name meant nothing, then all of a sudden it did and I laughed a little, breathless with relief. Useless was her name for Eustice, a photographer friend of ours who lived with a postgrad pathologist who was pursuing her internship at "U of G morgue," fishing it lower, "it's not like they're gonna miss it or anything. I mean, what's one less hand? They get 'em off the streets all the time. Useless takes pictures of them."

"Hands?" I leaned over her shoulder, studying with pale interest the hand's Caucasian skin gone muddy yellow, its regulation wrinkles, the marks where it had been separated from its host body. It pressed against the bag in a way that made me glad I hadn't eaten.

"Vags. Vagrants," delicate eyebrows drawn in a studious slant, faint radiation of beginner's crow's-feet around those eyes, I gazed at them, now, as I leaned closer still. "They die, nobody cares, his stupid girlfriend cuts them up and studies them or something." She swung the bag gently, side to side, strange pendulum, and I caught at her coat, tugged it.

"Be careful," I said, "you're awful close."

She shifted, not actually changing position. "I wanted to take pictures, before and after, you know? But Useless wouldn't let me borrow his camera unless I told him what I wanted it for."

"But he gave you the hand okay."

"It's just a hand."

A dead hand, I thought, and had to smile, it was all so weird that it was actually funny. Relaxing back, or as relaxed as I could be around the Funhole, taking my weight on my haunches and looking at Nakota, the lines of concentration around her lips, her touch on the fishing line so sure, fingernails bitten past the skin line. For as long as I'd known her she'd bitten her nails, chewing them the way a child sucks a blanket, dull-eyed intensity. These days she must really be gnawing them, and I wondered if the hand had bitten nails too. I'd read that nails kept growing, after death, a little while. "Who bites the nails of the dead?" I said, silly sonorous voice, and was rewarded with one of Nakota's rarest smiles, a grin of genuine amusement.

"I do," she said, and went on fishing.

The hand was down far enough that it seemed small to me, tunnel-vision gaze into the black, Nakota paying out the line as smoothly as a reel. The hand's skin looked whiter against the dark, the plastic bag translucent, its one visible aspect the green closure line at the top. Down and down. Write when you get work.

Then Nakota started, smiled a very different smile: "Something's happening," she said, and I saw her fingers tighten around the line, saw its visible sway in her grasp. Her face was suddenly grim, a businesslike frown, she must have thought she was losing it; her knees braced more firmly against the floor, I straightened too, quick nervous anticipation of possible need; like a fire extinguisher, in case of emergency break glass. Emergency, that was certainly the right—

A smell like a giant's rot came like a train from the Funhole, so amazingly foul that even Nakota gasped, grip slackened on the fishing line, face folding like a fist in self-defense and I sank back, shirt fumbling-pressed to my nose and mouth, as the hand came crawling jauntily up the line, some fluid beading lightly on the stub of its wrist, and I screamed into my shirt and grabbed Nakota's arm; her control of the line wavered, the hand swung in drunken ovals over the abyss, then quickly corrected with the élan of a circus acrobat and climbed higher, nearing the lip of the Funhole and I yelled, "Nakota, get rid of it!" and she swore at me, no words but a sound like an animal and refused to let go of the line.

"Let it go!" I shouted again and gave her forearm a stiff downward slap, causing the hand to grip more tightly to the line as if the motion had frightened it. I slapped her again and the hand jiggled in corresponding panic, I moved to slap her a third time and she backhanded me, hard and blunt, the hand swinging up and wide and free of the Funhole, slamming into a pile of empty Clorox jugs like a bowling ball down an alley, scattering the plastic jugs with a wet thump and me skittering to my feet, grabbing Nakota who hit me again, her whole face blotched with rage, dragging her to the door where we stood, me pinning her arms down, she kicking me backward in the shins.

Nothing happened.

She stopped kicking me.

Still nothing happened. I let her arms go and she immediately punched me in the face, very hard, darting at once to where the hand had landed. I touched my face, gripped the doorknob, waited.

"It's dead," she said. I kept waiting.

"It's dead," she said again, insistently, holding it up by the line. Gentle swing and it *was* dead, unmistakably, limp and sorry and somewhat the worse for wear.

"Well," she said. "I'm gonna throw it back in," and before I could begin to move she did line and all.

She saw my face, God knows how it looked, God and Nakota, and she laughed. A little shakily. "Don't worry, it's not coming back out. Like a black hole, remember?"

"I hope—"

"I *know* I'm right." A pause, her lips in wistful twist, an expression so not-her that I felt, for a frightened moment, that more than the hand had changed. "I wonder," still tilted, small hands on her shoulders, "what it looks like. Down there."

"Next time use an eyeball."

And her face began to crumple, a muscular change and she burst into an incredible hoo-hoo braying laugh, I had never heard her laugh so hard or so loud, it sounded like bottles breaking and I had to laugh too, she collapsed across me, arms hooked like crooks around my shoulders, her whole body shaking with the velocity of her mirth. We laughed our way out of the room, all the way back to my flat, laughed ourselves into the shower and screwed in the coolish spray, thready blood in the draining water, her skinny elbows protruding around me like the featherless wings of a bird.

TWO

Gone as usual in the morning, and me left behind and naked, inner thighs lightly scaled with the dried spoor of our lovemaking: she liked to stay on top afterward and let the juice run down, and I liked whatever she liked. Imagining in the shower that I could smell her still, the angular scent of those secret bones, had she always smelled so fierce and so good? Recalling those gone times, old memories lit by the fire of the new, I did not this time wonder how long it would last; I was too smart for that now. Take what you get, and don't think. Of course it could never be that easy, but there were moments, like now, that I could successfully pretend that it was, and I had no inclination to try to peer past those moments. I'm not one who wants to know the future: at the best it spoils the present, with longing or dismay, and at the worst, well. Who really wants to find out how tight the sling is, for your own very personal ass, who wants to know how deep the shit will really be? Not you. Not me either. Because it's rarely bliss saved up, is it, when you finally get there. I'll take my now, waking with a lover's scent still on me, around me, take my hopes before they're maybe tragedy; a good morning is still a good morning, even if it leads to apocalypse at night.

For once up early enough to have breakfast, so I did, an oily tuna sandwich wrapped in half a paper towel and eaten in the solitude of the morning hall, second-floor hall but you probably knew that. Looking at the door; Thinking of the Funhole inside.

Other devotees it surely had, in its inexplicable history as weird-ass god-thing, and what sacrifices? No one had Nakota's brute gift for imagination, but no doubt the process that was the Funhole would accept lesser treats; odd that we had never found evidence. I couldn't believe that no one else in the building had stumbled over this particular piece of real estate. It would be—not "nice", but good, in some fathomless way, to talk with someone else about this, particularly if they were even slightly more normal than Nakota. Or me.

Read your own poems, I told myself, and smiled, a thin scoff. I still wrote them, or rather found them written; I rarely remembered the act of writing since I was usually shitfaced when I did it. I couldn't bear to try reading them, and was too ashamed to let anyone else see; my muscleless talents as a poet had peaked in my moody English Department years, declined still less poignantly as I pushed with the grim fatalism of the true asshole to make a living from my "work." Nakota was right: I had no business mocking her weird sculptor friends.

Footsteps, aiming down the stairs, and I pushed off hurriedly from the wall, stuffed the last of my sandwich into my mouth, nonchalantly swinging around the chewed-looking newel post as the walker passed me by, a skinny black-haired white man just this side of boy, head down as if in communion with a daily tragedy too dense to share even by acknowledgment. Which was okay by me: I've never resented being ignored. I watched, waited for him to push his way out the big downstairs door, then hustled myself back up to get my name badge and my coat. Be on time today, I thought. Or even early.

Still I found myself dreamy, imagining the drivers beside me on the road as fellow participants in an odyssey the nature of which we were never meant to guess, tasting here and there of the surreal to a greater or lesser degree, depending on nature or circumstance or both. My, aren't we the mystic this morning, but I did not exactly laugh as I normally would have, and at red lights I studied them, those drivers, with a compassion I never felt, looking past their morning stares or blunt car-phone smiles, past all I saw on the surface, the divination of an eye accustomed to much stranger sights. Nakota would have dismissed them with less than a sneer; I wondered what would happen if they came to the Funhole, unsuspected font of the bizarre. Would the pressure of its strangeness weigh them, as we two were weighed, would they run from it, pray to it, doom it in their minds to nonexistence by virtue of its relentless incredibility?

The mood stayed with me all day: things at work acquired a significance: a customer's choice of video, sure, you could read runes in that any day of any week, but I saw, in this new state, deeper, encountered signs I had never before known: the slick sound of a Visa sliding across the counter, the feel of the counter itself, the way the endlessly playing monitors flickered in and out of blackness in the existential spaces between *Streetgirls II* and *Dead Giveaway* and *Dog Gone Wild*, the scent, even, of the money paid or the customer's fingers or the very air in the heat beneath the fake marquee lights, all of it told me things, showed me things, and gifted somehow by the Funhole—*was* that the source? —I saw, if not the meaning of patterns then patterns of meaning, and for me that was enough.

The mood holding, I drove not home but to Club 22, sat drinking a Pabst until scowling Nakota's shift began. Her frown did not lessen for me but she came to me, not at once but that too had portent: she knew, didn't she, that I was there for the duration, that I could wait.

Thin in dusty black, the leather of her work shoes cracking along the stress line where sole met upper, hair scooped into a deeply unflattering topknot: my love. Did I say that? Again?

"Hey," I said.

"What're you drinking that shit for?" knocking at my bottle with one sharp knuckle, tiddlywinking it so it rocked in place. "At least drink something human."

"Are you coming over tonight?"

Interest in those opaque eyes, I had known her so long and in the end so poorly. "Why? You got an idea?"

I shook my head, mood pointing lower, picking at the dull gold foil, Miller High Life, right. I got some high life for you. "I just, I thought you might like to come over for a while."

"I don't think so. I have to check some things out," and she turned, sloppy tray, heading for three solitary drunks lined at the bar like listing gravestones. Old-fashioned Christmas lights behind her as she served them, blinking on and off in a causeless rhythm more reminiscent of power spurts than festive design. I drank my beer and went home.

Pausing on the second-floor landing, listening to the woozy shrieks of what, anger or pleasure, it was just sound to me, somebody doing something in one of the flats. Close by the Funhole, would living next door to it cause an issuance, a distortion, in your daily rhythms, would you brush your teeth with mare's milk, would you crawl around and dart your tongue like a rattler? Would you bite?

I wanted very much to go stand by the Funhole door, put my ear to it, listen with all my might, bring paper and pencil, yeah, write what you know. Instead I went up to my flat to eat stale shitlike peanut-butter-and-pita-bread sandwiches and contemplate, with my new and moody gaze, the warped fluttering Bosch triptych hung sorry in an unworthy light: *The Garden of Earthly Delights* with its incipient birds and copulations, none more beguiling than the standard of strange that was my daily life. Still I found I appreciated them, all of them, more fully than I ever had, demons and rabbits, butterflies and spikes, loved them more and felt bad that my copies weren't even proper prints, just magazine pages, symbolic somehow I knew but not why.

I fell asleep with a headache beginning to eat away at my seamless wanderings, woke up to a ghost of the same headache and a couple pages of writing that began with the phrase, "The giant said you gotta give to get." Truer words, etcetera, and with a cooler heart and growing headache I rolled them in a graceful ball and threw them out the open window.

Nakota's day off, so to speak, had borne new fruit: she was over ten minutes after I got home from work, glittering with her news, not bothering to sit, this was apparently too important. "Listen: I got a new idea."

"Son of a *bitch*," struggling with the bent edges of a microwave dinner, unable to separate foil from plate. "I'm sorry. I'm listening."

"What if," grinning, palms flat on canted hips, and certain of applause, "what if we put a camcorder down the Funhole?"

My fork was bending against the foil. I smiled, at a loss. "Sounds good."

A chilly look, not entirely dimming her cool wattage but certainly a pall. "Think about it," in a tone suggesting that though this might be beyond me, it was still my duty to try. "You're the one who gave me the idea. An eye, you said, and I thought, right: a *camcorder*. Turned on, recording everything. *Everything.* It'd be like going down there yourself, almost. Almost as good."

I shoved the dinner into the microwave, turned it on, sat across from where she stood. "Nakota, it's a good, it's a great idea, but we don't have a camcorder, and we can't—"

"Two words," holding up two fingers, slim as candles.

I waited.

"Video," bending one finger, "Hut." The other. For once, I argued. I mean really argued, which at first genuinely surprised her, then angered her to a high cold pitch I had rarely seen. We went through all the steps: I couldn't do it, they'd find out, I was a worse thief than a liar and I was a lousy liar, she knew that. "They're paranoid about their camcorders," I told her. "There's only two to rent, there's no way one wouldn't be missed. This isn't some big chain store," trying not to yell, again, "this is *Video Hut* for God's sake, they bought those damned things with their own money, they take them home on weekends to take pictures of their kids!"

"Borrow one then," but I had an answer to that, too, imagine me as the answer man: the up-front rule was No Borrowing.

"Then I'll do it myself."

"Nakota, no."

"I can't believe," her voice low and slow and venomously cold, "that you're not with me on this, that you can worry so much about getting caught, about that shitty two-bit job—"

"I have to eat," I said. "Every day."

"I'll do it," she said again, "myself. Or," more coldly still, "I'll do it without a camcorder."

She said this like a duelist with the laughable advantage, but oh yeah, I am stupid, it took me a second or two to figure out what she didn't mean—a camera—and then what she did. And *that* she did. Explicitly.

I said absolutely nothing, stood there with my mouth still open on my next brilliant point, looking into those eyes that looked into mine with the calm confidence of the winner, because either way, either way she had won. I still said nothing but she saw somewhere in the slump of my features my acquiescence, and as soon as she saw it she did not smile but gave me a nod that was almost worse.

"Let me know," she said, "if you need me to help."

In the end it was almost stupidly easy, fitting I suppose for someone as clumsy at larceny as I am—I was never even a shoplifter, for God's sake. The late-night Saturday shift was universally despised; it was no trouble to volunteer, and best of all I could do it on paper, penciling in my guilty initials beside the perennial request.

When Saturday came it was no trouble, either, to volunteer to count out drawers: I was assistant manager after all. I counted each twice, nervous, irritating Nakota, who stood, camcorder in hand, hip-cocked and sport-coated in the fluorescent radiance of the back room. The rest of the store was near dark, small pockets of security light here and there, except where they really needed it, right?

"I'm not *taking* this," over my shoulder for the hundredth time. "We're gonna do this, and get it over with, and bring it right back."

"Yes, Mommy," but distracted, without any real heat, she was too excited. When the drawers were counted out and locked in the safe, I turned out the back-room lights, stood blinded in the sudden absence of dazzle, she beside me more blinded still.

"Ready?" impatiently, but she squeezed my arm, not even, I thought, a sop but genuine excitement, wanting to share it with me, coconspirator and part-time stooge. Locking up, her hand still on my arm, in her pocket—I saw this at a red light—three oversize Hershey bars, stolen from the fake concession-stand display. She saw me looking at them and smiled, big mock shrug.

"Want one?" It was good, too.

Back home she ran up the stairs, literally, soundlessly, as I trudged one floor past, leaving her to it. Your show, Nakota.

It seemed a very long while to me, ensconced in the bathroom, taking a much-deserved shit, and suddenly her pounding on the door and me yelling how it was open and there she was in the bathroom, holding the empty carton of a videotape.

"Rolling," she said, and for a moment we said nothing, only looked at each other, imagining the red idiot eye staring down into all that dark, awaiting whatever sea change was inherent in the trip.

"Beer," she said, a quick positive nod and for once it was an idea I could agree with, wholeheartedly, even while shitting. She stood there, leaning against the damp-bubbled wallpaper that depicted sick lavender seahorses at play in a sleazy gold-leaf sea, her eyes almost closed, lids minutely twitching as if she dreamed.

All at once a distraction, in the form of me standing, post-wipe, pants around my ankles and with her eyes open she knelt right there on the bathroom floor and took me in her mouth.

Oh did she feel good. Bony hands cupping my balls as she worked me, hair swinging in hypnotic rhythm and I grabbed that hair, that head, pulled her tight to me, her nose, I felt it, softly bending against my body, my breath rising, groaning hard and quiet when I came. Slow, slow she pulled away, wiped her slick mouth like a fed cat. I leaned against the sink; puffing out a spent breath, and saw her lean elbows-over the toilet and expertly expel a milky stream of semen, gazing up at me as she did and daring me with that gaze to complain.

"I can't stand that shit," she said when she was done. An almost smug smile. "Nothing personal."

Yet she was almost burlesque in her—niceness? Nakota? She went out as promised for beer, came back with a whole case, whuffing as she humped it inside. She wouldn't let me help. Or pay.

"My treat," she said firmly.

She even drank one, sitting next to me, cozy on the open couchbed, reading aloud from Flannery O'Connor and laughing in the least appropriate spots. I patted her skinny thigh, listening to that charmingly artificial reading voice, a schoolmarm voice I told her and she smiled, nodding, not displeased by my comparison.

We got almost all the way through "The Enduring Chill," my head nodding like a baby's, sweetly drunk and her voice a serenade and I woke up with a start, terribly thirsty, all alone. But I heard the toilet flush and saw her come out, wearing only panties, groping a little even in that familiar space to find her way back; she had dismal night vision. She climbed beside me, under the blanket but sitting up, and I felt without thinking that she tolled the hours like a human alarm clock, waiting for her video to ripen. "How long?" I said, guttural beery voice, and she said, "Pretty quick now," and next I knew I was alone again, and she up and dressed and nervous, fiddling with my balky VCR, the camcorder safely propped against the couchbed. "Here," I said, muzzy in the midst of a hangover, my descending foot disturbing a small phalanx of empty cans, too many beers. "Let me."

"Hurry up."

She couldn't even take the time to sit. Staring at the screen and me trudging back to the couchbed, wanting water but wanting to wait, just a minute, see what was up; I get curious too.

A clocked minute of static—a long time to sit and watch nothing, I was all for fast-forwarding but Nakota glared me down—then a sip of absolute blackness, *recorded* blackness, rich and menacing as an X ray of a cancer. Nakota, lips parting to say something but the thought drowned in the flash of an image: something like bloody stalks, caressing the screen like hands behind the glass, so greedily intimate even Nakota gave a tiny backstepping whoop. Then as if a barrier shattered, ferocious fun, whatever provided the images warming to this game: a vast black grin like the Funhole itself become its namesake, black asshole-mouth studded with teeth or bones like broken glass and in that Pandora opening Nakota breathless and me with my mouth hanging wide open, village idiot at freak show, a vertiginous glide forward as upon the screen came things I didn't want to know about, oh yes I'm quite sophisticated, quite the bent voyeur, I can laugh at stuff that would make you vomit but how would you like to see the ecstatic prance of self-evisceration, a figure carving itself, re-created in a harsh new form from what seemed to be its own hot guts, becoming no figure at all but the absence of one, a cookie-cutter shape and in but not contained by its outline a blackness, a vortex of nothing so final that beside it the Funhole was harmless, do you see what I'm saying, the Funhole was a goddamned carnival ride next to this nonfigure and all at once what I wanted least, least, far less than to be struck blind or any kind of petty death was to see the figure turn (as it did now) in slick almost pornographic slowness and show me, *show me what there was to see*

and I had to turn away, Nakota finally slacklipped too beside me, had circumstances at last gotten too strange even for her? "God," barely a word, in a self-protective spasm I covered my face with my hands and I heard her little shriek, shock-show dénouement, and when I looked again the tape was buzzing blank, show's over, folks, nothing to see here.

The whole thing had taken maybe five minutes.

Nakota: I could see her hand shaking as she pushed at her hair, see her visibly swallow, imagine the dry click of her throat for mine was the same, the same. "Do you think—" she said, and stopped. I thought she might say something else, but instead she ejected the tape, pocketed it with the same reverent care as one would a beloved relic, picked up purse and sport coat. Gone. She never turned to look at me, and for once I barely noticed, didn't care, because I had some big fucking fish to fry, yeah, and the flat was too crowded with her in it, too crowded with me in it so I got up too, dressed and gone, picking up in almost absent passing the camcorder. I would return it, yeah, but to hell with work for today. Videos, I'll give you a video. Not for the squeamish. Category, um. Let's say Foreign Film. Or Comedy, depending, all depending on your personal true-blue bent and if you're benter than most this'll be a thigh slapper. Maybe more. I'd slap my own thigh if I could remember how to work my hand.

After Video Hut, my careless key: driving. Around and around, almost no gas so I had to stop somewhere. A greasy booth at White Castle, hamburger squares gone cold before me, my hand tight as a tourniquet around the coffee cup, size of a urine sample, tasted like hell but then I'd seen hell, hadn't I, or hell's heaven, not the same dif-ference at all.

A kind of a bag lady stopped by my table to ask if I was done with my hamburgers. She smelled distinctly of gas-station washroom soap. She had on three T-shirts and a jacket that reminded me of Nakota. I shoved the burgers at her. "Help yourself," I said.

"I can't," she told me. Which made a lot of sense to me. She took my hamburgers and sat two booths away to eat them. I wondered what she'd think if I showed her the Funhole. You think you're on the fringe of society, huh lady? I'll show you the edge of the fringe, it's even out on video now.

I sat there until they told me to leave. Must have been close to two hours, I wasn't wearing a watch. When I got home Nakota was there, playing it again. I wasn't sure I wanted to see it, so I sat down and took her hand in mine, very firm, didn't give a shit if she wanted me to or not. She didn't seem to mind. Or notice.

"Why is it," as the preliminary static went by, her almost whisper, "that it seems, you know, *weirder* on a tape?"

"Because it is."

I don't know what about it seemed weirder to her; certainly the rean-imation of a dead man's hand is pretty fucking weird, as weird as the spontaneous rearrangement of insect parts or the eclectic combustion of a mouse. To me it was the affirmation that the Funhole was not a thing or a place but an actual process, something that was happening, and that the process could be, was, actually transferrable to tape. On another level it was somewhat like an operation. Or a death. There's this video at work, you probably heard of it, *Faces of Death* it's called, the penultimate moment captured on VHS. Same principle: you know, everybody knows about death, but to actually see it, wow. Dickbrains are daily blown away by this, no pun intended. Maybe for me this was the same: the Funhole, bugs mouse hand holy shit and look, *look*, here's how it really happens! Look!

For Nakota, who knows, no telling or even guessing with her, but she seemed truly stunned in a way I had rarely seen before. It was some kind of affirmation for her, too, but of what, again who knows and she wasn't

talking. Maybe, I thought, we were both hypnotized. Mesmerized, in
the original sense. Or maybe we were just the particularly stupid brand
of geek who doesn't believe it till it's on TV.

I sat still through it all. I watched the part I had not wanted, before,
to see, and was sorry I had. She didn't look sorry but she didn't look
good, either. From the pocket of the sport coat she took her cigarettes
and two small yellow tablets.

"Want one?"

I shook my head. "What are they?"

"Kind of crank. I've been takin' them all day." She dry-swallowed
them; I've never been able to get over how she was able to do that. It
almost gags me just to watch.

"I'll stick with beer," I said. There was still a lot left. I gave her a glass
of water and she got up and stirred two packets of sugar into it, shaking
the packets to ensure she got every last granule.

"Why'd you do that?"

"Why do you keep your sugar in packets?"

"If I buy it by the bag, the bugs get it."

"So let 'em." She drank the glass down, not even stopping for breath.
Then she grinned, foxhead grin. "I feel like I'm underwater," she said.
"And that I'm burning."

She put the tape back on. She played it over and over again, until I
couldn't watch anymore and sat quietly getting drunk. When I looked at
the clock on the counter, I was surprised to see it was only four o'clock.
I wouldn't even be home from work yet. I'd forgotten to leave a note,
but it seemed so worthless I didn't care. Maybe the Funhole had finally
gotten all the way inside my head and was driving me painlessly crazy.

I got so drunk I fell asleep on the kitchen floor. When I woke up
the first thing I did was crawl to the refrigerator and get another beer.
Nakota was still in her perched posture on the couchbed. The TV
light was the only light in the room. Raining outside and that the only
sound, it really was like being underwater. The world's most piquant
aquarium. And you are there.

"You're watching that like porno," I told her. It came out so garbled
I wanted to laugh, but she was, a ritual masturbatory excess, maybe

she even was jerking off. The perfect avant-garde stroke tape. Boy was I funny tonight. Too bad no one was laughing but me. Or even listening. Nakota sure wasn't. I fell back to sleep with a mouthful of beer, woke again to the toll of a monstrous headache, beer soaked and clammy on my shirt and skin, TV buzzing and Nakota fast asleep, back curled like a question mark and hands, childlike and defenseless, loose-fingered against her cheek as a shadow grew on her face like a cancerous smile.

"Did they ever say anything?"

Nakota drinking Sweet'N Low and mineral water, elbows resting on the slippery bar, trusty rag between us as my own elbow nudged my empty beer bottle. Near Monday midnight at Club 22, just Nakota and me and the lonely scattering of hard cores she served in her bitchy desultory way. Just now their particular glasses were full, mine too for she poured again, draft this time, cheap but what did I care, for me it was free.

She lit another cigarette. Black smoke, yeah. "Did they?"

"What, about the camcorder?" I shook my head. I didn't apologize and she didn't mock. Will wonders never cease. Not as long as there's a Funhole, they won't. "I don't think they noticed, but if they did they're not talking."

"Every time I see it," dragging on her cigarette, "I see something different."

I didn't. I nodded as if yes, I agree, but I was lying, surprising how easy it was to lie. I didn't tell, then, or later at my flat, when she came drifting to the couchbed, me already on the troubled cusp of dream, the lines of her bare body sculpted by innocuous TV light, she'd left it on to find her way but not on the Funhole tape, just plain shit TV, commercials flashing like headlights. She pulled at the quilt, low enough to insert herself, place her coldness to my warmth but I was cold, too, cold all the way inside. I held her, her fast breath on my chest, felt myself harden but did not move and she didn't touch me further, a shared delicacy so complete as if by agreement. When we woke, not morning but lightening, the cold air tinting pink, I was so hard it hurt and still I did not move, but her hands found me, in silence and cold, a few hot strokes and I came and as I did she rubbed herself, half on me, tight against my thighs and I heard her come, a tiny croaking cry, and she said without taking a breath, "Watch it with me."

I didn't say no. But I didn't watch.

I was right the first time: to Nakota it was like a stroke tape. For a mindfuck.

Since the tape's inception she was in my flat as much as even I could want: Zen and poker-backed, focused on the screen, day after day and no more disappearing acts, staying on till morning. Once in a while she would still be there when I left for work, lying prone and passive but nothing peaceful in those eyes, behind lids that shivered as if she dreamed an endless dream. The tape was always playing unless I shut it off. I was getting very good at ignoring the images onscreen, unless my gaze was caught at that critical point where the figure turned. Then I must watch it, whether I would or no, and in the end feel as I always did, hurt in some spot where I could not see to measure the depth and severity of the wound.

After work, the first few days of snow behind us and already I was sick of it, dirty piles at curbside and people driving as if they had never seen the fucking stuff before, the heat in my flat no real heat at all but a kind of half-assed damp warmth that warped my magazine prints and left the floors dry and cold: coming home, newspaper, half-eaten lunch in grease-spotted brown bag, see domestic me. What's for dinner, honey, Funhole soufflé?

Nakota, in front of the TV as always, but no glance at my entrance, no acknowledgment that anyone else was in the room; just a slow, slow turn, rising to her feet like deep-sea ballet, moving the few steps to the television as if it were miles she traveled, and there kneeling before it to press, gingerly and gentle, her cheek against the glass.

I almost expected—what? a sizzle of flesh? a blinding burst of light?

her to get sucked right into the TV? Of course nothing happened, nothing visible I should say because that's the tricky part, isn't it, that's where the rub comes in. The worst wounds are internal, I should have known that from my own experience, but I'm the type of guy who doesn't learn.

She sat like that for a while; I let her; I saw no reason not to. I stopped staring, put my things away, although it didn't seem right to start cooking dinner or anything; how *does* one behave at an ecstasy?

Finally, after I had read the paper, nervous twitch of newsprint every time I thought she moved, finally I went and shut off the tape, shut off the TV, helped her stand—she seemed to need it—and back to the couchbed. She sat down, docile enough, and I stood looking down at her, wondering what to do now. Suddenly she opened her eyes very wide, bugged them at me in a way that would have been comical any other time, and said through a big threatening grin, "That's right, pamper the madwoman, you fucking idiot."

"Yes, your craziness," and to my wary smile she laughed, a normal sound or as normal as she ever got, lit up a cigarette and asked me if there was any mineral water or anything to drink.

"I'm not going to work tonight," she said. "Tom asked me to but I told him no."

So the evening, bed, no sex, her skinny body cool to the touch and dropping into sleep like iron into sand. I sat up to read awhile but could not wholly concentrate, the words jumbling into other words, sentences into diatribes and paragraphs into convoluted polemics on the pressure of instinct, and then the words changed again into symbols I could not read and I knew I was asleep and dreaming, and I was not disturbed even though the words changed again to writhe on the page as if they were pinned there and me some spiteful collector who would have them no matter what. They spelled out challenges, feeble defiance, and I laughed and slammed the book shut, over and over, enjoying my rhythmic cruelty to such a monstrous degree that I finally woke, scared, sat up to wipe at my eyes. And saw Nakota was gone.

The door was open.

It took me two seconds to grab on jeans, catching my pubes in the zipper and it hurt and I barely felt it, galloping like the cavalry down the stairs saying "Shit, oh shit" like magic words and even from the landing I could see: she hadn't even bothered to shut the storage-room door, hadn't bothered with the ten-watt light. I turned it on, I wanted to be able to see. Whatever it was.

And a sight, oh, was it.

On her knees, oblivious and naked, braced arms on either side and hair dangling straight, about to stick her head down the Funhole.

"God *damn*," too horrified to think what else to do, to worry that I might hurt her, I slammed into her like a truck and knocked her sideways so she crashed like the tethered hand had done, smack into a pile of junk and shit flying everywhere and back she came, crawling like a crab, teeth bare, brows arched and tiny tits jiggling and her eyes absolutely blank and I grabbed her and she bit me, I mean bit me like a dog and blood and worrying at the skin of my hand so I had to jerk it away and in that second boom, back to the hole. I yanked at the back of her neck, panic strength and she made a little sound, I'd hurt her that time for sure and a little, a tiny bit of life came back to her face and I squeezed where I'd hurt her, use the pain, use it.

"Nakota," squeezing again, "stop it, *stop* it, you hear me?"

And everything came back, eyes and all but not right, not quite, I saw it and my grip eased but just one wary notch. Blood on her teeth and almost crying, I had never in my life before seen tears in her eyes, "I have to, Nicholas, let me go."

Muscles, humming in my arms, vibration passed from her body to mine, God she was strong. "I can't."

Tears and blood. "I *have* to, Nicholas. My *head's* down there."

"Oh, Nakota," and I thought She's crazy, this has driven her crazy. What do I do now. "Let's go upstairs, okay? Let's go upstairs and I'll—"

"I need my head back!" and a lunge, *God* she was strong, fierce jerking elbows and kicking feet and snapping teeth as her mouth worked, long slippery thread of spit and trying to get at me and I held her, tight, tight, I wanted to drag her out and away but the way she fought, the force I had to use just to keep her from breaking loose, I was hurting her already even though she gave no sign she felt it. I would have to really hurt her, maybe even knock her out (though I had no confidence

I could actually do it, I had never done anything like that before), and meanwhile she was wearing me out just fighting me, fighting me, fighting me, and finally I yelled, "Okay, okay! Just stop, okay? Just *stop*," and I gave her an extra-hard shake, her head snapped like whiplash and she got quieter, still panting but quieter.

"I need my head back," she said.

Oh God. I tried to talk to her, talk her away from the craziness but she kept straining past me, little whine in her throat like a sick animal, mumbling about her head and pushing with all her strength against my body as if I was a wall or door she must surmount to be free. This would go on all night, forever, until she wore me down and I had no doubt she would. Eventually. She was the queen of eventually.

"Stop it," was I going to have to really beat her up to stop her, oh God please don't make me do that. "*Stop* it, Nakota, just—" Whine and panting, like wrestling a dog, snapping at me, so this is what it's like when someone loses her mind, uh-huh, pushing and pushing against me and all her muscles alive and she kicked me, I should have expected it, the classic move, and as I jackknifed, groping for my balls, she bounded past, a literal leap like ballet and the pain, yeah and the anger made me able to grab a part of her, some skinny part, and sling her with all my strength against the wall. She hit like a door slamming but the momentum was too much for me, balance gone and I was too close, too close to the Funhole, so black and calm below me as I pinwheeled in perfect silence, the moment as long and exquisite as a car wreck

I'm going to fall right into it

and nothing from Nakota, I had knocked her finally silent, no help there hold on I can't I'm losing it

God

and with a plunge like a scream I fell full length, body wrenching like a twisting fish and my right arm, thrust out for desperate balance, at last gone deep inside.

She got her head back, all right.

THREE

Nakota as nurse. We both needed nurses, she more than me, though my bitten hand was already outrageously swollen, "What kind of germs you got anyway?" weak joke that got less than a smile, lips twitched around her cigarette. Black smoke, stinging in my eyes. Her motions were slow, crippled grace, she moved about the flat like you drive a wrecked car, even her hair looked wounded, dirty looking and dragged back in a twist-tie bow. We had taken all the aspirin in the house and were starting in on the Nyquil.

It was almost morning, overcast dawn, sure to snow again today. Me in bed, Nyquil in one hand, beer in the other, Nakota bent shivering over the stereo. On her bare back, just above her ribs, was a disconcertingly heart-shaped bruise. You only kick the shit out of the one you love.

"Hurry up," I said, "you'll freeze." She found what she was looking for; it took some looking: loud kickthrash music, fitting obbligato for our little dance; ladies and gentlemen, I give you the Funhole Waltz. Back across the room and it hurt to watch, bruises like clouds, massed and banked all over her but especially on her arms, where I had gripped her harder; the memory of my tyrannical panic made me wince, but I knew for once I had been purely and unarguably right. An odd feeling. Not pleasant. You can get used to being wrong all the time; it takes all the responsibility out of things.

Climbing into bed, into the warmth; we had piled on every blanket in the house, we needed that heat. I cuddled her with careful arms, gentle of her pain, offered her a sip of Nyquil. "Pleasant bouquet," she said. Her speech was slurred.

When she handed back the bottle I flinched in the taking, and she turned her head, slow. "I thought it was the other hand," she said.

I did too, but there on the right palm, a hole, a definite hole, and an ugly scared suspicion rose like dizziness: oh God please, not a souvenir. I did my duty. Please don't do this to me.

I compared hands. The left one, the bitten one, was puffy, purpling, you could see it had been torn. The right one had a puncture in the palm, a round wound with round gray edges. As we looked at it a minute drop of clear fluid, thick as syrup, welled up but did not drip.

"Did," her voice sharpening now, sitting up straight oh you sick bitch, she was *excited*, "did something—hurt you?"

"Shut the fuck up."

My voice was shaking. I wanted to hit her again, turned away instead. Eyes closed, remembering only the fear, possessed by fear at the lip of the Funhole, so great and the feeling of *clenching*, then hearing her distant moan and pushing myself back and away, crawling to where she sat still against the door. Crying without tears. No new head to present to her, but her own seemed to be working okay at that point. Back upstairs to a burning shower, it seemed we couldn't get enough warmth, enough different kinds of medicating, Nurse Nakota pushing pills in my mouth. Now back to normal, cheering my contamination.

"Did something down there—"

"I said shut the fuck up!" and I slammed my hand down on the bed, quake of covers and the Nyquil splashing green as chartreuse and a pain that made my eyes spring to watering, oh *God* that hurts, Nakota subsiding but with shiny eyes, I closed mine so I wouldn't have to look at her.

"Leave me alone," I said. And she did. But I felt her thinking.

Old saw proved right: it *was* better in the morning, bruises, swellings, aches and all. All but my right hand.

Alone in the bathroom, back against the unlockable door, examining my hand in the weak fluttering light: like checking a bite from the devil, yeah, almost scared to touch it, and sore? Oh it was. I ran cool water on it, then warm; the skin there reddened a little under heat, but otherwise there was no change.

Nakota knocking, "I gotta get in there, Nicholas."

"Wait a minute," pressing a little harder against the door. I held my hand close, close to my eyes, small sloping grayish wound like a miniature, scale-model

don't say it

"I gotta *pee*, Nicholas!"

Stepping away from the door, letting her in, holding my hand close to my side. As she pissed I dressed, hurried in absurd uneasy fear to grab keys and get out, yelling "Bye," over my shoulder as I slammed the door too hard. In the hall, panting too hard. All my motions on cartoon speed, revved up, I forced myself to walk very slowly down the stairs and I did not want to stop at the Funhole door, of course I most certainly would not be stopping there because the handle felt so good, so good in my sore hand, and inside it was warm, warmer than the hall, warmer than my flat even, the heat seeming to emanate, of course, from the Funhole itself and why wouldn't it, hmm? Why wouldn't it.

Murmuring to the darkness. "What did you do to me?"

Warm. A tension I had not fully noticed seemed to drop from me all at once, my shoulders slumping in relief, so warm. My hand was wet, soft sweet dribble of fluid, it too was warm.

"What's going to happen to me?"

No answer, no oracle. Just the mouth of the Funhole, warm breath rising, I noticed in a dreamy kind of way that its smell was stronger today, a rich and complex odor, maybe it was a kind of incense, a spice smell, maybe it was

maybe it was happy with the taste of my *blood*, you fucking asshole get away from there, get away!

Out. Out and hurrying down the hall, no tension in me but the tension of fear, good clean healthy fear, all the way outside where I teetered and slipped on the snowy pavement, ice beneath and instinctive hands outstretched to save myself, slamming down hard enough to knock out my breath, both my hands hurting so that I felt instant tears dripping instantly cold. It took me fully half a minute to even sit up, and when I did I saw the crows, big black wings in thoughtful telephone-wire posture, apprentice urban vultures. It seemed just as my glance found them they flew, not toward me but up, mobile clouds before the weak and desultory sun.

I stopped at a drugstore, sat in my car applying careful Band-Aids to my lovely new hole, and was in fact only twenty minutes late to work, a circumstance pointed out to me with exquisite scorn by the manager and as gratefully received by me. Let the day begin, I thought, and my hand throbbed in damp cool agreement.

No more video, I told her.

Imagine the scene. But I did it anyway, threatening her with a calm authority I definitely did not feel, inside I was shivering but I told her no, no, you want it, you take it somewhere else. "I don't want what happened to happen again," I said.

"It won't." Sullen soft-voiced rage, eyeing my wounded hand—the right one, of course; she had no eyes for the one she'd bitten, no, that was too normal for her—her own hands shaking so from temper that she could barely light her cigarette. "I'm not scared."

"I am."

More sullen still, "You know I don't have a VCR."

"That's tough."

At a loss as to how to adequately punish me, cigarette clenched between her teeth and hands tightening, untightening, far more angry at my calm than she would ever have been at my anger: "You're absolutely spineless, you know that? Worthless spineless gutless"—extensive litany of my crop of failures, and as she tolled them all I thought of the deeper failures, things she did not and never could know, things she might—would—consider unworthy of memory, things that to me carried with them regrets with edges still so bitterly sharp that even the thought of them brought the same bright instant shame; watching that mean little mouth moving, moving, cigarette burning unnoticed and silent splash of ash, knowing that oh, yes, I had done banal and infinite wrong, but this time, for once, I had not.

Finally, frustrated: "I'm taking this," shaking the tape at me like a fist.

"Go ahead."

And gone, ash fragments left behind, spoor that I swept into my palm and dusted out into the cold night air, imagined I saw it settle on the snow below to form patterns like the runes she always said she saw, insect wings, all the insects buried now in peace under this selfsame snow.

Nursing my hand, sitting at night—alone, did you have to ask?—and examining its growing soreness, the way the, what, infection seemed not to spread but to deepen, the gray edges of the wound now blackened. All my other, transitory souvenirs of that night had healed, even Nakota's bite marks, all of me good as new or as good as I was going to hope for. But not my right hand.

It wasn't getting better, either.

I kept it covered, no sense displaying the war wounds now is there, graduating from Band-Aids to gauze and tape for as it grew worse, it just plain grew: its circumference widening as gray went black, the skin there slick, now, as plastic, *expensive* plastic, nothing but the finest rot for me. Fluid still came from it; that was the part I hated most, goddamn fucking drippy stuff, mostly a dribble but at times such gush that it soaked the cuff of my shirt, and me sometimes at work and trying to make like I spilled my Coke or something, I mean how many Cokes can you spill? And it smelled, yeah, but not like you'd expect: a changeable odor, sometimes so garbage-rank it turned my stomach to change the bandage, sometimes so sweet it almost smelled—tasty. Even Nakota, on her cold infrequent visits—I caught her looking, nose wrinkled like a cat's, but too proud, certainly, to ask.

Which was another, much larger problem, far more painful than my stupid artificial decay, far less curable. She had left me: for punishment, of course, over the video, which she was assiduously watching elsewhere, had to be since I hadn't seen it, much less watched it, for over two weeks. (And where was she watching it? Had she actually gone out and bought a VCR? Not a chance. Then with whom? And how did she explain it, if she bothered at all? Swallow those questions, I thought, swallow till you choke but don't ask.) *God* how I missed her, and not when you would think, no lonely nights spent snuffling into my bachelor pillow, yanking at my stiff bachelor dick. Instead it hurt most at the times she was there, wrapped in the ratty sport coat she now affected constantly, pipestem jeans and too big Keds jammed with men's ankle socks and always wet, her hands always cold looking, lips chapped past red to a nasty-looking ash color; occasionally they would split, I saw blood in the cracks. It made me want to cry, I realize that sounds ridiculous but that's how I felt.

She would sit back on the couchbed, knees crossed, staring at me and my constant prattle and me staring inwardly, wondering too at my own transparent jabber, all of it saying so clearly Come back. Come back and don't be mad anymore.

But still I couldn't give in.

Even though I knew she had to be watching it elsewhere, knew I was saving her from nothing and in fact maybe making it worse for her without me to watch her, then what? I was a pretty shitty guard dog but I was something anyway, to stand between her and her own recklessness, I had kept her from so much already. Maybe that was the problem, too, or the backbone of it, my veto of the video the last straw for her. God who knew. All I knew was that even if it kept her from me, I had to keep saying no because I could not stand, could not *stand* to have to watch her constantly, wondering if tonight would be the night she would sneak off and me have to chase her, maybe hurt her, to make her stop. Or worst of all she might get away from me entirely. Kill yourself, Nakota, if you have to; I love you but I never could stop you, really, only slow you down. But I reserve the right not to have to watch. Anyway—trying to comfort myself, wretched notion but—anyway, she seemed much less zombified now, as if the hours (I supposed) of unsupervised addictive repetition had cost the video some of its cold hypnotic charm, what were once vices etcetera. Stupid—I keep saying that, don't I?—but a necessary fiction for me to keep going. If I failed her—again—if there was no way out of it, it was at least not as an accomplice.

This reasoning worked until she would stand, not smiling, and say, "Let's go." And she leading, me trailing, off to the Funhole.

She came, of course, not for me but for the Funhole, and this was maybe the most mystifying; I was sure there were many times, most times, she visited without me, her schedule could easily permit this, she could have rented a flat in the building for all I knew. For me the wonder was why she bothered taking me along at all. No questions from me, though. See her rarely, touch her never, but if that was all I could get, then I was going to take it and be, if not glad, then sorry, but in silence.

Down the hall. Staring into that dark mouth, closer now, both of us, she hands in pockets or on her knees (always, always a chill for me to see her do that, remembering) and me behind her, her knight in twisted armor, awkward picking at his bandaged hand as his lady fair beheld her grail.

In silence, always, and always parting at the stairwell, she hurrying off brisk and wordless, me to trudge upstairs to try to concoct a distraction, something, once I even pulled out my pathetic roll of poems. Beer, too, but you know? I didn't want to drink it. Instead I would sit at the window, eyes closed, breathing cold air until I fell asleep. Waking with cramped shoulders, piss-full, my hand hurting, hurting.

Nothing got better.

The doctor's office, faint bleachy smell, nervous on the red plastic sofa and reading a *Redbook*: "Is Your Mate A Workaholic?" No, but my lover—ex-lover has an annoying habit of trying to stick her head where it doesn't belong. Or is that more of a *Cosmo* article? Ho, ho, ho.

"Mr. Reid? Nicholas?"

Follow the nurse, his ass round and womanly, his uniform baggy and blue and clean. Blood pressure, pulse, temp. "I understand you're having a problem with infection? A hand wound?"

"Yeah."

Reaching for my clumsy cover-up job, bandage palimpsests and I shook my head, pulled my hand away, hiding it like a little kid behind my back: "I'd rather, you know, if the doctor just see it. I mean," lame little smile, "it kind of hurts, to touch it."

"Fine." It wasn't but I got my way, which is what counts. If I had to put on a one-man freak show it was going to be by invitation only, thank you very much.

The doctor, skinny hands the color of weak coffee, grizzly gray hair. Bluff and bored, let's get this over with. Cheer up, doctor, I thought, peeling at my bandages, this ought to make your day. A medical marvel.

He didn't say a lot, at first, asked questions a little then a little more, touching my hand with those bony fingers, pressing my knuckles, the meat below the thumb.

"Hurt here?"

"No."

Press, press. "Hurt here?"

"No."

"How about here?"

"No." I felt I was disappointing him. On the wall behind him was a calendar, peaceful winter scene brought to you by Searle: Please Buy Our Dope.

"How—"

The pain was so unexpectedly blunt that I jerked my hand away, tears in my eyes; some of the wound's fluid splashed him, honey-colored drops on his fresh white coat. Cradling my hand against me, unconscious soothe of outraged flesh, and he asked me again, "How did you say this happened?" Not, note, how did it, but how did I say it did. A distinction, but I pretended not to make it and patiently told my lie again: a puncture wound from a very dirty metal rake handle. Why I said rake, living in a flat, I don't know, but it was my bullshit and I stuck with it.

"Uh-huh." He wasn't buying it but wasn't going to call me on it either.

"Well. This is a very unusual infection, Nicholas. It has to be kept very clean. I'll have the nurse give you some instructions for care," as if my wound was a temperamental tropical pet whose very rarity demanded my attendance. He gave me a prescription for something, cephalosporin, sent me on my way. I paid cash, which made me further suspect, wandered off like a criminal with my spandy new bandage and my guilty pain.

It snowed all the way home, dull relentless flakes, more and more against my windshield and my wipers not up to the job, driving through a landscape smeared and troubled and my sore hand aching, aching against the wheel. Back home I tore off the new bandage, let my hand sit palm-up on the open windowsill to touch without catching the steady reach of snow. I slept there, and when I woke, in the early dark, my hand instead of being cold stiff as the rest of me was a lustrous pink, the flesh pliant and warm and I touched it, wonderingly, and as I did a spurt of fluid as thick as jelly burbled out on the iced inner sill and in its yellow clot I thought I saw swimming a bright and winking eye.

Listless afternoon checkout at Video Hut, bandaged hand clumsy and cold, somehow, at the fingertips, was my circulation going or what. Learning to use the laser pen with my left hand. Learning to drink coffee with my left hand. Learning—it cost me some pinpricks—how to pin my badge on. My fellow grunts past asking now "what happened," ignoring me and my wound with equal nonchalance. Just the way I like it.

No snow today but cold, oh yeah, I could feel it coming off the big front windows, feel its demand every time the door opened. Beside me, new grunt in short brown braid and badge askew, asking under his breath, "What kind of dumb shits come out on a day like this to get *Booby Prizes*?"

"Or *Mommy's Little Massacre*." Ignore the faint ooze beneath my bandage. Open door and "Look at this one," I said, clandestine nod at a definite damage case, big guy in cracked brown leather, pale all over, pale like a corpse. "Bet he's not here for the H&R Block tape."

"Scary looking," and just as he said it the guy turned, he couldn't have heard but he turned, came walking straight toward the register, closed stride, and my new buddy melted backward, me left alone with my laser pen and my fucked-up hand, saying, "Can I help you?" in a less than forceful tone.

"Are you Nicholas?"

Flat, flat voice, not especially deep, and when he leaned hands on the counter I saw the pitted skin, hilly nails with years of black grease beneath. Up so close he was paler still, so white I thought Albino, though his eyes were a watery gray. Weird long lashes. He blinked a lot.

"Yeah, I'm Nicholas," I said. "What can I help you with?"

Closer still, dull gas-station stink off the leather as he leaned down to me to say, "The Funhole."

I stared. I think my mouth was open, requisite dummy stance but I couldn't help it, I kept staring and he said, more flat and quiet still, "'S okay. Shrike told me all about it."

"Who's Shrike?"

Faint impatience now, which I suppose I can understand, here he was with his great mystic password and I was reacting as if he'd just stolen my brain. "You know, *Shrike*. You don't have to be nervous, man. She showed me the video."

Well. It wasn't a bad name for her, Shrike. And she'd showed him the video, had she. So: this must be my replacement. Talk about eclectic. Looking more closely, "Randy" stitched in that lumpy universal red on the shirt beneath the leather, a tiny bisected skull, gold-toned and grimy, hanging from one grimier ear. White-blond hair, very clean, the cleanest thing on him.

"So," I said. "What'd you think of it?"

"Oh man," leaning even closer, and now that flat voice had passion, "what a fuckin' *trip*, I couldn't believe it. We must of watched it twenty times. Shrike says the more you watch it, the deeper it goes, goes in *you*, you know?"

"Uh-huh."

"I watch it and I think, Now this is God, you know?"

"God. Yeah." Lord of the fried. I smiled, involuntary sour twitch and—man of many moods—Randy laughed. "I knew it," he said. "I knew I'd like you, man."

What an accolade. Shut up, I advised myself, he can break you in half. We stood there smiling at each other for a few more seconds, me wondering what the hell to add to this surreal bonhomie, but Randy had no worries, he knew exactly what he was about. Leaning even closer, one more inch and he'd be right in my face, conspiratory murmur: "So when can I see it?"

"See what? The Funhole? Haven't, hasn't Na—Shrike taken you there?"

"Oh yeah, we saw the *room*."

What the *hell*? "But you didn't go in?"

"Yeah, we went in, but *you* know what happens."

When absolutely cornered, I reach, always, for the truth. "I don't know what the hell you're talking about, I really don't. You went in the room, that storage room, but you didn't see it?" Slightly affronted, leaning back and his gaze suspicious, was I fucking with him or what? "It's like Shrike says, you have to be there."

We stared at each other, this was making no sense at all to me when suddenly my mind translated his words into something even more senseless: not "you have to be there" but "*you* have to be there," meaning me, which meant nothing. What did I have to do with seeing the Funhole, and why would Nakota say I did? She was a liar, sure, a twister, but what could she possibly get out of such a silly story, and what exactly had she said to convince Randy that what he saw would somehow improve with my presence?

"So." Randy crossed his arms. Big arms. "When can I see it? Tonight?"

The sensation of being boxed in, trapped in a cusp moment of purest choice, warred with a weird diluted glee, what the hell, right? What the hell. It's not my goddamned hole anyway now is it, not my personal property, it doesn't have my name on it. Whatever happens won't be my fault.

"Sure," I said. "I get home about six."

"All *right*." Randy's smile restored, I thought he would actually shake my hand but instead he punched my shoulder, lightly, a gesture so adolescent that for a minute I misunderstood and stood, my own grin fixed, waiting to get smacked again but this time less tenderly. "I'll give Shrike a call. See you later, man," and gone, cold air blowing in his passing, and watching him all the way to his car, wondering, still my stupid grin until my friend the deserter came up to me, tapped me on the back.

"Friend of yours, Nicholas?"

"Guess so."

I reached, seemingly without my own consent, for the phone: call Nakota. Then: no. No I won't. Let her find out from him. Still grinning, put the phone down, and as I did I saw my bandage, soaked and bubbling, a rich reddish gravy leaking fresh across the counter and I blotted it, fast swipe with my sleeve, went at once to the bathroom to peel free the clotted gauze and rinse the wound, the hole, the running water not as fast as the leak, drainage they call it, this was drainage all right. "*Look* at that shit," I said to myself, finally not even rinsing but just letting it run, run, if it was blood, I thought, I'd be bleeding to death.

It went on so long it got embarrassing: somebody, the new guy knocking at the door, "You okay in there?" and me watching the flow, mumbling something; at last he went away. Finally, without slowing, it just stopped. With my left hand, clumsy but getting better, you know what they say about necessity, I extracted my little Band-Aid tin of gauze and pre-clipped tape, made a new bandage, watched a careful moment to make sure it wasn't going to start up again. Nothing. Nothing but the white innocence of the gauze, the crisscross tape, my sallow flesh.

The rest of the day dragged. Was I actually excited about my new job as ringmaster, hur-ry, hur-ry, hur-ry, step right in to the greatest hole on earth, you betcha. For once exercising my bullying rights as assistant manager, I made the new guy close up, drove home too fast for the weather, slewing and skidding, arriving a little before six.

Cold enough, in the entryway, to see my breath, cold enough to stiffen my normal hand as it tried to work the key, lumpy feel of my fingers and impatient, I used my right hand, ignoring the pain for that moment, sorry I had the next. Boom, boom, migraine throb in my palm and I had to sit down, right hand cradled in left, coddling my cut-rate stigmata and the knock on the door, loud and brisk, already?

"Come on in," I said, too quiet, had to say it again but by that time they were, big ol' Randy eager enough to slobber, and Nakota, cheap black windbreaker, hair in disarray, surlier than ever. She went to the refrigerator, came back scowling, no mineral water of course. That idiot grin was back on my face. It felt great.

"You've met," Nakota said, as if that were somehow my fault.

"Want a beer?" I asked Randy. "Let's take 'em with us."

He got two Old Milwaukees, had his half-drunk before we got downstairs. Nakota, no dear, I will not let you lead, this is my dance. You made this bed, so lie in it. Buddy buddy down the hall, and my hand on the door, no flourish, it didn't need one: "After you," to Randy, and—am I smooth?—a quick step in front of Nakota, cutting in, cutting her off, I almost stepped on her. Grinning over my shoulder.

"Fuck you very much," she said, less than a whisper; I winked at her.

My beer can was empty. I tossed it in the corner, heard its faint metallic rattle, nudged Randy. "Should've brought a couple," but he wasn't listening, no, he was on his knees, humble worshiper, saying—I had to get closer to hear—"*Look* at it, man, look at it, look at it," his jacket's shoulders hunched and damp with melted snow, white hair hanging down like tattered fringe.

Me on his left, and Nakota of course between us, her face, what, peaceful? Sort of, or as peaceful as she ever got; "fulfilled" might be a better word. Bending low as if at a water hole, ignoring both of us, drinking in the smell and it was truly staggering tonight, an almost liquorish reek. Was it a taste in the mouth, for them as for me? Did they feel my rich foreboding, my sudden nervous itch?

"Look at it!"

Nakota's breath, in and out, in and out, I could see, even in the dimness, the tiny quiver of her breasts beneath the windbreaker. There was new blood at the corners of her mouth, not even dry yet.

Breath going in and out.

"Look at it."

In and out.

My hand hurting, irritating, like a beating heart, in time almost with Randy's rhythmic exclamations, shut up, I felt like shouting, shut up you stupid bastard, in and out and "*Look*" and all at once it was *funny*, funny in a way it had never been before, in fact hilarious, and beneath its influence, in a gleeful spasm of lunatic bravado I stood, flexed my knees in runner's burlesque and began to jump, fast and then faster, back and forth across the Funhole, Jack be nimble, back and forth and sweat ripe on my forehead, what fun, back and forth, "Look Ma," yelling, "no hand!" and back and forth now in slowing pirouettes and Randy's arms grabbing me, his grip on me much like mine must have felt to Nakota, her face now pointed toward me, and I saw, with a clarity that calmed me, that she was frightened.

Randy's face was blank, but his eyes were wide, so wide I saw the veins, and I laughed, a descending little chuckle because I was realizing I had just made pretty much of an inexplicable dick of myself and wanted to salvage something of it with a joke, in fact I had no idea exactly what had been so overwhelmingly funny just a minute ago.

"You were floating," Randy said.

"You should see me dance," but I saw he meant it, no metaphor, Randy would not reach for a metaphor, now would he? No. No, he would say what he saw.

"You were, you were, what's the word—"

"Levitating," Nakota said. Her voice was very dry.

"No no," weak josh, "I'm just very fast," but they weren't buying, they were barely listening, they were staring at me. Finally Randy turned to Nakota.

"You were right, Shrike," he said. "Boy were you right."

I looked at her, but she was looking at Randy, and then they both looked at me and Randy said, with a peculiar inflection, "You better lay down for a while, man. You don't look too good," and the fact was I didn't feel too good either, so back we went, me lying on the couchbed with a fresh beer balanced on my stomach, Randy beerless across from me, Nakota running tap water in fruitless hopes of making it cold.

"Just drink beer," I told her.

"What'd you *do* back there, man?" said Randy. He took a big swallow of beer. His earring jiggled. "What *was* that?"

"Nothing." I was embarrassed now, I wished they would just quit looking at me and talk to each other about the Funhole, the weather, their curious tastes in sex partners, *my* curious taste in sex partners. Anything. "I was just acting stupid, okay?"

"You were levitating, Nicholas." Nakota, sudden appearance over my head, looking as if she too had mastered the trick but no, she just took a seat on the couchbed back, looming down from there. "You were hanging in the air over the Funhole for at least thirty seconds. At least."

"Bullshit."

Randy said, "More like a couple minutes," but she shook her head, how often had I seen that dismissive shake, used exclusively when she knew she was right, absolutely knew it, and I was scared, now. Scared of the way they kept looking at me. Scared of the way I couldn't exactly remember exactly what I had done.

"You were right about him," Randy said to her. He drank off his beer, reflexively crushed the can. "Gotta take a leak," he announced, distracted politeness, shaking his head still in private wonder and moving off unerringly in the direction of the bathroom, maybe his bladder had a homing instinct. Door barely shut before I heard the vast luxurious stream, and I said quietly to Nakota, still above me like a gargoyle, "What's all this shit you fed him, about you need me for the Funhole?"

"It's true," she said.

"My ass. For God's sake, you've been coming here yourself for weeks, you know you—"

"I can come here all I want," she said, "but nothing happens."

"What do you mean, nothing happens?"

"I mean," with cold emphasis, "*nothing happens*. It just sits there. It doesn't have a smell, it doesn't—it's not *active* without you, Nicholas. You're a catalyst. You're—"

Alarmed, I tried to sit up, to speak away her words, she was scaring the shit out of me and she wouldn't stop: "Would you like to see *our* video, Nicholas? Randy's and mine? We did it with his friend's camcorder. Fifty minutes of pure static."

"Come on," grabbing at a straw, the merest twig, anything, "I wasn't even there when—"

"You got the camcorder the first time. You sat with me to watch it. You said for you it never changes, it's always the same image."

Heart beating in time and I could feel my hand itching, itching hard under the bandage. "So what?"

"So it's not like that for anyone else. Me, Randy, Vanese—"

"Who's Vanese?"

"His girlfriend. We all see something different, *all the time*. But not you."

"I don't believe you."

"I don't care." And then, leaning down so her hair brushed mine, "I didn't want you to know. Ever. I didn't even believe it myself at first until the first time I tried it alone—"

"When was this?"

"Few months ago."

"A few *months*?"

"Nothing happened. Nothing happened with Randy, either. I could bring an army in there and it wouldn't make any difference. That's the point, Nicholas. Nothing happens without you."

Randy, beer in either hand. "Here," and he even opened it for me, put it in my hand but I didn't want it, I didn't want them there, either of them, maybe Nakota most of all. I felt tired, almost sick, and I didn't want to hear any more bullshit, I just wanted to nurse my hand in silence and be left well enough alone.

"Go home," I said, closing my eyes. "Shrike. Go home, Shrike."

I heard Randy stand, heard the subtle creak of his boots. "Ask him if I can bring one," he said to Nakota, who bent to me again.

"Nicholas, Randy wants to bring one of his pieces."

Still eyes closed, "Pieces of what?"

"Sculpture, he's an artist, a metalworker. You saw his stuff at the Incubus, remember? He wants to set one up by the Funhole, is that okay?"

"Why are you asking me?" I sat up, staring at them both, the beer toppling, splashing cold against my ribs. "Why are you asking *me*? It's not mine, I'm not in charge of anything here. Do whatever you want. Just do whatever you want!"

"Listen," Nakota to Randy, gaze still on me, "we better go."

"I'll bring that piece by, man," and they left, then, finally, closing the door with an odd gentility and me left alone with my new terror, the rest of the night spent talking myself out of what Nakota had said, talking myself as far away from it as I could get.

When I woke my pillowed arm was numb, sticky-slick and, blinking, I saw my hand coated to the elbow with fluid as neat as a glove, a coy pink with tiny clots of deeper color spattered in some pattern which in my overwhelming disgust I chose not to decipher; I ran to the bathroom, literally ran, as if my arm was on fire, plunged it into the sink and turned the hot water on full blast, head averted like a fastidious driver past a smoking wreck, till I could feel the water on my plain bare skin, a plainly painful heat. I shut it off, toweled my arm, and found all of last night's beer rushing willy-nilly up my throat so, bending, I had to take care of that, too.

Wiping up, back to the couchbed and without a voluntary glance tearing off the sheet—pink, too, and wet, that much I had to see—jumbled ball and straight to the trash, no thanks, I puked once already this morning. Deeply grateful to discover it was Wednesday, my day off, my content evaporating when knock-knock at my chamber door and Randy's hesitant behemoth voice: "Hey, Nicholas? You up, man?"

Shit. If I could have broken his neck I would have, just for the pleasure of the silence after the snap. "Yeah," rubbing my frowsy face, vomit breath and less than half a phony smile. He carried something metal, silver and black and about two, two-and-a-half feet high. Looked something like a ladder as seen on the verge of a whiskey pass-out. Or maybe that was just my woozy perspective. Say what you see.

"*Dead End,*" Randy said, nodding at the metal thing, and I remembered in a halfass way the bit last night about bringing over a piece of his art, apparently this was it. Actually it was almost interesting—a ladder, yes, but crooked, twisted, the rungs less stepping spots than dirty tricks, descend at your own risk was the first-glance impression, but I was really in no mood to critique anything, so I tried to indicate this by what I was hoping was an innocuous nod. I did it a couple times for good measure. Randy didn't say anything, just stood there, so I said, with another nod, "It's really nice. Really."

"Should I just put it in there?"

"Yeah. Go ahead."

By the time he came back, I had had time to wash my face, drink some water. He stood in the doorway, shook his head to my offer of coffee. "Gotta get back to work." He was wearing the "Randy" shirt and a pair of jeans that I saw at second glance were not actually black but black with grease. "I got my truck outside." My all-purpose duh look; "Tow truck, man. All-Star Towing. My day job," and he smiled, shrugged. "Gotta eat, you know."

"Me too. Every day."

"Well. I'll see you, man. Maybe later on tonight? Shrike said something about it."

Maybe in hell, Randy, you and Shrike both. "Sure."

When he had gone I sat at the kitchen table, drinking coffee and trying again to convince myself that all Nakota had said was worse than bullshit, just her own weird little way of fucking with my brain, and Randy, why Randy was obviously suggestible. By the time I was through with my coffee, I felt much better, and after a shower I felt almost good. Out, I said to myself. Climb out of this rathole and go do something. Very cold but no wind, that kind of winter calm where every step is magnified, my friends the crows in bleak formation and me crunch, crunch, through the bitter crust beneath; it felt good to walk, hands in pockets, head down and breath leaking in thready white through my reddening nose, walking in a winter wonderland. Very few other people out. I stopped and got a newspaper, took it to a Burger King where I sat with a large coffee and read, feeling the peculiar unhappy serenity induced only by the steady perusal of disasters too remote to do anything about but feel wretched; it put all my stupid petty worries to rest. No, I am not Funhole Messiah, I just know too many weird people.

So of course I went to see Nakota.

She didn't smile when I came in, artificial dark of Club 22, some weepy fake country tune on the jukebox. But she nodded, a grave almost formal gesture, and raised an empty beer glass with another nod.

"No thanks. Just a Coke," and that was free, too.

"Randy come over yet?"

"First thing this morning."

She smiled, little snarl of amusement. "He was hot to get that piece to you, *Dead End*, right?" I nodded. "He sure was impressed with you last night. What'd he do, ask you to lay hands on it?"

"No." It *was* ludicrous, I had to smile, and her smile, her real one, joined mine, Nakota-Shrike, is there nothing you can do that I won't forgive? Please, stop trying. "I don't know about you," I said. "I just do not know."

"Know what?" Too much syrup in the Coke. Too much, suddenly, in her smile.

"I don't know why you bothered giving Randy that bullshit story. And all that about me levitating, I mean come on," but I wasn't smiling anymore and she wasn't either, her whole face so careful that I felt the fear again, rich as vomit, the flicker behind her eyes all at once the birthing flicker of the figure, the video-thing; I pushed the Coke aside. "What is it with you?" I said, leaning not forward but back, away, gibbering in me that same feeling as when I must turn away from the screen. "Why does everybody have to be as crazy as you are?"

"I'm not the crazy one, Nicholas. Or would you rather use the word 'possessed'?" I didn't answer. Tilted head, and the smile she gave when she was particularly delighted by something gone badly wrong: "You really did it, you know. Whether you believe it or not."

"You," my shaken whisper, "are out of your fucking mind. Leave me alone, all right? Just leave me alone," sliding off the stool, pushing out into the ice and dazzle of the afternoon, skittering on the sidewalk but not falling, no, maybe I could just fly home. Stop it, are you going to go to her for sanity, she's crazy as a shithouse rat and always has been. Stop it. I leaned against a newspaper box, a pain in my chest, the cold air too cold in my lungs. I was three blocks east before I remembered my car.

Barely working the key, the engine whispered several times before finally starting, maybe I could call my good buddy Randy for a tow. My right hand, my "bad" hand, curled in my lap like a dying pet, all at once an ache unbearable, like a burn, a fresh and agonizing burn and I ripped the bandage away, to do what, don't know; staring, I sat there, watched as a structure of crystals as fine as beach sand grew of its own accord from the wound, minute ziggurat that filled up like a beaker with blood, my blood, and suddenly I began to scream, a soundless and infinite howl as I beat my hand, whipped it over and over against the steering wheel, again and again until the muscles of my arm tightened with exhaustion's heat and I let my arm, my hand fall limp to the seat; it had absolutely no feeling at all, not least in the wound, and I was glad. Crying and glad and I drove home one-handed, went upstairs, wrapped the whole thing in a towel and sat to watch the news, drinking a crusty glass of ancient Tang scrapings. By the time the weather came on I had stopped crying.

Why, though, didn't it hurt?

I had hit it hard enough to break bones, certainly I had tried my best. But there was no pain.

Look at it.

No.

Go on. Look at it.

No.

Conscience, arguing for or against? Curiosity is a horrible thing. I pulled off the towel all at once, one big scared conjurer's whoosh, and there, ladies and gentlemen, is the rabbit in the hat, is

a hand, perfectly normal and uninjured, with a hole in the palm the size of a quarter and black as its big-daddy namesake, for God's sake say it out loud you've got a goddamn Funhole of your own growing right out of your body yes you do oh yes you do

and that's *why*

and in my panic I found myself walking, back and forth, holding my arm at a ridiculous stiff angle, keep that thing away from me and back and forth before the windows, I must have been going for quite a while because the news was long over and a sitcom was on. Laughter. A commercial for an airline. Pet food. At least put a bandage on the fucking thing, that way you won't have to look at it. if I can't see you, Mr. Hole, you're not really there.

But at least it was constructive action, at least it wasn't pacing like a psychotic rat, and at least I didn't have to look at it anymore. It was hard to do, I was shaking pretty much all over, and when I heard knocking for a minute thought, auditory hallucinations. Then: no, stupid, it's just your new disciple. And that made me laugh, and got me to the door.

He had beer, good beer for a change, and he was alone. No grinning bitch in tow to mock my festering disintegration, to remind me by her crooked shine of everything I wanted most not to know, and that in itself was worth the price of admission. Plus now I didn't have to sit alone thinking crazy thoughts.

"Sit down," I said.

"Cold fuckin' weather," he said.

The weather. We talked about it, he told me what a bitch of a day he'd had, every car battery in town must have gone dead overnight, one call after another. He wasn't Aristotle but he was a live human being and he could tell a decent story and pretty soon we had the stereo on and he was telling me about his art.

"Seems weird, you know, I always hated art class in school, bunch of shit. But I love working on my sculpture. I've shown 'em, some of them, at the Incubus. You been there, right?"

Killer clowns, and a pocketful of bugs, those were the days. "Couple times."

"Yeah, well, it's not much of a place but it's a start, right? It's not like I'm actually makin' any money," and he smiled, a surprisingly shy smile. Drank more beer. "I wouldn't be driving a tow truck, you know, if I was."

"Well, I don't work at Video Hut for the intellectual stimulation either."

Dead End was one of a series, he told me, some of the pieces incorporating more than metal—"One's got a skull," *Dead Set* and a hairless headful of curlers, of course—and *Dead Reckoning*, that was a metal eyeball attached to a telescope; I didn't have the heart, or the balls, to bring up the fact that dead reckoning meant navigation precisely without the use of a telescope or any other device. Call it artistic license.

"*Dead Dipping*, that's got an acid beaker, it's a kind of process, right, and this new one, *Dead End*, it's like a ladder, it's like all the way to the bottom—"

"I noticed that." My voice was pleasantly slurred from Randy's good beer. I liked Randy and his good beer too, I liked the way they both distracted me from things I would rather not have to think about. liked the way I was getting empty-stomach gutfuck drunk on Randy's good beer, as far as I was concerned he could talk about his art all night long if he had a mind to and even if he didn't I did.

All the sitcoms were gone and so was the news and so was everything else, some kind of cut-up movie buzzing on the TV and Randy's beer was also gone and he was standing up, in fact two of him were standing, saying something about going out to get more. And I was agreeing that this was a fine idea, and there we were, on the stairway.

And there we were going the wrong way, going down the hall instead of down the stairs, and a very small part of me was banging its head in frustration and terror against the furry walls of my great and perfect drunkenness, and we were shushing each other like giggling idiots, which in fact we were and wasn't it *fine*, though, wasn't it *fun*? And my unsore hand, my good bad hand, on the doorknob, and inside the sweetest smell in the world, a siren smell like heaven and beer and open pussy and summer all the time and Randy beside me, did he smell it too, saying something and I nodded at him, yes, yes, working at my bandages and I couldn't quite get them off, the tape snarling on the gauze and it was pissing me *off* so I ripped and worried them with my teeth, spit them down and off, oh what a kind relief and I stuck my hand down the Funhole just as far as it could go, as deep as it could get, down that sweet-smelling friendly hole and did it feel *good*? Oh God you know it did. And I wiggled it around, yeah, and I didn't really feel anything because *it* was feeling *me* and it was a wonderful thing, I couldn't imagine why I'd been so scared before, it was just what was meant to happen, what wanted to be.

"—*please*—"

Not my voice, no. Was there someone here with me?

"—*on*, man, listen to me, you got—"

Oh my yes, Randy, my good friend Randy, and we'd come here for him, hadn't we? Yes. Yes, don't be selfish, at least listen to what the poor son of a bitch is saying and boy is he sweating, is it hot in here or something?

"—*Dead End.*" Yes indeed this boy was *sweating.* "Look at it, man!"

He sure likes to call me man, doesn't he, and the idea made me smile, a lazy smile and I turned my head but it was sort of hard to see so instead I turned my body, slow one-eighty rotation and my arm was the axle, the dear hole the fixed point around which I spun, feet in the air and graceful as a swimmer and sure enough, Randy's sculpture was doing something very *strange.* No wonder he looked so scared.

"Is it melting?" I asked.

"Don't touch it anymore, okay, Nicholas?"

"I'm sorry," I said, and I was. "Did I break it or something?"

"No." Everything about him was shaking. Even his voice. "But every time you touch it, part of it—melts, okay? So don't touch it anymore."

He was right, I saw that he was right: where my hand had presumably been, on the crooked metal rungs, were somehow indentations, melted to resemble the footsteps of something very strange indeed. And down its length, he must see it too, that greasy nacreous shine, that signature video light. What next, the figure itself? Climbing?

"Nicholas?"

"All right," I said—I was nothing if not agreeable—but all at once I started to feel very weird and I realized it was the beer, it was being so drunk, I was going to throw up and for some reason this struck me as hilarious. Pukin' down the Funhole. Even Nakota couldn't match that. But if I did then I would have to throw up on my own arm and I didn't really want to do that, so I reached out my free hand to Randy and asked in my agreeable voice, "Would you please pull me the fuck out of here? Because I think I'm gonna barf."

I did, too. It was amazing.

Alone.

Cold.

On the bathroom floor, my head very near the toilet bolt, its rusty crusted sharpness pressing with a kiss's delicacy against my left ear. All of me aching but in particular my right arm, my nose full of snot and all the light in the room wrong, somehow, too bright and too pale.

Why was I lying on the bathroom floor?

The memory did not come in pieces but all at once, and when it did I retched, sorry little sound, there was nothing left in me to void. More than anything I did not want to look at my hand, no, I don't think I can do that. No.

"Nicholas."

She scared me so much I whacked my head against the toilet, she was the last person I wanted to see, I was so glad she was there. She squatted, tilting her head, and reached to gently turn my face toward her.

"Big night last night," she said.

Tears. Isn't that just what you would expect from a fucking self-destructive self-pitying derelict and she was getting them, I wept as I rose from floor to knees to standing slouch, she tried to lead me to the other room but I resisted. Hot water, rub the whole bar of soap on my face, hold it with your left hand if you please, please. "Randy called me. He was here till about six, six-thirty, he would've stayed longer but he had to get to work. He said—"

Palm up, left palm: the universal gesture for "save it." She left me there to wash, and I scrubbed at my face. *God* how I hated myself. Look in the mirror, you dumbshit.

I looked at my hand.

Half-dollar hole. At least.

There are no words to tell how I felt at that particular moment. I used up the rest of the gauze, quick and clumsy, found Nakota making instant coffee. She stopped to watch as I dressed, goose bumps and my cold legs stepping like a nervous dance, and then she was beside me, motioning my clothing away and down, unbuttoning with sure fingers her own baggy dress.

Warm skin beneath the comforter and the heating motions of her flesh, lips against my throat, teeth tugging at the hair on my chest, nipping a line down my belly and then taking me, still half-soft, into her ovaled mouth. I rubbed with one tender fingertip the skin around her lips, my eyes closing in pleasure and dumb-animal relief, and held her head against me gently, gently till I came. In silence then I lay beside her as she used my left hand, my thumb, to come herself, then lay in that silence with me, her head almost on my shoulder.

Finally into my near-placid near sleep, her insectile voice: "Randy said you melted his sculpture."

I didn't answer.

"It's steel, Nicholas. Do you know what the melting point of steel is?"

Wearily, I knew what was coming: "No, Mrs. Science, but I bet you do."

"Three thousand degrees Fahrenheit. Give or take a degree."

Well.

"He said you levitated again. With your arm in the Funhole."

I didn't speak. I had nothing to say. "Nicholas," urgent, sitting up, and I saw the cold wash stippling down her skin, she didn't notice, "there's something so *big* happening to you, why do you have to get fucked up to let it happen? I wish it was me," and that, of course, was the whole camp follower's crux. Which made everything she said suspect, not that it wasn't suspect enough, but then again at least she wasn't running screaming away from the freak I was becoming, at least she could still blow me for old time's sake or whyever the hell she did it. Not love. Probably wanted to suck off the hole in my hand but was too shy to ask.

"*I'd* know what to do with it."

Ah, God. And I had almost gone in headfirst to save her. I put my right hand deliberately on her face, squeezed with my painful fingertips her bony cat's chin.

"I don't want any of this to be happening," I said.

"It's a little late for that."

"I want it," as deliberately, "to go away."

"The Funhole's not going anywhere," and the way she said it, the calm gloat of her gaze, gave me an intense urge to smash her face straight through to the back of her skull and horrified, I almost jumped out of bed, somehow *feeling* the way her skin would split, her caving nose and lips blown back by the force of my fist, my right fist. "Leave it alone," I said. My voice was shaking.

"You can—"

"I said leave it alone!" and without wanting or meaning to I had her by the hair, pulling her face close to mine like a caricature of a bully, "Leave it alone!" and I watched her face go careful and blank and I cried out, wrapped both arms around her and held her tight, *tight*, saying over and over into her hair, "I don't want to go crazy, I don't *want* to go crazy, Nakota. I *don't*."

"You're not," she said. "This is really happening."

Of course Randy had his own interpretation of the whole circus, none of which I was interested in hearing, but there he was at quitting time, tow truck idling as I counted out my drawer, his whole manner so eerily respectful that seeing him was worse than listening to Nakota's coldhearted rant. He stood, one arm on the counter, the other jingling his keys. Blink, blink, those pale gray eyes.

"Sorry I had to leave the other morning, man."

"No problem."

"I had to get to work, you know? Otherwise—"

"Randy, really, it's no problem." I lost my place and had to start counting again, out loud, keep your conversation to yourself. Patient, yeah, with my impatience, waiting me out.

"Hey listen," hulking diffidence, "you doin' anything tonight?"

"No, and I don't really feel like doing anything either, Randy, all right?" Suddenly I was angry, mad enough to show it. Sorry We're Closed, no sideshow tonight. "I feel like shit and my fucking hand hurts and all I want to do is go home and take a shit and go to bed, okay? Is that okay with you?"

In the following silence my anger shriveled. I looked away, out the window into the ten o'clock dark, shifting wind but not as black as it gets, no. He pulled you out of the Funhole, you dumb ungrateful piece of shit, remember? Sat by you and watched you puke. Talk about only a mother.

"Hey." I turned back, wanted to put out my hand but, embarrassed, couldn't decide which one—there's a unique dilemma for you—and settled for a stupid shrug. "I'm, I'm just—shook-up. If you want to stop by later, come on ahead."

"No big deal," he said. No smile, but not pissed either. "I wanted to check on *Dead End* mostly."

Oh yes, that's right, the art they said I melted. By my fiery touch. *Shit.* "Sure." I felt so incredibly tired all of a sudden. "Listen, I don't mean to be a prick. I just—"

"Don't worry about it," with a great and sudden gravity. "If all this shit was happening to me, I'd be plenty worried about it too."

Whatever else he said lost me, but those words went all the way home, in the flat and sitting in the dark and thinking, thinking. Worried, yeah. A simple idea but a good one. I thought of myself weeping to Nakota, loose-mouthed and sloppy and sick looking, and I was swept with a feeling of self-disgust so intense that I had to leave my chair, stand and pace it away, away.

But it wouldn't go away.

So I did.

FOUR

She owed me a favor, this woman, I had almost forgotten her name but I still had her phone number. We had lived in the same building once, years ago, never lovers but fairly good friends; she liked to go to movies and drink beer and in those days I liked to do those things too, so we got along pretty well. I had once loaned her money to get her car out of a police pound; whether she had paid me back or not was a moot point. On the phone her voice was friendly but not too, which was exactly what I wanted.

"Can I stay at your place for a little while?" I said. I had the bottom of the phone balanced against my hip, at my feet half a ripped gym bag already packed, I was that sure.

"How long," Nora, her name was Nora, "did you want to stay?"

"Not long. Week, maybe."

"Still remember how to get here?"

"Better give me directions."

My car was making a fairly suspicious coughing sound—I don't know shit about cars, so every unknown sound it ever made had the power to spook me—but it was a clear night, extremely cold, and I was making pretty good time away from the city; maybe I could get to Nora's before it died.

She lived out past the 'burbs, not real country, or "rural" as Nakota always called it in her sneering way, but far enough so there was a kind of space around things; that was what I was hunting. Get far enough away from everything and maybe I could get away from myself, too. Maybe. Because otherwise there would have to be another kind of running, yeah; don't think about it now. Windshield wipers, monotonous back-and-forth, my radio the victim of random static. Driving through an immense quiet. Just don't think about it now.

I had left a note for Randy stuck in my door, advising him that Nakota, Shrike had a key, and at any rate the other door was always open, the Funhole was nothing if not twenty-four hours. "Good luck with your art," I had added at the bottom, then felt silly, but I didn't have time to write another note, so I left it there. I didn't add anything for Nakota.

The drive took a little over two hours, the last ten minutes puzzling out my way; Nora's directions were spotty and memory was worse, but I saw a place I did remember, kind of a makeshift rifle-and-archery range, the pale circles of the targets visible in my headlights as I slowly made the turn; this is the place, yeah. Great huge heaps of snow, skinny long driveway one car wide. Her house was still that same babyshit-yellow color. The porchlight was on; it was yellow too.

Nora opened the door for me before I knocked. She was a little, what, not fatter but rounder, her belly a soft small pouch, her long hair short now, little yellow fringe around her rounder face. We didn't bug hello, but her handshake was two-handed, warm fingers in my cold touch.

"Nicholas. How're you doing?" stepping back as I shed my coat, politely stamped my snowless feet. "You want anything? Coffee?"

The coffee was much too strong. The light in the kitchen was too bright. Apparently I would be dealing in absolutes here; the idea made me smile. "That's better," Nora said. "You look almost alive now."

That surprised me into a laugh, and she laughed, too, but not a real one; she would be wanting, of course, to know what the hell I was doing here, and once she found that out to her satisfaction, then maybe she could laugh. I had no intention of telling her the whole truth or even a major part of it, but I had to tell her something.

"I had a big fight with Nakota," I said.

The magic words. Her mouth pulled into a line that was absolutely flat, as flat as her voice saying, "Ah." She had known Nakota as long as

I had and hated her, why I wasn't sure, with Nakota there were endless reasons. Nakota, so far as I knew, had no real idea that Nora existed. "Well."

"Yeah, well."

"You're still seeing her, then, aren't you."

"Not tonight."

Now: a real laugh. She had a weird almost silent way of laughing, it defined her again at once for me, brought all of her back. She pushed her spiny chair back from the table, almost soundless against the old red linoleum, put more coffee in our cups. "God, what a bitch she is," comfortably. "Her real name's Jane, you knew that, didn't you."

My hand awkward on the cup, saying almost nothing as she talked, caught me up with what she was doing: quit her job at the hospital, working the graveyard shift at a nursing home, Sunny Days, "Can you imagine? *what* a name," lots of work to do around the house when she had the time—she was putting in a vegetable garden next spring, big one—and skiing too, cross-country, there was always time for that.

"So you don't see many movies anymore, huh?"

"No, I sure don't." I'd seen her looking, and now she asked: "What happened to your hand?"

"Accident," I said, letting my gaze move sadly away from hers, which wasn't hard; she took it the way I'd wanted her to, wrong, and said no more about it. I have always depended upon the tact of others, uh-huh.

Turned out she would be leaving in the morning, early, to do some skiing with friends. I imagined her friends: blond, bluff looking, jeans and down vests in sensible colors, yelling to each other over swipes and passes of clean snow. It was like a cockroach dreaming of the smell of disinfectant. She kept talking but all at once I found I was waking from a doze, she was taking the coffee cup from my hand.

"Nicholas, hey, you fell asleep." Before I could say anything, "Don't worry about it, long day, long drive. My fault for keeping you up talking. I'm sorry I don't have a bed for you, but the couchbed isn't too bad. Probably," pulling down the blanket, bilious print and warm looking, "you won't be up when I leave, so help yourself to whatever you want, food, whatever; there's some stuff in the freezer too. There's a spare backdoor key hanging right by the door, so you can get in and out." There may have been more but I heard none of it, slept instead in a circle of dreams, none of it restful, none of them kind.

The quiet of the morning woke me; at home there was always some kind of traffic, day and night background. No snow falling, but a kind of overcast that might linger all day, same dour gray into the night. Into the kitchen, the warmest room in the house. It must cost a shitload to heat a house this big, no wonder she kept it cold. My hand throbbed as I made coffee, pouring water and my motions slow, sliced an orange. The acid of the juice found a sore on my tongue.

As I ate, slowly, like a convalescent, like one of Nora's patients at Sunny Days, I thought of all the things I had avoided during my poet days at school and beyond, days of waking late and drinking early, wandering through life with my one constant a constant shrug: regular jobs and regular people and regular hours, all the commonplace pains and terrors that, by fleeing, I had somehow replaced with these others, this whole grotesquerie that was—yeah, c'mon, say it out loud, there's no one here to hear you—driving me out of my mind. Driving me crazy. Because I had no way to cope with it, no way to understand why what had begun as ignorant dabbling had evolved into all this.

What had I done wrong?

What had I wanted that made this happen? Nakota's taunts and Randy's silent doggish respect, the bugs in the jar with runic wings, the video and its glimpsed emissary figure, the hole in my hand, the void in my head that led me into this, now there was a real Funhole, where the darkness came in. Was the darkness always there? Was all it needed to infiltrate a lack of determination to keep it out? and had I really done all this to myself, by myself, by being the little I was?

I was so *tired* of hating myself. But I was so good at it, it was such a comfortable way to be, goddamn fucking flotsam on the high seas, the low tide, a little wad of nothing shrugging and saying Hey, sorry, I didn't mean it, I didn't know it was loaded, I didn't think things would turn out this way. It's so easy to be nothing. It requires very little thought or afterthought, you can always find people to drink with you, hang out with you, everybody needs a little nothing in their life, right? Call the specialist when you do. You don't even have to call, chances are I'll already be there, you've just overlooked me because I'm in a corner, crouched like a dustball, a cobweb, my busy little spaced-out grin and oops it seems I've stumbled on some sort of exalted hellhole, Funhole, do excuse me while I let it out, while I let it into my body, while I let it run my life because *somebody* has to, right? somebody has to take the goddamned brunt even if it's a void.

Even if it's chosen me.

Because how bad can it be, right, if it wants *me*, how dangerous? If it will settle for a tool this poor HOW BAD CAN IT BE.

"God," thick mucus voice and tears running out of my eyes, "oh God," and I wept into a paper towel, crying hard in the kitchen's warmth, my body half-folded against the table, retching sobs like vomit. I cried a long time, past pain until I felt so empty nothing hurt, nothing anywhere, if I had died I could not have felt more husked. A walking depletion. "Aren't you the poet," I said out loud, my voice a hush in the larger silence, and I wiped at my eyes, then almost smiled, weary, when it hurt: orange juice in my eyes, burning like gasoline. You dickhead.

After eating I went slowly back to the couchbed, more comfortable than mine at home and larger, the blankets certainly cleaner. Nesting there with my right hand on my chest, its returning pain a pulse so metronomic that for whole moments I did not even feel it, instead only the sensation of great emptiness, as pleasant in its way as the bare cessation of pain after a protracted illness. Asleep again, till the place where I lay woke me with its warmth, the strong slant of the afternoon sun pointing straight at me, on me. I lay there, completely empty, in the sunlight. When the sun went down I got up to piss, drink water, back to the nest. I felt I could spend my life there, or die there, it made no difference really. Typical, I thought to myself, of myself, but even the hatred was gone, washed out maybe by the force of its own corrosion, replaced by the great nothing, a void far deeper than any Funhole could ever be.

I lay there for three days.

I got up once in a while to piss, the intervals lengthening as the hours passed, dark or light in the hallway and me trudging back to my nest, my chrysalis, that sense of emptiness filling, little by little, with a certainty, a necessary idea of what fulfillment, for me, might be. What to do. What do you need. I asked myself, and the answer came, filtering through my weakness, perhaps even enhanced by it. What do you want?

Dreams. Out of focus, surreal in their ferocity, blunt contrast to my daytimes of staring up at the ceiling, at my leaky hand, at the pale water stains and minute drifts of dust in the corners of the room. One dream in particular, its edges blurry-bright, one long stretched face like a frame around my terror, a frame from the video as if I lay behind its very eyes, the eyes of that animate nothingness, woke me weeping, left me so wet with sweat I thought for one half-conscious moment that I had either pissed the bed or died bleeding; night sweats, that was called. Evidence of extreme weakness. As if I needed any.

The next morning I woke to see my right hand twitching slowly and violently, like a large and dying insect, floundering hard against the flat pillow without producing any sort of feeling in my flesh. It was like watching yourself in someone else's dream, so incredibly bizarre that it was almost entertaining; I was very much past giving any kind of a shit so I watched it, wondering if some weird necrosis was taking place, my hand cut off, so to speak, from its fathering Funhole and dying as a result. "My hand and my dead hand," I said out loud, and while it flopped and twisted I sat watching, smile turned to grin, found I even had a hard-on and grinned at that too.

My hand stopped, and I laughed, a little dying cough, the way you finish laughing, in stages, at one hell of a joke. I used that hand to dial the phone, ignoring the immediate and surprising pain this caused, forcing my finger into the retro rotary dial to call work and tell them I wouldn't be coming in anymore. This was no secret; in fact they wanted very much to tell me first. My last check was in the mail, the manager said, sounding pleased.

"And you won't come in my mouth, right?"

She didn't get it. I hung up and went into the kitchen, sat in my underwear eating Cheerios out of the box; they were very stale, almost like Styrofoam or rice cakes, apparently Nora didn't like Cheerios very much. Still in my underwear, my mouth full of half-chewed Cheerios,

I began to search the house for the .22 I knew Nora had, she used it for target shooting, well I had a target in mind.

It wasn't hard to find, either, just where you'd expect: under her bed, plastic box of bullets beside. A neat bedroom, tidy little piles of paperbacks and sweaters, above her bed a shitty-looking plaque, obviously handmade, its burned-in sentiment peculiarly appropriate to my mood and mission: "When Life Gives You Lemons, Make Lemonade." Well, life had given me shit, and I was making a compost heap. Or more succinctly, life had given me a Funhole, and I was making a grave.

It took me a few minutes to figure out how to load it, I'd never loaded a gun in my life. Few more minutes to position myself at the end of her bed. Eyes open, or closed? Death's etiquette. Let's try not to screw this one up, shall we? And I felt not even happy or good but at least not bad and that was surely more than enough and certainly much better than I deserved.

Open your mouth, I said to myself.

The tip of the barrel lay on my tongue, holy metal. The light in the room was exceptionally bright, even on my closed lids. Maybe, I thought, this is what people say car wrecks are like, even to swallow seemed to take forever. My mouth was full of saliva, my heart all at once beating fast and light.

I remember thinking, Why, I've made a choice. I don't want to be part of this anymore, and I'm, I'm opting out. Imagine. An actual decision, and I was very much enjoying my novel sense of resolve and picturing, in a self-indulgent way, the manner in which the bullet would come flying up the barrel, when something new came to me: shame.

Not disgust. I was intimate with that. Not self-hate either because I was, if not done with it, then so possessed by it that I could no longer feel it, as a perfect swimmer no longer consciously feels the sea as an element apart. But: instead a profound and simple shame, a sensation as immediate and irresistible as pain or heat. In my big, my unique moment of decision I was behaving as needlessly as stupidly, as *typically* as ever, because by this action I would bring trouble on Nora, big trouble, on a person who had actually tried to help me, who had given me what I asked for.

Typical.

I lowered the gun.

That's just like you, you cheap piece of shit.

But not the shame.

And not the action prompted by the shame, either.

I put the gun away. I went downstairs and cleaned the kitchen, the cereal and yesterday's dried orange rinds and slightly smelly coffeemaker, thinking all the while. Another novelty. Not running from the bad feeling, not avoiding this new shame. Feeling it, as deeply as I felt the fresh pain in my hand, the victorious ache. In the glare of the shame I saw that if I must be myself, if there was no changing the aimless scramble that was me, if I must be in the end a victim, then: yes.

But not this way. Not at another's expense, or at least not an innocent other. Because that was mutable.

But then why not jump off a bridge? An empty bridge, no one around for miles? Why not find a broken bottle and an alley, cut my wrists with one and bleed to death in the other? It's not that simple, is it, all this selfless shit is just too much to swallow, come on now there's no one here but me and my new insight, leaning against the kitchen counter, almost sick, now, with the ugly clarity, this breakthrough pocket of pus and deceit, no more of this shit that it's Nora, don't pull your shit on me.

What do I want. I thought. Transformation? *Do* I want, at all?

And knew that what I most wanted was not to know. Wanted instead to be ridden, not mindless but adrift, still, in the eddies of my helplessness, there is such *peace* in helplessness, it's better than death any day, you're still able to enjoy the ride. It had nothing to do with anyone else, not even Nakota, maybe, though as nothing as I was, I knew I loved her, that much was no shame. But. She said it didn't work without me, and without wanting to I believed her, finally, without beginning to understand why this should be so. But. If I really loved her, if it really was quiescent without me, why not then stay away for good, let it shrivel or bloom as it would without my presence?

But you know the answer to that, I thought, don't you.

Because in the end we are what we are, we want what we want, whether we know it or not. Whether we care to resist or not, or whether in the end it's worth resistance after all.

And the bubble and shine of the air in the kitchen, as if a faint was in the offing, well why not then, why not? and a rich ache slicing up the path of my arm, to my throat, to my stupid head, a claiming pain that said, Why don't fret, you've made the *right* choice, you've done the *right* deed. Ah, God, I thought, pushing by main force away from the counter, pain, sick stomach and all, Funhole imprimatur, sanctified by the weirdest thing in the world. St. Nicholas, but don't expect any presents from me.

After the kitchen, the living room, spartan movements as my nest disappeared into a green plaid couch and a folded blanket. Shaving, my hands all one tremble, doing it slow. Showering, using Nora's gooey shampoo. Dressing. I put all my things away in my gym bag. I wrote Nora a note, thanking her, saying I was sorry I had to leave before she returned, saying I would call her sometime soon and we would talk. This last I knew was not true, but it was kindly so I said it anyway. I didn't want her to think I had used her simply for a hidey-hole, even though I had, wringing, the last dry drop of juice from an old, old favor, one she had repaid as a matter of course. Of course.

It was extremely cold outside, much colder than it looked, not brittle to the eye but lush, the slopes and gullies of slickly crusted snow. It took me a long time to scrape my windows, slow even back-and-forth motions, the frost and ice curling away from my cracked yellow scraper in neat little half circles. I stopped to get gas, using almost the last of my money to do so. A handful of change to make a phone call, standing shoulders hunched against the cold, my breath frosting the mouthpiece. Five rings. I counted each.

"Mhhh. Hello."

"Hey."

"Who's this? Is, Nicholas, is that you?"

More wide-awake by the minute, Nakota's voice sharpening, I could so easily hear her frown. "Where are you?" she said, and I said, "Be at my place in about three hours."

And hung up.

And got there in two.

My usual space in the parking lot, feeling not light-headed but something kin to it, walking up the stairs and seeing the tiny clouds of breath, my place would probably be a freezer. And it was. A dirty freezer. I threw a lot of stuff away, sweeping my arm across surfaces in a motion that any other time would have felt embarrassingly theatrical, but now, oh, after a two-hour drive in cold and total silence, thinking all the while, all my thoughts were gone, used up, burned up by the cold and I knew what I was doing, yes, or at least acted as if I did. For once.

I felt the Funhole as soon as I walked in the building, as I moved around my flat, felt it moving in me as a reptile, a snake, maybe, feels the motion of its coils, and was no longer disturbed by it, no. No. I had made one sharp decision, gone consciously back on it, and now the other resolution, made in the shadow of the first's decline, the mindless false Zen of to-know-and-not-to-know, was so strong in me it required no thinking, required very little in fact. Perhaps this was in keeping with my basic nature, somewhere in the neighborhood of a plant, say, or an animate napkin, yeah. I couldn't even insult myself anymore. I didn't care. It didn't matter. I felt like I was breathing methane, as if the cold was a living fire in my eyes. All the way home I had watched my hand, my naked bandageless hand, quick glances to see it independently twitch and shudder on the cold seat beside me, my dark stigmata very visible in the clear, clear light; any other time it might have scared me, scared me bad. But not today.

It was barely three hours when I heard her, cautious down the hall. Whom were you expecting, dear, Jekyll or Hyde but the joke's on you this time. The joke's on you because it's neither, it's someone different, it's someone you don't even know. I opened the door as Nora had, before she even knocked.

"Nicholas." All in baggy black, extreme thrift-shop raggishness even for her. Wearing her windbreaker in this intense cold. She smiled, it was a real smile. Naturally. I had gone off with the keys to the toy box, and now I was back.

"I have to do something," I said. "I need you to help me."

"What kind of help?" Eagerly. *Eagerly*, picture that. Was I angry at her? No. Yes. You want me to be a fool, the Funhole's conduit, clown prince? I can't be anything, now, other than this one thing, and if you'll hold on just a minute, I'll show you what it is.

"I want you to move in here," I said. She opened her mouth to speak but I cut her off. "I don't care where you sleep," which right now was true, maybe I never would care, I didn't know; all I knew was now. "I don't care about anything except having this flat paid for, which I can't do because I lost my job."

"You—"

"I want you to move in as soon as you can. If you can't afford it, get Randy in here too."

"He lives with Vanese."

Vanese. Oh yeah, the girlfriend. "Fine. Get her too. Cheaper by the dozen."

"Nicholas, are you sick or something? Did—"

"Be in here by the end of the week at the latest. What is it, Tuesday? That gives you three days. You don't have much stuff, you can do it."

"*Nicholas.*" Insistent tone, her hand on my arm more tentative. "Is something wrong?"

"I tried to kill myself," I said, and flicked off her touch; still, a tremor. "It worked."

The Funhole. Roiling, and in the swallowed glimpse behind my eyes, a foreign smile in my personal darkness, a figure. Welcome home.

It took her less than two days to get her stuff in, and I was right, there wasn't much. Cartons of books mostly, some crummy clothes, a plastic sack of toiletries. A twin bed with a mattress so fragmenting and decayed I took one look and refused to let her bring it in.

"What am I supposed to sleep on, then?"

"The springs. The floor. Out in the hall if you want." I stood arms crossed, looking at her as she stared warily back at me. She was not the type to blossom under hard treatment, under any other circumstances she would have told me without preamble to go fuck myself, but there was something manifestly afoot and she definitely wanted all the way in. I knew she thought that my stark change in behavior meant I had finally gone straight over the edge; whether she believed me about the suicide attempt I didn't know. I knew what I knew and I was done puzzling, I was done with a lot of things now.

An immobile day, that long cold Friday. No food, I didn't feel like eating, as if my sense of purpose could only be nurtured and sustained by physical emptiness. I sat in my chair by the window, left hand cradling right, watching what went on down below, people driving and walking in the worsening weather, the spattering of snow now the first breath of a real storm, it was going to be bad, they kept talking about it on the radio. Six to eight inches, they said. Maybe more.

Nakota kept the radio on, kept prowling the flat, waiting for what? Directions? A sermon? A quickie fuck? I hadn't touched her since I'd been back, hadn't felt like it, though there was a part of me that would have been extremely pleased just to hold that skinny body, hummingbird heartbeat against my chest, faint whiff of cigarette breath in the air before my face. But I made no move toward her. Another appetite blunted. I didn't talk much either. Every once in a while I'd look up and catch her looking at me, head faintly tilted, understanding nothing. There was no way she could know what I was thinking.

"Don't look at me," I said once.

She ignored me, but there was something, then, in her glance that I didn't like. If she was going to start respecting me, she had picked one hell of a time. The idea was almost funny but I wasn't in a real laughing mood.

About six-thirty, the flat dark, only the green radio light: "Is Randy coming?" I asked her. Outside white sky, a downpour of snow. When she answered, her voice startled me; she was much closer to me than I'd imagined, sitting close enough to touch.

"Him and Vanese," she said.

"The more the merrier." I had a weird urge to smoke. "You got a cigarette?" and she lit one for me, passed it to me, her fingers careful not to touch mine. I hadn't smoked in so long I hit the cigarette like a joint: horrible sensation, that hot dry feeling in my chest. The nicotine made me dizzy. I blew smoke in the air and couldn't see it because of the dark, tried to feel it with my fingers. I blew smoke on the hole in my hand and felt nothing.

"Nicholas?"

"What?"

"What's going to happen? I mean, what're you going to do?"

"Throw you headfirst down the fucking Funhole. Shut up, Nakota."

Although I didn't feel particularly angry when I said it.

It was nearly seven-thirty when they knocked: I heard Randy's voice, a lighter voice murmuring behind. Nakota leaped up as if the room was on fire. She'd been waiting, patience steadily withering, for them to come—she never could stand waiting for anything—convinced their arrival heralded the Main Event. Which was quite correct. She literally banged the door open.

"Took your sweet time about it, asshole," she said, very bitchily, she'd been saving it up for days. Had to unload it on somebody since I was temporarily off limits.

"Hey, it's a fucking blizzard out there, okay?" Randy in the doorway, tentative: "Can you put a light on or something, man? It's darker than shit in here." And behind him, the source of that lighter voice, standing silent; and her silhouette as thin and insubstantial as paper, a cutout doll.

"Do what you want," I said.

They came in, hooded eyes blinking in the changing light, Nakota refusing to move for the woman, they pushed shoulders, the kind of juvenile territory shit I thought only men fell for. Apparently not.

"You the guru?" the woman said to me,

Vanese, coming closer, wary highstep, the moves of a person who can cut out in a hurry. Hands in cheap leather slash pockets. Big carved cheekbones, big red plastic earrings. Biggest of all were her eyes, deeper brown than her skin, that same wariness clear in their darkness. "If this's as weird as Randy says, I don't know."

"It is," I said. "And I don't know either. You staying?"

"Yeah," from Randy. Her shrug. "I guess."

"I got your note," Randy said. "Shrike said something, you quit your job?"

"Yeah." I looked at him, at Vanese, fingers moving in her pockets, picking at something, a cuticle, a sore. Longest at Nakota, scarecrow, my heart's desire still. Leeched by the force of the days past and to come, pilloried, walled up but still: desire. Who can fathom that, deeper than change, deeper than the Funhole maybe. "Come on," I said, looking only at her. "You wanna see something, you're gonna see it."

Down the hall, our little band of pilgrims, refugees before the fact. Vanese tried to ask me something but Nakota shushed her so violently that she subsided, though not without a glare. I could feel something, not pain, in my hand, a sensation like pins and needles but less distinct, a buzzing in the flesh. It was that hand I put to the door, and when my careful palm touched the knob I felt not a jolt, as I'd somehow halfass expected—too many horror movies. But the buzzing—now a flicker, like fire in my skin, as if you could feel a burn without the pain, as if your flesh could melt on the bones. Like wax. Like steel.

The room was cold. Why not: everything else was, the hall was ridiculous, but it was still somehow a surprise. I hadn't been in there since that night with Randy. Days. Randy's sculpture, to which he scurried as soon as I got out of his way, was unchanged, or at least I saw no difference. Vanese took a place by the door; still careful, but her gaze went back and forth, the Funhole and me and Randy and Nakota and back to the Funhole again. Nakota ignored everything, knelt beside me where I stood, at the lip of the void. Her hands lay palms-up on her thighs. Maybe she wanted a hole, too, just like mine.

I felt so good.

It was not a sensation I associated with the spot where I stood. Empty, all of me, even of breath for I let it dribble out as I got to my knees beside Nakota, worshipful posture but I didn't feel worshipful, no, that wasn't the point at all. Never had been. Emptiness. Yes. Because that's what the Funhole was, wasn't it, that was the key and clue: a negativity, an absence, a *lack*. A depression, that's what a hole was, no matter how dark and lively, no matter how ultimately full. Even an empty road leads somewhere, right?

But this time, feel it.

"Watch me," I said, aloud but only, really, to Nakota, and in a motion that had, to me, that same kind of half-speed car-wreck intensity, I thrust my arm in full length.

Feel it.

I did.

Not what you would think, no, not suction or even a true sensation, but if you could touch an insubstantiality, a fever dream, rub hallucinations on your skin, if you could cradle your own mind when you dream, trace the hills and gutters of the brain's landscape—there really is no explaining it, I'm sorry but it's so. Even they, who were there, even Nakota who was in all senses closest to me, well. They didn't really get it either. *I* didn't get it all, but what I got, going into it with empty eyes open and empty hands at the ready, was horrifyingly intense, not so much empowering but the sensation of such, I heard my own voice howling as if I was in pain but I wasn't, you see, I really didn't feel anything bad at all even when I looked down between my open orbiting knees and saw the steel of Randy's sculpture running over the skin of my knuckles, dripping down to fall not into the Funhole as one would think (and one *would* think) but flying off in a strange arc as if repelled, dropping somewhere to the right but my vision didn't go, didn't really go that far. Nakota was trying to touch me, I could see that much, but she wasn't making contact or if she was I wasn't feeling it. I had my other hand, my right hand, out of the hole now, some other part of me was inside, or maybe not because I was falling, losing altitude we call that, God *damn* sometimes this was funny. Sometimes I was funny. But apparently not now because I heard voices, they sounded scared or screaming or something and I was trying to stick my right hand, my palm, my hole into my mouth, trying to suck the blackness there, it had a greasy bad smell like the

Funhole itself but would it taste sweet, so sweet, would it lie on my tongue like honey, drip from my lips like blood?

"I wish you would all be quiet," I said. No one heard me. Maybe I didn't really say it at all.

I was on my back on the floor. I could taste the iron of blood, I was having a great deal of trouble seeing. "Uh-oh," I said. "Randy, did you beat me up?"

To my great surprise I found they could hear me, and I saw Randy's face, astonishingly red for that white skin, I didn't know albinos could get that red. "I'm sorry," he said, "Nicholas, man, I'm sorry but—"

"He thought you were going down," Nakota said, not looking at Randy; without another word I saw, I knew she thought it perhaps the premier idea of all time, certainly my greatest hit, and was inevitably angry beyond telling that Randy had arrested my descent and yet maybe a little glad too. Why dear, I didn't know you cared. Although of course she didn't; all she cared about was being the first one down.

"Was I?" My mouth felt very loose, a bad feeling. I tried to spit and gagged on blood. "Let me up," I said. The back of my head hurt, too.

"Nicholas, I—"

"Shut up," Nakota said, with such viciousness that startled even me, but she made no motion to help as Randy and Vanese lifted me to my feet, walked me down the hall and up the stairs to the flat. Randy began a halting monologue that lasted until I was sitting on the couchbed, a wet dirty washcloth pressed like a membrane against my mouth, which refused to stop bleeding, saying essentially the same thing: that he had not meant to hurt me, that things got so weird so fast, that trying to eat my own hand was one thing but when it looked like I was going headfirst into the Funhole, well.

"I'm sorry, man." He looked sorry too.

"Don't," shaking my head, wanting him simply to stop saying it. He was a good one for repeating himself, Randy. I leaned back on the couchbed, closing my eyes for a moment as Vanese, nail clippers in hand, worked to cut the tape for my ragged new bandage; I was all out of surgical tape and had to settle for electrical tape, which was so very old, I told her, that all the glue was probably dried and therefore worthless. I definitely did not want to have to look at my hand. The idea—not the memory, for at that moment I couldn't accurately remember anything—that I had tried to suck on my wound was making me so retroactively sick that I felt I might have to vomit if I thought about it too hard.

"Why'd you do that for?" Vanese asked me, in the unconscious scolding tone of an older sister, rip rip rip at the tape. "No telling *what's* down there."

Nakota, arms tightly crossed as if that was the only way to keep from slapping the shit out of someone: "That's pretty much the *point*, isn't it?"

Rip rip. "I don't see you volunteering to go down there."

"I *tried*."

"Uh-huh."

"She did," I said. I felt consummately shitty. I felt like I might cry. I wished I could get better very fast so I could run downstairs and do it again. There is no rational way to explain that, because it was no rational wish, but it was intense as a bodily need, demanding as hunger or desire. "A hard-on of the soul," I mumbled, and laughed into my washcloth, sticky and damp with blood.

Randy was miserable, there in his neutral corner; he probably felt worse than I did, which would have taken some doing, but his was a malady of action, mine obviously a cruder sort of melancholy, the weltschmerz of a man who has just had his clock cleaned. "Hey Randy," I said, through my baggy lips. "Get us some beer." For no reason, or rather, her reason, Nakota laughed. And it wasn't for me asking for beer, either.

Randy found four beers in the refrigerator, opened them all. Nakota looked at hers as if he had just offered her bottled spit. *Warm* spit. "No thanks," she said. Vanese took hers with an absent nod. She must have been an older sister, or a mother or nurse, her whole attention was so absorbed by the task at hand. So to speak. Either that or she was just very conscientious. Or anal retentive.

"Does that hurt?" she asked me.

"Very much," I told her, although it was by no means the most painful part of me. She shook her head, to herself, set down the nail clippers and picked up her beer. A long swallow. She had a pretty throat, Vanese.

It hurt to drink, but the beer tasted good. I wiped my mouth and face one last time and put aside the washcloth. "Still snowing?" I asked Randy.

He looked out the window. "Yeah, pretty bad. Blowing around some." Vanese joined him at the window, said something, quietly, to which he shrugged.

"If you don't think you're going to make it home," I said, "you can stay here."

Randy looked at Vanese, questioningly, and with her own shrug she nodded. "All right," he said. "Thanks, man." More diffidently, "You feeling any better now?"

"I feel fine. I feel like more beer." Nakota looked at me, nodded contemptuously toward her untouched beer. Randy immediately got his coat on.

"You going home?" I asked, surprised, and he said, "The least I can do is get you some beer, man."

"It's too bad to drive," Vanese said, but Randy shook his head, irritated at her objection; she returned to her seat beside me on the couchbed. For some reason, again her own and having nothing to do with jealousy, this pissed Nakota off.

"Why don't you go with him?" she said pointedly to Vanese.

"Why don't you go to hell?"

"Ladies, ladies, please," I said, possessed all at once of a weird good humor, "come on now. If you must fight, at least use your fists."

Randy laughed, big loud resonant horse laugh and I smiled, as much at the sound as my joke, my mood, twisted lips and Vanese smiled back at me, an astonishingly sweet smile that took all the wariness from her big eyes. Even Nakota smiled. And then we were all laughing, the whooping laugh of relief, the way you laugh when they show you the X rays and it's nonmalignant, for now anyway, and the doctor has a small but distinct booger hanging out of his nostril and you and everybody else in the room can see it and as soon as he leaves you laugh your ass off; like that.

Randy took a while coming back with the beer. Nakota turned the music back on. Vanese, still beside me, tapped her knee in time, her nails were chewed past the quick. I drank all of my beer and Nakota's too. Nobody said much but there was still, like smoke in the air, a feeling of fragile camaraderie; foxhole love. Funhole love.

Not only beer, but a couple bags of chips, some candy bars. Randy stood shaking off like a dog in the doorway as Vanese took the wet-spotted bags from him. I wiped at my mouth; it was still bleeding.

"It's fuckin' nuts out there," Randy said. "I didn't even take the truck, you can't get down the streets." His pale hair was mottled dark with melted snow. He ripped open one of the chip bags. Vanese took a bottle out of the smaller paper bag, offered it silently to Nakota: mineral water.

We all got drunk, except Nakota. Vanese turned out to have a talent for caricature mimicry; as she enacted the scene in the storage room, our parts—Randy horrified bully, Nakota ("Shrike") exaggerated bitch, me entirely out of it, and she, Vanese, scared shitless—became horror-movie funny; we laughed again, less hysterically, with more real humor, told what we each remembered and laughed about that too. Survivor's humor, maybe. *I* thought it was funny.

It was very late, there was still beer but Vanese had fallen asleep, mouth open in a little *O*, Randy was close to it. Nakota, in an atypical gesture, offered them her spring bed. Randy shook Vanese awake enough to transport her there, they both crawled atop it, shoes and all. Vanese's mouth never closed once.

Nakota stripped in the middle of the room, she had to be freezing but she never showed it, walked over to my bed and got in. If I had waited for an invitation to join her I would be waiting there still, but that was her: take what's not yours and don't share. Especially with the owner. Weaving a little, a lot, I flopped down—my anesthetized body twingeing—and pulled the covers up.

"Sleeping with your clothes on," she said. "Typical derelict."

"Of course I'm a derelict. Derelict laureate of the Funhole and don't forget it," as her hands found me, purposeful stroke of my small flabby cock, "and don't fuck me either, it hurts too much."

"If it doesn't hurt," she said, death's-head above me in the dark, "you're not doing it right."

FIVE

When Nakota found I planned on actually staying, as much as possible, in the storage room, to watch beside the Funhole, I saw for once
her complete and enthusiastic approval; it was a disconcerting thing.
Vanese thought it was a terrible idea, tempting fate on a daily basis.
Randy was horrified.

"That's suicide, man!"

"Shut up," Nakota said. She was smiling. "He knows what he's doing."

Actually I didn't, not entirely, but I knew what I had to do and this
was it. I didn't think of it as suicide or even particularly dangerous,
although that was arguably a dumbshit thing to think in view of past
occurrences. I just knew that I was going to do it.

Around the living room, morning-after faces on Randy and Vanese;
Nakota of course like the cat that just ate shit. Randy in particular looked
utterly bleached, like a dried-up chicken bone. Vanese had looked better
in last night's dark but she still looked pretty good, even scared, even
mad as when she turned on Nakota and said, "Why don't you stop
badgering him and go stick your own head down there?"

"Why don't you mind your own business?" loftily, cream-fed queen
too cool to bicker with the rabble.

"He's not your business. Nobody's your business, you're too worried
about your own ass. What you want." Vanese was really pissed. I thought
she was going to start swinging or something.

"It's nobody's business," I said, quietly, it was hard to talk this morning. My instant coffee tasted like the devil's asshole. I drank it anyway. All that blood and beer, and half a pound bag of Raisinets, little hamster turds bubbling in my stomach like animate shit. "Nobody has to watch out for me."

"Well *she* sure won't."

"Nurse Nancy," Nakota's grin. "Little Miss Pop-up Book. Vanese, don't you have somewhere to be?"

"I gotta get to work." Randy, shaking his head, suddenly as miserable as he was last night, surveying me on his way to the bathroom. "You don't look real good, man," he said, but sadly, a long sad piss without closing the door. Vanese got up, joined him, closed it for him.

"What a pushy bitch," Nakota said, but still coolly.

"Oh come on." At once I felt irritated with her. "You know she's right. Why be pissed about it?"

"I'm not pissed," dismissively, getting up to hunt for matches. She blew smoke at me, smiled with her blue-white teeth. "I'd like to get the camcorder, if I can. I think this needs to be recorded, I—"

"What're you, *Wild Kingdom*?" Vanese again. Randy was slicking his wet hair back with long nervous strokes. He nudged her and she stopped.

"Take care, man," he said to me, and then in passing, "Mind if I bring another sculpture?" Vanese stopped like slammed-on brakes. "You too," she said to him, with a disgust so palpable I felt obscurely flattered. "Some friends." She walked out without him.

"Bring one if you want," I said.

Embarrassed now a little. "Maybe tomorrow." As they left, Nakota smirked. "Short leash," she said, lighting up another of her shitty cigarettes.

"Just shut up for once," I said. All of me, the beaten parts, ached with a slow bruisy throb. Vanese had made my bandage too large and too tight, unwieldy, it chafed the skin of my wrist so I pulled it off, lay my hand palm-up on the table, sat with eyes shut and breathing quietly until Nakota said, "Look."

I looked. Fluid was seeping slowly from my hand and wiggling like sperm across the table.

"Shit," Nakota said admiringly.

I closed my eyes again.

My preparations for this one-floor pilgrimage were pretty slipshod, but again, that was sort of typical and, untypically, I knew I wouldn't be needing much. The proverbial pot to piss in, or on, depending on my aim; a pillow and blanket; pen and paper, unlined drawing paper, a big pad of it bought at the drugstore, it was meant for kids. It had a bear on it. Nakota started to make fun of the bear and I told her to go fuck herself, right out loud in the store, I said if she lived to be a thousand she would never begin to approach the unconscious purity of that bear.

"Well, that's your department, isn't it?" It took me a while to figure out that she meant unconsciousness, not purity, but it should have been obvious.

Dressing in decent black for work, brushing her hair, she asked what I was going to do with the paper. Don't know, I told her. I just feel like I need it. She put on her sneakers. They sagged at the sides. "You must walk funny," I told her.

"Funny, right." She was working more hours now, had to, to pay for the flat. She always bitched about how crummy Club 22 was and how the only people who ever came there were career alcoholics, which I maintained was a redundancy, and besides she was far too temperamental to ever work at a decent place. She was unimpressed with my reasoning. As usual.

"You going in there tonight?" she wanted to know. Pulling on her crusty sport coat, a castoff, I later found, of Randy's. Pushing hair out of her eyes. Her hair was getting longer; I liked it. I didn't mention it because if I did she would cut it at once. "Will you be in there when I get home?" She hated to miss a minute.

"No. I'm going to watch the door tonight, see who goes by there or what." We'd discussed it, she and I, not a few times; seeing the cleaning stuff so dirty, so completely undisturbed, had convinced us that no one used that room anymore. Used it for storage, anyway. If there were other devotees, well. It's a fact-finding mission, I had told her, with grave humor. If there are cults operating here, I should know about it. Maybe they'll worship you as a god, she said, with one of her little sneers. Maybe they will, I said; it was a joke but I didn't laugh.

After she left I carried my stuff downstairs and inside, careful not to look too long at the dark serenity beyond, careful not to linger. But: what are you scared of? I thought, why so cautious when that's the very thing you'll be doing for the next week, weeks, whatever, for who knows how long. For however long it takes. Whatever it is.

Still I hurried. Shut the door. Then sat, ragged towel discreetly folded beneath my soon-to-be-numb ass, on the freezer-cold landing, eyes half-closed, typical empty slouch like most of the people who lived there; we used to joke that in my building, the tenants were the vacancies, and lucky for me it wasn't hard to play at being nothing.

I figured no one would notice me and I was right. I sat there for most of the day, leaving once or twice to piss, get a cup of coffee, run some hot water over my hands just for the painful pleasure of flexing them for a minute or two. Then back to my station, observing the people who stepped past and around me as if I were a thoughtlessly discarded bag of thankfully odorless trash. Which was okay by me. As people passed I watched them, my covert gaze and wondering, Do you know about it? Have you ever opened that particular door, have you ever even noticed that it's there? Skinny girl in too big dress, old man with Brillo sideburns, how about you? How about you, guy with firestorm zits and black leather, looking like you'd like to step on my hand, there, as it lies so close to your bootheels? Are you going to? You won't like the stain, believe me.

By ten o'clock I was satisfied that our original conclusions were correct, but I had one more test to try, one I couldn't make till morning so, unbending joints and tendons as unwieldy as rusted hangers, I lurched gently upstairs to sprawl on the couchbed, massaging my numb feet and watching the tail end of a documentary about wasps. It was actually pretty interesting. I liked the male wasps, the sunning stud wasps on sycamore leaves, tiny terrorists taking the air. Best of all though was the wasp beetle, whose yellow and black coloration mimics that of the wasp, no real terrorist at all but merely masquerading. The kinship of the image made me smile; it reminded me of myself.

Nakota announced her arrival by some five-star bitching, everybody was assholes, her boss was an asshole, the customers were the biggest assholes on earth. Apparently the big ordeal was some guy puked on the bar and she had to clean it up. I laughed, which only made things worse but I didn't especially care.

"Go ahead and laugh, you stupid shithead," she said, blowing smoke at me. Bitterly, "It was all green."

"Listen," nudging her, "you know what? I sat out there all day and I didn't see anybody pay the slightest bit of attention to the door."

"Good," but still pissed, wanting to find something to complain about even in that, not ready to be glad about anything yet. "When're you moving in?"

"I have one more thing to try, tomorrow morning. We'll see how that comes out." Actually it was pretty mundane, but a good idea, I thought, a commonsense thing to do, the thinking of which pleased me. Early the next morning I called the building manager, a guy I had seen exactly once, left a message I was having some trouble with the pipes in my kitchen and would he please send somebody around to look at them; I gave the number of the apartment nearest the storage-room door. It was the building's only storage room, we had early on made certain of that. Not that it truly mattered: nothing in the building had ever been repaired or replaced within living memory, there was certainly no live-in maintenance man, and the clientele being what they were, no one was going to bitch too much about anything in return for the simple security of being left completely alone.

I sat in my accustomed spot and waited to see if anyone would come looking, for tools, whatever: the quintessential fool's errand maybe but maybe I was quintessentially suited for it. And then again, what else did I have to do? Watch the video?

All day, nothing, or nothing but Nakota's escalating impatience, like sitting next to a jiggling container of acid; unstable. When she left for work we weren't speaking, which was restful, and we weren't speaking much anyway considering I was on the landing most of the day. Evening, I went in, not satisfied but resigned to my results: there was nothing in my upcoming vigil to fear but the Funhole itself.

I drank so much hot coffee, cup after cup, wanting to pour it directly on my aching stonecold ass to speed the thaw, that I knew I wouldn't sleep for hours, maybe till morning, which was okay because a day of sitting, two days really, is not exactly exhausting. I watched the news with the sound off. It was more frightening that way but more obscurely comical: Was this flat-faced white man, sweating in his suit, perturbed about a big matter or small, time or money, life or death? Was this tight-assed anchorwoman's oblique frown in response to a football score or a natural disaster, was it the passing of a tyrant or a kidney stone that caused her smile?

Halfway through the phone rang; I expected Randy but got Vanese. Long pauses in her speech, she was diffident, asked how I was doing; I had to smile, I hardly remembered my bruises. Being hurt was no big thing and I wanted to say so, but it sounded so he-man I couldn't. Instead I told her about my new system for watching the news. It made her laugh, a little, but she wasn't really calling to talk.

Finally, after a longer pause: "You didn't do it yet, did you?"

"No." I felt like a doctor, trying to soften the report of an incipient malignancy. "Maybe tomorrow."

"You ought to think this through, Nicholas. I mean I know it's not my business, but I saw, well you know what I saw."

I was what you saw that scared you, I was the thing you don't want to mention. "Vanese," as kindly as I could, "don't worry about it. Really. Nothing's going to happen, okay?" It was a stupid lie and we both knew it, and it killed the conversation. After I hung up I sat in the dark wondering how I could inspire worry, why she would bother to call. Older-sister syndrome, yeah. She probably sat around worrying about stray dogs running loose on the freeway, too. And then I was ashamed, to think something so cynically dismissive of her kindness, was I that big a shit that I couldn't even appreciate simple human concern?

It helps, I told myself, to be human in the first place, and then of course in walked Nakota to further prove my lack of humanity. "Well?" she said, and "Nothing," I said. "I start tomorrow." It sounded like I just got a job or something. Kiss me, honey, I'm off to the Funhole.

She smiled, blue teeth, sparkling eyes and all. A celebratory blowjob, perhaps, or at least a surcease from bitching? Yes. And no, but as I lay there, her mouth upon me, my eyes almost closed and skating on the verge, I thought of how I might feel that same time tomorrow, or next week, or whenever whatever epiphany I sought finally overtook me, and to my distress this idea, this disintegration, triggered my orgasm and I cried out as I came, then closed my eyes tight, tight, if I can't see the monster then it can't see me. But after all I was my own monster, wasn't I.

"Shut up," I said aloud and to myself. Nakota did not speak, ignoring me, intent on her own orgasm; she probably wouldn't have answered me anyway. I felt a passionate impulse to cry, hard tears that would hurt like splinters, coming down. I didn't. But the want stayed with me, hour after hour as Nakota lay asleep beside me, skinny jigsaw form blanketless in the cold and that burning, burning in my throat.

And woke in the night to find myself, crouched, lips open like some mindless nursling, hot face close upon the cool glass of the shining screen as Nakota had done before me, but in—and I knew with a certainty past instinct—much more intimate union. And the figure upon it, dissolving, transforming, crooning in soundless glee as it moved to press, perhaps, its empty cheek upon my own.

"Huh," no word, just barely sound, a huffing groan of shock as if, waking, I found myself thoughtfully tilting an acid beaker, about to drink a vial of virus. Jerking backward and away, a clumsy stutter of movement and I sat back, hard, fresh and smelly sweat on the shiver of my skin, and behind me something, a beer can, fell with a soft metallic crash; Nakota heard nothing, slept on, skin and bones in slumber.

And the image a glimmer, the pure malignancy of its darkness suddenly abloom in comic flickerings, but hey! that's not all, folks. Left-handed, I shut off the TV, hurried back to bed to lie helpless and awake, watching the screen with one sideways eye, the way a dog watches the foot that kicks it, the way the insect watches the huge avenging hand.

Supplies, yes, my pot and blanket and pad of paper, creeping off in the dark dawn—I hadn't slept and finally didn't want to, what better way to approach the Funhole than with aching eyes and preternatural insomniac nervousness. Wrapped in my blanket, the pad to my chest (bear side in), I sat with my back to the door and thought, too embarrassed to say it aloud: Well, here I am.

Here I am.

Dusty floor. Randy's sculpture. A smell like, God help us, baking bread, a robust yeasty stink, good enough to eat. A very thin bug, all minute feathery legs, ran a wide path around the Funhole. I watched it go, wondered suddenly why I had so rarely seen insects, mouse droppings, any indication of life that should surely have flourished in a room so undisturbed, why wasn't there a shitload of cobwebs here? Ever? And of course I knew why, stupid questions to pass the time until, what. Until you're assumed in a pillar of cloud, until all the blood in your body turns to gold, until you go crazy from your own dumb solitude and throw yourself in a grand suicidal gesture not down the hole but out a friendly window?

What a melodramatic asshole I was turning out to be.

I took out the bear pad and started doodling, and the next thing I knew Nakota was kneeling before me, bright eyes and shaking my shoulder, hunting no doubt some kind of transformation. "Well?" she kept saying. "Well?"

"Well nothing." I was exhausted and pissed, all I wanted to do was sleep. "Let me sleep," I said, and pushed at her, it was like pushing away a nosy determined dog. "Just get the fuck out of here and let me sleep," and I pushed her again, harder, and she slewed sideways, making no motion at all to arrest her slide, ended splayed before the lip of the Funhole with a nasty smile on her face.

"Good move," she said. "That was a close one, wasn't it?"

"Who gives a shit," I said, and meant it, meant it too when I said, consciously cruel, "It doesn't want you anyway, Nakota. Shrike. *Jane.* It wants me."

And it was so. And it was said to hurt her. Which it did.

And I didn't feel bad. Which scared me, as much as the sudden rich throb of my wound, an approving twinge, gladhand so to speak and remorsefully, I reached out for her, saying something, I don't remember, and she took my proffered right hand and squeezed, hard and vicious, driving her fingers into the most painful circle of my flesh, squeezed till I literally gasped and in blind reaction hit out at her, hit her in the face. I looked at my hand, horrified to see my fingers spotted with her blood.

"Congratulations," she said, and I saw she was laughing.

"Please," I said. "Please just go away."

She did, but not for minutes, long minutes with her bright eyes watching me as I assumed my sorrowful crouch, sat with head finally averted so I did not have to see. When she left I checked the door, could it be locked from the inside? No, or the outside either. I would have to fix that.

When I slept again my dreams were painless, oddly dry for such a literal position, there on the lip, the rim, yeah, of a bottomless drink of dreams. Dumb stuff: about my car, a movie I'd watched with Nora, a beach I'd once slept on, wrapped in some woman's worn-out rain poncho. That last dream was more vivid, when I woke it was to the scent of the plastic poncho, the cold gritty rasp of the sand against the back of my hand, I had used it for a pillow. How cold it had been that morning, gray unspectacular dawn and me standing, weaving, still half-high and pissing into the calm waters of the lake. Up the hill to the all-night party, which by that time had degenerated into three drunk women talking about TV shows and a guy passed out on the front porch. I had found a bed and slept in it, and in four hours woke much as I felt on this Funhole floor, cramped and more exhausted than when I had lain down. The bear pad pressed, now, into my cheekbone, and I cuddled it like a toy as I fell back to sleep.

Hunger woke me the third time, my body clock saying it was probably afternoon. Nakota had gone to work. In the empty flat I made a shitty meal of burned eggs and half a bowl of vegetable soup, there was hardly anything to eat but I could hardly complain since I hadn't been to the store in, what? Days definitely, probably longer, who knew what Nakota was eating. The flesh of others. After spending all that time in the dark, it was hard to think of going out, of venturing into the frigid day. Maybe tomorrow. Cautiously, who knew what I expected, I turned on the TV. Nothing not normal. If I stayed in the storage room at least I'd never have to see the video again, unless of course it started projecting itself on the walls, my own personal drive-in, stop it, just stop it. On the news they told about a man who had had a stroke at the wheel of his car and as a result flattened two kids on bikes. Three people dead and nobody to blame.

Lying on my back on the couchbed, one hand behind my head, feeling grubby and too listless to actually do anything about it, and thinking I could hear music, somebody's radio, a tune with a bass so subliminal that I could not hear it, could barely feel it as a whisper in my bones. Maddeningly beautiful. and faint as an insect choir, like standing in the dark and glimpsing—the barest peripheral, an image behind your eyelids—the passing of your one desire, close enough to nuzzle if you could only fix its motion, see it all the way.

Fainter. And nobody's radio. Funhole music.

I hear you.

Back then to the dark, boneless slump before the hole, the gloryhole, lying beside it like a lover too timid to reach for what is offered: God it was cold in there. Gray light coming in under the door. And that sound, no more distinct for proximity, same sweet ghost howl not so much siren song as the song that charms sirens. Pillowed again with the bear pad, all my body sore still from the vigil. Aching in my hand like the beat of my heart.

And if I slept, it was a sleep like fugue, and in that sleep Randy's sculpture began to twist, elegant stance before my eyes, I never touched it but it moved. Moving, nothing so clear as in time to the music but connected nonetheless, its strut like the dance of stalking bone, the weak directionless illumination a shine down its elegant lengths. And me witness through my closed eyes, my dreaming gaze transfixed and then abruptly waking to a pain so outrageous that tears dribbled down my cheekbones, I tried to sit up and found I could not move my arm, my hand, it was like being staked down, crucified to the floor. From my hand a fluid clear as water snaked its living way to the Funhole, and instead of running into its depths formed a transparent black rainbow above it, gaining in radiance as more fluid left me and the pain trebled. I writhed against what held me, I moved my head back and forth as if that would somehow help, rainbow and wall and rainbow again, and Randy's sculpture suddenly bounded straight and horrifying up in the air as if it would fall, impaling arc, directly into my chest. A coughing scream, no I won't look and I felt a little echoing thud and looked again to see the sculpture sitting chummily next to me, its metal dripping only slightly, mingling with my hand's extrusion to form a silvery mix that did not alter the rainbow's color but gave the bow a jaunty flex that it demonstrated by moving in definite time to the music, which instead of swelling grew dimmer still, maddening as the knowing shine of the sculpture beside me.

I cried, from pain, from relief that I had not been harmed, or not more than was bearable, and the fluid from my hand turned as luminously black as the rainbow and my tears too dripped down black and I cried harder, scared, scared, I still couldn't move my hand.

And Randy's voice, obscured but still audible: "Nicholas? You in there, man?"

"Yeah," weakly, trying to get my voice back.

"Yeah."

He came in, slowly, bringing with him a definite smell of the cold outside, a different odor, lushly astringent, a better world. He carried another piece of sculpture, steel baby swaddled in newspaper. "Nicholas?" tentatively; I realized with dull surprise that the light was either off or burned completely out, I had grown so used to the dark.

"Here," I said. "I'm over here. I can't get up."

"Are you all right?"

"I can't get *up*."

His first look was, naturally, for his sculpture; he noticed its new placement, of course, it was hard not to; noticed too the new configuration: I saw him shake his head. Crouching over me, his own smell was of beer, more faintly grease and gasoline." Shrike said you were doin' it," he said, a nervous, reverent smile. "How's it going anyway?"

"Pretty damn bad." Nodding at my hand, twitching it to show it couldn't move, but, surprise again, the pressure seemed to melt as I twitched it, dissolving altogether to allow me to sit slowly up, muscles burning. Wiping black tears from my face, their trail as tangible as sweat, as blood. "I feel sort of shitty, to tell you the truth."

"I bet you do, man." Somewhat embarrassed, but eager, yes definitely that, he took the wrappings from his new sculpture, showed me its sharp diagonals and high-boned dull silver skull. Lovely. Just what I wanted, a death's-head to keep me company. Almost as bad as having Nakota there, and I only realized I had said that last aloud when he laughed.

"Yeah, right. She's pretty pumped up about this, you know!'

"I know."

"Vanese is *pissed.*"

I nodded, my head felt suddenly so very heavy, as if my own skull had turned to steel, ominous loll in the flimsy carton of my flesh.

"You want me to stay here awhile?" He shrugged himself deeper into his jacket. "It's pretty cold in here, you know?"

It was not the kind of thing that, once immersed in, you kept on feeling; as if possessed by cold you overcame it. I shrugged. "At least come out and get something to drink," Randy said, but unsure in the offer; the Funhole was a taskmaster of some kind, he knew enough to know that, but whether it required regular hours was still beyond him.

Silence. Diffidently, but with raised-eyebrow inspiration, "You could come out for a while, you know, come with me to the Incubus. There's an opening, free beer, you know? Maybe some food. You want to!"

Oh Randy, this is so sudden. And when I smiled, his face withdrew, a little, not frozen but closed, the quick way you close a closet door in the dark: what's really behind there? And I realized, with a larger incredulous smile, that he was afraid of me.

"Sure," I said. "Sure, I'll go."

Hair still shower-damp, ice cold against my bare neck, following Randy into the crowded heat of the gallery, my step not so much unsteady as inherently fragile. Even though the lighting was sporadic at best, smoke-dense, it seemed incredibly bright; I kept blinking, almost as much as Randy. The Mole Men, out to take the air.

He grabbed two cups of piss-flat beer, directed me with one elbow to the hors d'oeuvres: withered tortilla chips piled around a bowl of mean-looking salsa. I took a chance. The salsa tasted like chunky kerosene.

"Almost as bad as the art," Randy said. His beer was already gone. "Can you believe anybody has the balls to show this shit?"

It was pretty bad. I mean, my name may not be Art, etcetera, but this stuff—huge cockeyed depictions of women with tits bulbous enough for a scotch ad holding big cigarettes like guns with smoke coming out of their pussies, with titles like *The Tobacco Industry Wants You*, or—my favorite—*Fat Kills*—I mean, come *on*.

I said to Randy, "Why can't you do stuff like this?"

"I didn't know it was gonna be this bad," and when I laughed, he did, too. "Let's get some more beer."

In our blue-collar dishabille, Randy's gas-station jacket and me in my usual junkwear, we stuck out; all the rest was fake leather lab coats and baggy white pants, heavy red lipstick and combat boots, clustered in a bunch mouthing the same party line, laughter choreographed and thin. "Art fucks," Randy said, with intense disdain.

We took folding chairs, plunked them square by the keg, and passed a pleasant hour making fun of everything we saw. Smoke made my eyes dry. The beer tasted so good I was grateful. Randy laughed a lot, mostly at things I said, but from time to time I caught him looking at me, sideways and shy.

"These people, man," waving his cup in a careless drunken circle, a blurt of beer slopping free, "these *people*, man, would have no fuckin' *idea* what you're doing, you know?" My shrug made him more insistent. "No, man, I'm serious, I mean they would have no clue."

"Why?" from behind both of us. "What's he doing?"

Tall, was my first blurred impression, tall and skinny and wrapped like a sandwich in one of those dumb-looking lab coats. He had a kind of mouth that looked as if it were constantly sneering, but it was just the subtle effect of a particularly weird overbite. He came around our chairs, stood in front of us, in front of me.

"What're you doing?" he said.

"None of your business," Randy said.

"Who're you, Randy, his agent? I mean the man can talk for himself, can't he?" He stuck out his hand, a little too fast to be friendly. His fingers were damp. "Malcolm," he said.

"Nicholas Reid." I resisted the urge to add, King of the Funhole. A stupid giggle escaped me anyway.

"So," cocked-hip stance, half smile, "what *are* you working on, Nick, that the rest of us wouldn't get?"

Nick. "Performance art," I said. Randy was shaking his head, I thought at Malcolm, but then I realized it was aimed at me. "Wild shit."

"Wild shit." Malcolm said it with an air of irony so heavy it reminded me of Randy's steel skull. "Where do you show your stuff, or perform, or whatever?"

"I don't know," I said, slow drunken grin, "if you're ready for this."

"I'm always ready for a new experience." "Nicholas," Randy's earnest gaze, one hand out as if to ward my words, "don't even bother with this guy, okay? You don't want—"

"Okay," I said to Malcolm. "Gimme a pen or something." I ignored Randy, or at least his growing dismay. My scribbling was just legible, green ink smearing on somebody's badly done flyer. "Just come by one day, and I'll show you something you have *never* seen before."

Some woman, behind and beside Malcolm, on first glance a cut-down twin, on second just another lab coat, no overbite but a smile like a guard dog's. "I wouldn't bet on that," she said, and gave a snarky little chuckle. "I mean we have seen it all."

"Oh, I doubt that," I said, my own smile downright beatific, grinning at a joke she could not possibly get or Malcolm either. Randy either, for that matter, Randy who sat unhappy and grim, sucking down the last of the beer. "I doubt that very very much."

"If Randy's into it," someone else's sneer, I didn't accurately see the speaker, being now occupied by the sudden slant of my traitorous eyelids, "how weird can it be?"

"Fuck you," said Randy, but without his usual verve. I made a little honking sound, disguised laughter very undisguised, mocking their slit-eyed knowing ignorance, the arrogance of slim experience that truly believes when you've seen one, you really have seen them all.

Well. I can name *that* tune. "See for yourself," I said. "Come one, come all."

Empty-stomach drunk, yes, and the isolation, yes yes, but still there was no excuse, I should have listened to Randy, now driving home, glum weave through sparse and icy traffic, I should have seen for myself that Malcolm was exactly the kind of fuck who would take me up on it. I could have made something up, I told myself, I could have said I was a mime. My stomach ached from the beer, from nervousness and hunger.

"That was stupid," I said for the tenth time. "I'll say I lied. I'll say I was drunk. I *am* drunk."

"Won't work, man." Randy's blinking was so incessant that I was afraid he couldn't see to drive. "He'll just start sniffin' around on his own, him and those smartass art-school pricks he runs with." We shot past a big rattling truck; Randy was passing everybody. "Goddamned posers. They believe anything he tells them. If we have to, we'll stuff the fucker down the Funhole."

I shook my head, smiled to show I knew it was a joke, which of course it wasn't, but there were some things I just couldn't do, even me, even now.

"He'll probably be waiting on the fucking doorstep," and sure enough, a car I didn't know, dumpy blue Toyota parked in my Dumpster spot: but it was Vanese, pinched mouth, shivering behind the wheel.

She was out of the car and into Randy's shit in two seconds, and I saw, from her posture and her hands, the way her body kept reaching for him though she was obviously pissed off out of her mind, that she was terrified; she thought he had come here just to drop off a piece, but the hours passed and she thought, yeah, something bad, had to be, sitting there with a crazy man and she came to check and the lights were out and nobody, nobody was home.

"What'd you think?" Randy, yelling back in the dark. "I went down the fucking *hole*?"

Which was exactly what she had been thinking, even a drunken piece of shit like me could see that, but apparently Randy couldn't, he just kept yelling even though I tried to calm him down; which naturally made things worse. "Don't you start, man, you fucked up enough for one night already," and Vanese, instantly apprehensive, "What's *that* supposed to mean?" and Randy bellowing, in the voice of a man pushed past frustration into some unbearable new state, "Fuck this shit, man!" and slam, bam, gone in a weaving trajectory, he would have squealed his tires if he had thought of it but he was beyond thinking now.

Vanese was crying, upright and brittle with tension, one band pressed against her face not to hide the tears but it seemed to catch them, as if each was bitterly precious, as if each, like a hologram, held the whole sad moment entire. She cried almost without sound, deep sobs that occasionally ended in a soft glottal cough.

"Vanese," I said. "He'll be okay."

She shook her head, the pessimism of a woman who knows.

"Really. He'll be okay, okay?" I didn't know what to do, I couldn't leave her there but I was freezing, I had to piss so bad my kidneys ached. I made her come inside, insisted her through the door and up the stairs, but she didn't fight me as hard as she could have; she was too tired.

On the couchbed, shaking. She in fact was freezing, I saw it in those long jerky shudders. I put the blankets around her, coat and all, tucked her in with clumsy drunken care. "I'll make some coffee," I said.

"You can't even make sense," through teeth that abruptly began an almost comical chattering, but she was trying to smile, it was a joke. "Let me," and she moved to get up.

"Sit down," I said. Forceful. What a man. When the coffee was done I sat next to her, helped her hold the cup. "Another few minutes and you would have had frostbite," I said. "Why didn't you just wait inside?"

"I did, for a long time. But that hall's so cold," feelingly. "In the car I had heat."

"Why'd you turn it off then?"

"I didn't. I ran out of gas."

I shook my head, lectured her on her stupidity, a lecture that veered somehow into a confession of my own: me and Randy at the gallery, and my incomprehensible boasting, something you've never seen before. "Vanese," sagging back, "I am so dumb."

"You are," shaking her head, amazed. "Malcolm. And the Malcolmettes. *Shit.*"

"I know," trying to shrug, "I know I know."

I didn't, though. I spent the next few hours trying out various scenarios on Vanese, things I could tell Malcolm, and with sorrowful expertise she shot them all down. Malcolm was a wily boy, she kept saying, Malcolm was smart. Malcolm would see through my bullshit, I wasn't much of a liar anyway, and if for some reason he didn't, one of his cadre would, and anyway I couldn't dodge forever. It might be better to just break down and tough it out.

"You mean just show him?"

"Why not?"

"Why *not*?" Because it's the real black hole, Vanese, because it's unpredictable and uncontrollable, because anything could happen. Because I don't want to be responsible. Because it's a pathway, and I wanted to go alone. Because it's mine. "Because it's not a good idea," I said; firm, but ultimately lame. She said so, and then there was really nothing else to say.

When Nakota heard about it, the next bleary morning when she woke me coming in, all she did was laugh. One hand poised in the act of shedding a shoe, the other against the couchbed to hold herself steady, and those strange teeth wet and bare in a long sustained crow, she finally had to sit down she was laughing so hard. At last "Oh, Nicholas," wheezy with mirth, patting my blanketed thigh in mock congratulation, "nobody can fuck things up the way you can. Malcolm is—"

"You know him?"

"We used to be lovers." There was something unsettling in her use of that term, I had never thought of her as actually having a lover. Screwing people, yes, absolutely, and the weirder the better. But a lover? No.

"He's an artist," she said. "When he isn't selling clothes. He makes these kitschy plaster death masks," pulling off her other shoe, settling down beside me. One pointy hipbone gouging softly as she moved. "He thinks he's God, and all these little assholes, his groupies, they're all a bunch of goddamned yes-men and all they do is follow him around. Like puppies looking for their mother's tit." A dry sniff, careless toss of the other shoe. "Fact is he's a pretty shitty artist, but nobody can tell him that, or at least not till recently. Richard—you know Richard, down at the Incubus? no?—anyway Richard says Malcolm can't show there anymore, his stuff's too cute. Malcolm was *extremely* pissed off," smiling as at a droll memory. Guess you had to be there.

"So what's all this got to do with me?" I didn't really want to know, I'd heard enough on the subject already, but it was one of those questions you have to ask.

She was going to answer, her mouth opened a little, and then closed in a different kind of smile. "You'll find out, won't you?" And nothing else, fell asleep beside me skinny and superior, her chin digging into my left forearm, the idea of my discomfiture and eventual self-induced downfall no doubt sweet as a lullaby, drifting her into whatever black excesses passed for her dreams.

Slowly I raised my right arm, palm downward, let my unbandaged wound drip and bubble as it would, onto the bare skin of her shoulder; what fell was syrupy and gleamed in the seeping dawn, like the droplets of poison that fall forever in the face of chained Loki; and what fell, clung. My arm tired and carefully I lowered it to my side, fell asleep watching the fluid not so much dry as coagulate on her skin; when taints collide. If I coated her in it, head to toe, would it serve as her chrysalis, would it make a new woman of her? She could stand to be a new woman. She could stand to be a new anything. But maybe in the grand tradition of mad science I should try it on myself first. And maybe not.

Noon when I woke. She was still asleep. The fluid lay undisturbed on her shoulder, a shiny clot, much prettier than when it came out of me. Cautious not to wake her, I slipped from couchbed to shower, from shower and hasty dress to Funhole, nauseated with hunger, still barefoot, my clothes clinging to my half-dry body. Wet hair and cold, so cold, lying beside it, I still hadn't remembered to buy a lock for the damned door. The air, the Funhole's private atmosphere, almost porous with odor, rich and faintly bad like spoiling food. Internal incense, the smoke of constant praise.

"Tell me," I murmured, my lips almost touching the dusty floor. "Tell me before he gets here."

SIX

No time to waste, Malcolm. Leather lab coat, stink of smoke, grinning at me from the salt-scarred pavement. Head wolf, come confident alone without the pack. Daylight was no good for Malcolm, total dark was his milieu. His sunglasses were crooked. "Where're you goin'?" he said.

"Right now I'm going grocery shopping," not stopping but slowing, a little, giving him the moment to join me if he was going to. "You can come with me if you want."

"Grocery shopping," with a lilt meant to show amusement, or maybe merely shitty. He fell into step with me, or rather linked his ironic amble to my perpetual slouch. I bet he even shaved ironically. "I usually let my girlfriend handle all that."

"You said you were always ready for new experiences, right?" Sliding into my car, letting him wait a minute before I unlocked the passenger door. "Have one on me." Nyah nyah, I can do irony too.

Silence between us made me nervous, as nervous as the frigid planes of the day around me. Above the choking sound of my heater, I said, "Are you off work today, or what?"

"I'm an artist," now definitely shitty, but willing not to chew me a new asshole for the sake of belittling my ignorance. Under other, less complex circumstances, I could have had a lot of laughs out of this guy. "I'm always working."

"Uh-huh." Into the IGA parking lot, an acre of slush and abandoned carts, cars parked at strange angles. Inside was even brighter than out-side. The cart I chose had a twisted front wheel; I kept helplessly hitting aisle displays, other carts, even Malcolm once or twice. "Beer," I said, cart inventory, "mineral water. Crackers. Eggs."

"Real domestic type, aren't you?"

"Peanut butter."

"How can you eat that stuff?" pointing at my no-brand peanut butter with genuine disdain. "Peter Pan's the only good kind."

I had to borrow two bucks from him at the checkout. Malcolm smoked all the way home, pretentious Gitanes, clenching one between his teeth when he talked. His sunglasses were still crooked. He criticized every song on the radio until in self-defense I put on the all-news station; then he mocked the news. As I parked, I thought about Randy's plan to feed Malcolm to the Funhole. "Randy's right," I said, one bag in my right arm—newly bandaged hand throbbing in dull rhythm, shit I had forgotten to buy gauze—two in my left. Malcolm didn't offer to help.

"Right about what?" he wanted to know, following me up the stairs.

"About you."

"And what does Randy say about me?"

"That you're unique."

He laughed. "I bet he does. Hey, Nick, let me tell you something about Randy. Randy's a grease monkey, he works for a goddamn gas station—"

"Towing service."

"Whatever. Him and his twatty little steel pieces, I mean come on, they all look like car bumpers, stop bringing your work home with you." He laughed and I didn't. "He's a failed sculptor, he's a failure at *life*. He just hasn't realized it yet."

"How's things at the clothes store?" I asked, pausing for my door key.

He didn't like that at all. "Who—".

"Nakota told me. Says you work at a clothes store, selling T-shirts or something. Hey, don't be embarrassed," with my friendliest grin. "We all have to eat sometime, right?"

"You know Nakota?" as if he was only waiting for my flimsy expla-nation so he could shoot it down. I told him she lived with me. Nasty, "She's never said anything about you."

"Shy," I said, and the evidence stared at us as I pushed open the door: naked and smoking, blankets around her waist as she sat reading old *Art Now* magazines, her sneer for both of us in proportionate degrees of unworthiness.

"Oh boy," she said at Malcolm. "I thought I smelled something."

"Missed me," walking to her, leaning over to cup one breast as if this would put my nuts in a permanent tweak. I started putting the groceries away.

"Get your hand off me," Nakota said, "I don't want to touch anything that's been touching your dick."

"Used to be I couldn't get your hands off it."

"Don't remind me. I still get flashbacks."

It was schoolyard bickering, stupid, but one thing was ominously apparent: Nakota did *not* like Malcolm. Not the usual halfass contempt she felt for almost everyone, but actual malice. Which made all this far more dangerous, gave me the sensation of walking not on ice but on something much more volatile, walking on the backs of giants. And she behind me. Wearing stilettos.

"So." Grinning at him. "Want to watch a movie?"

Oh boy. She never was one for wasting time. I opened up a beer, thought longingly of the mad quiet of the Funhole, lying there in my prayerful trance, why I was turning into a regular Nakota. Bedlam instead tonight, obvious in Malcolm's reply: "I don't watch films anymore."

"'Films,'" with one of her ugliest smiles. "I'll show you a fucking *film*, you roach." This endearment meant nothing to me, but Malcolm tightened up like someone had just shoved an icicle up his ass. "Nicholas, put the video on."

"Wonderful," Malcolm said, "home movies."

"You'll like this one," I told him. Now that it was inevitable—and let's not forget, kids, who put this whole doomed scenario into action, do I see a show of hands?—I was determined to have whatever weak fun I could. "Lots of action."

I hadn't seen it myself for a while, I was courting enough disaster as it was. I had no idea if Nakota was still watching regularly, but if so, it just didn't seem to pack the same wallop, or maybe she was wallop-proof by now. Maybe it had never been intended to pack the same wallop. Maybe it was just a lure, why not.

Malcolm's string of bitchy comments—he was one of the truly bitchiest guys I had ever seen—wound down shortly after the first minute. Silence was an uncomfortable mode for him but he was so busy trying to figure out how the hell we'd faked this that he wasn't ready for the real, and at the part where, Nakota claimed, it all diverged for everybody (but me; and yes, I saw it again, the cool beckon of that same figure, and had the same reaction, a curling-up inside, a mortal shriveling) (but this time, what? something worse and I shrank from the naming, pulled back as if from some unfathomable contamination that had already gone fatally far), the climax, so to speak—then he froze, mouth literally open, and open it stayed long seconds after the tape was over, disappeared into buzzing gray silence.

I rubbed my eyes, drank a little of the beer. Nakota smirked. Still Malcolm said nothing.

Finally, in a tone stripped of all falsity, burned down to a nub of hungry essence, he turned not to Nakota but to me: "I have to do you," he said.

"Do me?"

"Your face. Make a mask of your face, like that," gesturing at the TV. "Like the one in the video. I don't know how you did that, but I want to try to duplicate it if I can."

Nakota, strolling naked for a glass of water, taking Malcolm's matches from his shirt pocket. "Malcolm's famous death masks," she said. "Not sold in any stores. Not shown in any galleries, either."

"Will you do it?"

I didn't know what to say, fell clumsily back on the truth. "I don't know. I don't know if I want to."

"Nicholas has his own work to do," Nakota said. "He doesn't have time for you."

"Why does everybody in the world talk for you?" Malcolm said to me. "First Randy, now Queen Bitch here. Just tell me, will you do it or not?"

Nakota clearly wanted me to refuse, but I had no interest in pampering her spite. If it had been Randy asking, I would have said yes at once, but I didn't like Malcolm, I didn't trust him, it was like keeping half a snake in your pocket, a sicked-up vicious pet. Vanese's advice or no, to me it seemed the best idea entirely to get him out of here with the least possible damage. Worse, any time spent dicking around with a mask, even to pacify him, would steal my Funhole time, so much of which already went to waste in the unavoidable things I had to do to live. And I simply didn't want to do it, I mean who wants a death mask of their face? No. Bad idea, Malcolm.

"Will you do it?"

I shook my head, positively no, and said, "All right."

And then—I can't imagine what my face looked like, I couldn't have been more surprised if an animal had crawled out of my mouth, those were in no possible scenario the words I had meant to say—I just sat there in mute asshole gloom while Nakota and Malcolm leaped head-first into war.

They were pretty energetic about it too. It was easy to see what they saw in each other, although in modulated degree and for wildly different reasons; in fact it made me wonder what it was in Nakota I loved. Although that was a question whose answer I had never failed to find, and at this point it was almost comically moot, and anyway I had other, more simple problems to consider if not solve. Such as my inexplicable acquiescence to Malcolm's deathmask wish. Which seemed to somehow fill the bill begun by my equally inexplicable boasting that had brought the whole circus into lurid life.

About the point where Malcolm was screaming, "Because I'm an *artist!*" and Nakota was screaming back, "Yeah, you're an artist all right, a bullshit artist!" I left, closing the door behind me, not even bothering to do it quietly. They wouldn't have stopped for money.

The hallway was extra cold, but the odor of the storage room was ripe and welcoming as a womb, and with embarrassed pleasure I slipped inside, lay facedown beside the Funhole, my right hand resting lightly on its lip. I thought I heard from its deeps not music but the elegant drone of bodily organs, a sound so unimaginably soothing that I felt I could not only sleep there, I could sleep forever, till all of me was a death mask, a human catafalque turned to happy dust on the quiet floor. The last thing I did before I slept was remove my bandage, and let my hand dangle, a sweetly sordid treat in a smiling mouth.

Malcolm was, unfortunately, as good as his word. Next day and already bustling around the flat, apparently come to stay: dragging his stuff in, plaster and cheesecloth and tools in a fake leather case, talking all the time and me leaning up against the couchbed, hearing like an echo's echo, a trickle of dream that Funhole music, not command but insinuation; it was hard to concentrate on anything else. Especially Malcolm.

"—longer than you think," sketchpad too, expensive-looking charcoal pencils and sitting me down, bossy and rude and making me sorrier I had agreed to this, always assuming that were possible. My motives were unfathomable at best but this time it was all beyond me, I might have been predicting the movements of a stranger, and if I cared to try I would end with nothing more than a vaster confusion. Who deciphers the thoughts that come, windborne, from others' heads? And who gives a shit, once thought becomes action? We all know who gets the blame.

And all this time Malcolm talking, directing, overruling, my God he was a windy fuck. Making fun of my magazine prints on the walls, saying Bosch was a poseur and Bacon a fag. Making fun of my photograph of Nakota and saying it looked like a B-movie outtake. Telling me all about himself, since I obviously did not want to hear. Call it punishment.

He was pretty good, though, sketching. He caught not only my features but what I did with them, and I saw in his sketch a kind of premature aging, the stroking finger of a dissolution coming on me like disease. I'm dissolving, I thought, seeing not so much the lines, the gradual leech of life, but the laying-on of a kind of hyperlife, like a sugar carving melting in blood. Look close now: what's wrong with this picture?

He saw it too, but wasn't smart enough to recognize in his head what his eyes already knew. "You won't win any beauty contests," he told me, "which probably explains that bitch of yours."

"She was good enough for you once upon a time," I said, but very mildly; I had no interest in defending Nakota's honor, not that she had any. He dismissed that, it was a long time ago. "Sit still," he said. I did, still wondering why, was still sitting when Nakota came home, casual bang of the door, grinning at me.

"Tedious, isn't he." pouring a mineral water. "Malcolm, are you planning on moving in? Because if you are, I want your share of the rent up front."

"I wouldn't live here if *you* paid *me*," he said, but it was abstract venom, he really was absorbed in what he was doing. Imagine. Nakota was more pissed that he wouldn't fight than she would have been if he had—she was a person of simple wants—and in a sulk spoke to neither of us, punishing me, too, as a matter of course.

Which was all right with me, because I could still hear that music, and it was getting to be one hell of a strain to try to listen over everything else. With their mouths shut it carne clearer, it was almost pleasant to sit there in the cool silence, aching back and open mind, listening, listening—

To the quality of the silence as it changed and, irritated, reluctant to open my eyes, I did, and saw them both, she on the couchbed and he a few feet nearer, staring at the TV. Because the video was on. Of course.

She had done it to piss him off by distracting him, but then again it was her favorite show, too. They really did have a lot in common, much more so than she and I. Small mercies, right. I didn't want to watch but oh yes, there was no avoiding, and so I did, seeing again the same figure, feeling again that overriding mutter of dry disquiet but growing, grown, into something more that I could not name.

I thought, I don't need this. I don't need any of this, I can have the real thing, and I stood up and walked out, no need for an exit line either since nobody noticed I was leaving.

In the storage room I sat on the blanket, my bear pad close by like a toy, breathing in and out the rich bubbling stink of the air, watching from the corner of my eye as Randy's sculpture lifted one armlike stalk and began to move it back and forth, beckoning or warning but it was a little too late for both, wasn't it, and either way I didn't care. I lay with my cheek on the bear pad, staring sideways into the Funhole's depths, thinking through the music of processes both irrevocable and remote; call it reverse entropy; call it the Little Bang.

I don't know if they joined me, later, but when I woke up I was alone, so cold my skin hurt, the garbagey reek from the Funhole all over my hair and clothes, my blanket and pad. Olfactory spoor. A marked man. Upstairs Nakota's sleeping face frowned in protest as I walked past the couchbed to the shower, the blue TV light made dimmer by encroaching dawn.

In the shower I let the water run hard, especially on my hand, pounding through the syrup to the lessening meat beneath; if I had cared I would have been plenty pissed at what was happening to my hand, the damned thing was almost all hole now, and what happens when there's nothing left but bone, huh? Huh? I flexed it, forced myself to use it, to hold the soap, to wash. More syrup bubbled out, a twinkling gray like a bad special effect, refusing the water's best efforts to wash it away. Last laugh. As usual. It's hard being a conduit. No flowers, though, please.

Malcolm worked hard, I'll give him that. Unfortunately he had seized upon the continuous play of the video as essential to his work, and when I complained told me I was chickenshit, I had to learn to let go of my petty fears. This was so funny I smiled beneath the tickling cheesecloth; step two already, we had gone beyond the preliminaries more quickly, he said, than usual, he was obviously inspired by the megaweirdness (his phrase).

"I got you," indicating with nimble plastery fingers, "*there.*"

The sensation of plaster on the skin, even through cheesecloth, is like being buried alive in cheap cement, nose straws or no nose straws. Heightened of course by my petty paranoia, I did not like the video playing all the time, it was like leaving your front door open all night long and trusting to your own stupidity that nothing naughty would shamble in. All I could see was the inside of my eyelids, all I could hear was Malcolm's voice, muttering to himself as he slopped plaster and stared at the TV. I didn't like it, being there in such a stupidly helpless position while he worked on me, what if he decided the video was telling him to suffocate me? One nose straw was beginning to tickle with every breath. I tried breathing less often but that's more difficult than it sounds and I had to stop. And still Malcolm's atonal mumbles, and the faint sounds from the TV.

But it was definitely his medium, and never mind Nakota's kneejerk spite: he wasn't going to make anyone forget Rodin but he knew what he was doing, and in his sure and shaping hands the plaster became the vehicle for, if not the macabre transfiguration he seemed to hope for, then for me the seeds of simple change, if only by way, a subtle way, of observation a new kind of seeing previously unconsidered and now in an instant become the norm. Or maybe all the, what, megaweirdness was inspiring him more than he knew, maybe the constant black mutter of the video was telling him more than his ears could hear, more than my own attenuated straining could decipher.

And when we, he, had finally done for the day, the night, as I washed my red and itching face, over and over, who should show up but the Malcolmettes. Three of them, anyway: Eenie, Meanie, and Shitty. Or something. I was never all that shit-hot with names anyway and these three were strictly interchangeable. The only way I could find to distinguish them was that one's lab coat was a rusty-blood color and the other two were women. One of which, when she opened her mouth, revealed herself to be the one from the Incubus, the one who'd scoffed at my drunken promises of strange.

They didn't bother sneering at my apartment, it was beneath them to even notice such boring squalor, but they couldn't say enough about the death mask. Clustered close around it and nodding back and forth: Technique, they said, it was pure technique, pronouncing it like it was the grail of words.

"This compares with a Caldwell," red lab coat said, offensive thrust of nubby chin, please God, I thought, don't let him stroke it knowingly.

"*Easily.*"

"Or deVore," said the other, non-Incubus woman, who stood so close to me I could. smell the stain of her breath, without, of course, acknowledging me at all, though it was my plaster face she now examined so tenderly. The others nodded, Malcolm with a certain smug restraint, a Borscht Belt parody of Hamlet doing humble. "Midperiod deVore," the woman added, hasty caret-dip of head.

"Who the hell," I said, so pleasantly adrift, "is deVore?"

"You wouldn't understand this," she told me, simultaneously swiveling and stepping back so as not to accidentally touch me while she told me off, "but it's an honor to become one of Malcolm's masks."

"That would be why he works in a clothes store," I said, and just then saw Miss Incubus standing before the TV, head to one side like my dog used to do when she was hearing sounds no one else could. All I saw on the screen was static, but I shut it off anyway, brisk hard finger punch to OFF, too hard because I was scared. Of what she'd seen. Not for her, or not for her precisely, but wasn't it bad enough that Malcolm had seen it? Did we need to get all the rest of his crew in on it too? What a sweet Pandora's hell that would be.

And then of course, operating on the premise that anything, no matter how bad, can always get worse, here came Randy, and Vanese, who continued the evening's merriment with a deadpan: "Oh *my*," and Randy standing sidekick, hands on hips and mouth dour in a frown.

"Don't tell me you let this cocksucker con you into something stupid," no eyes for the other three, who returned the favor and, bored children, started playing with the stereo, trying to find something they liked, no doubt an impossibility.

"Hey Nick," Malcolm's over-shoulder grin, theatrical, did he think this was a movie or what. "Your watchdog's here."

I answered neither. What was there for me to say? I felt as if I were moving through water, a vast and calm preoccupation that in its way shielded me, protected me from the emotions of others, from the facts, and facets, of life. Such as now. The hell with them all. Except maybe Vanese. "He's doing a death mask of my face."

"Does Shrike know about this?" Randy's face was turning red. Vanese gave him a look of secret feminine scorn, walked past us all to make herself instant coffee. She wore a pair of strange delicate earrings, flat silver loops that seemed to drip and twist in some corrosive dance. I went to her, touched one gently.

"These are nice."

"Randy made 'em." She touched the same one I had, set it swinging. "Reminds him of the Funhole," she said. "Nicholas," lowering her voice, soft urgency, "you didn't let Malcolm talk you into anything, did you? I mean I know Shrike, Nakota whatever, I know she was here, but she's got her own agenda, you know what I'm saying?"

I most certainly knew what she was saying. "So what happened, when he got here?"

"We showed him the video."

She stared at me, past surprise, she even looked as if she might laugh, from sheer appreciation of our brazen idiocy, then shook her head, shrugged, and stirred her coffee. "It's your ride," she said. "Hang on."

Glaring at each other, Randy and Malcolm traded bon mots, none of which I heard, instead hearing not so much below as *through* everything else the, what, the voice of the Funhole, the sound of its workings, as music permeating their voices, the room, like water soaks a fabric yet leaves the fabric itself intact. I stood, head bent, and it must have seemed as though it was their argument I heard, that I cared who did what, that in fact I had any say in the matter at all. Everyone else seemed to think so. What was next? Franchise rights? Funhole Inc.? Didn't *anybody* understand what was going on here?

And of course stupid bastard Malcolm, "Is that right?" to Randy's ever-reddening face and moving to turn on the video again, to prove his point, stupid point, and as if abruptly waking I moved too, faster than they could react, and pushed his hand away.

"Leave it," I said.

My motion had momentarily surprised them into stillness, maybe they had all forgotten I was there, but Miss Incubus was first to bristle to defense, turning on me with what she no doubt thought of as a streetgirl's stare; Main Street, maybe. Anytown, USA. Brusque: "What's your problem?"

Malcolm laughed. "Believe me, we don't have time for that."

"Look," and back it came again, that underwater feel, but did you know, I thought, that I can swim? "Look, you don't know what you're fucking around with," I said to her, ignoring the prepracticed stare, they had all of them seen far too many movies. "You really don't."

"You know," she said, pushing right up into my face, "you're nothing but promises, you know that? Bullshit promises, *I* think."

"*You*, think? Jury's still out," and Vanese snickered as red lab coat turned on her and she gave him a look that was the real edition of what's-her-name's counterfeit glare, just as good as a pinch in the crotch and maybe better since it shut him up before he could speak, which is usually the best time, and under it all like a muttered secret that *sound* in my head, rushing like water but like no water I could finally navigate for long, swimmer or no.

"Listen," I said, including them all in my gaze, even I could hear my desperation, "this is really turning out to be—"

The door clicked open, and in the hall's cold-blown rectangle Nakota, one hand on hip: "Well well," stepping in to take over, "looks like the gang's all here."

Oh boy. Waiting to see what she would do, and not alone, I stood in that forking rush of water, one half of me almost hurtfully aware of the temper of the room, the other half dreamy-drowned in the flow, the surge, it was in the end a mercy that they could not hear it too. Nakota poured herself some mineral water, walked through half conversations to turn on, of course, the TV.

"Nakota," I said, "don't."

"Why not?" mild burlesque surprise.

"You know damn well why not," said Vanese, with the deep and instant irritability that only Nakota seemed able to rouse in her, "you stupid rabble-rousing bitch, the only one you ever think of is yourself."

"Shrike," Randy's hand, palm-up like some vexed saint's, "really, Nicholas's right. You shouldn't really—"

"Screw you all," she said, and tapped the tape to ON.

Well. I guess she told us, in fact her specialty, that pale poker face one large suppressed sneer. Rapt and stupid Malcolm, sitting fast beside her, his trio ringed behind him, Randy just as rapt and Vanese abstaining but then nobody could abstain for long, could they, with that witch light in the room? Of course not. Of course not. They sat like kids, open mouths, apparently Malcolm's all-day exposure had done nothing to dim the cold gee-whiz, they sat like rubes at a seance and one of the trio said, "God *damn*," and as if that was my cue I got up, obeying my own wishes for once, that riverine voice a carpet as I walked out of the room and heard Malcolm behind me, tardy distracted petulance: "Hey, Nick, where're you going?" and half of Randy's shitty reply, and nothing else because here they came, all of them. Call me the Pied Piper.

I ignored them when they talked, nothing mystic, I just didn't feel like answering. By the time we hit the door they had stopped entirely, all I heard was the churchly shuffle of their feet, basilica Funhole. We stood in the hall, our merry octet, three of them watching Malcolm who with the other three watched me.

I know what you want, I thought. But you're not gonna get it.

"You," to the Malcolmettes, "get the fuck out of here." They stared at me as if I had just become miraculously stupider than I was, which I had to agree would have been some feat, but then I was smarter than they were, wasn't I, I knew exactly what was behind door number one. "I mean it," no such warning in my voice, as flat in fact as my determination that they must not, not, be allowed to see it, not in fact be allowed near it, I was no goddamned ringmaster after all, was I? The video was bad enough, wasn't it?

"Go back upstairs," I said, "and watch your movie. Go on," and paradox Nakota turned on them and said, "Are you deaf?" with all the menace I lacked, backing them off a pace or two but that was obviously as far as we were going to get without a gun. I looked first at Randy, whose face was as blank as my voice, and then Vanese. Who shrugged.

"It's their funeral," she said.

Nakota laughed: "Hold the flowers," and slipped past me into the storage room, the three left behind instantly craning, what had been a square room full of nothing was now the most, the only important place to be; strange the workings of denial, you can see it in a school-yard clique, which this silly scene very much resembled. Malcolm next, fearless leader without so much as a glance behind, then Randy and Vanese and me last of all, one sweaty hand closing the door.

On the other side, "Watch this door," I said to Randy, and Vanese nodded.

Kneeling, self-conscious now, before the lip, untied my badly made bandage with my teeth. I heard Malcolm's stage whisper, the whip Vanese retort. Randy's distant grumble. And strongest of all beside me, the astringent odor of Nakota's devotion, the cold heat of her impatience, urging me on to her kind of action, let the games begin. "Ah well," I said, and heard the cobweb-echo of my voice, there in the hole. It was in no way a natural echo, but an entrancing sound, scary too since I knew damned well it was some kind of—I almost said side effect, and maybe those are the right words after all. I tried it again, different words, my mouth very close to the lip so none of the others could hear.

"Do you know me?" I said.

do you know me

want you

in a tone so shockingly intimate that my whole body flushed, I felt the warmth go through me like fever, like pain, as if your own mind could speak to you in a tongue you never knew you knew, but recognized at once; as if, foreign-born, came your first exposure to your native lan-guage, and those first words "I love you." And below that I was simply scared shitless, a postcard from the devil, or more ominously a collect call from God himself, will you accept charges?

I could not move, there was no thought in me for motion; could barely come closer but I did, surrounding the lip of the Funhole with my body, curling circular around it, face and hands dipping in the darkness and my right hand shook so terribly that droplets flew, danced beyond gravity in the new bloody light shivering around me, the drops gone circular too in a weird and crooked halo around my shameful head, and I think I cried, or cried out, because like fresh stigmata the pain in my hand became too strange to bear, and I yelled at them, "Get out" not because their safety was at stake (or because, in that moment, I would have cared if it was) but because I needed, I *had to have*, privacy. Aloneness. I heard like shadows talking Vanese's voice, the deeper faraway mumble of Randy and Malcolm, nothing at all from Nakota, and my own voice entreating them all in jumbled curses, ending every sentence "Go away!"

Vanese got them out, the two of them—there would of course be no moving Nakota—I knew it was her and I wanted to tell her I was grateful, wanted to give her my thanks but there was no way I could because I needed all my concentration, every rubbery scrap, because something was eating at me, something stroking my bones from the inside out and there was no cure for that but to give in, give over, crawl headfirst and kill me, fuck me, I don't care. Why are you so suddenly crazy, I asked myself, some tiny distant human part of me tight with terror and disapproval. I thought you could handle this, I thought this was a purely philosophical FACT-FINDING MISSION, and all the rest of me could answer was Pain.

And desire.

Because it kept *talking* to me, that voice, seeming to say things I had no right to hear, and there in the dark I lay naked to listen, one hand in the hole and the other on my cock, sweating, blood thin in the corners of my mouth, my eyes wide open as they never were, my erection one hungry center, a focus for my want. And that voice, oh my God, it used no words but what it said, what it said. As if things lay displayed that my dry daily brain could not have fathomed, would have dismissed from disbelief or terror, or both. Or worse.

And Nakota beside me, as insubstantial as the morning memory of a dream, some familiar chimera, that was her all right. She stood over me, saying something about the door, the video, maybe that the video was a door, breathy hypnotic gibberish flowing over me like dirty water and "I watch it all the time," she said. "It tells me things. I come here too," and closer still, perhaps to watch my new and juicy ornament, there above my head. "It tells me a *lot* of things," she said.

"Are you a hallucination?" I asked her.

"I want to be you," she said, and she showed me her teeth, her eyes were enormous in the bloody dark, I saw her shaking as she stripped, wet shoes and crummy uniform and tiny scraps of underwear, and she said to me what I said to the Funhole, to that cruel and luminous voice: "Fuck me."

By her hair, I grabbed her by her hair and dragged her down, not caring if we both fell into the Funhole, if we died there, oh Jesus I was worse than crazy and she egged me on, shrew hands locked to me like crampons in my flesh, climbing me, crawling me like an insect, a leech, all bones and teeth like fucking death, yeah, her mouth open on me and screaming something and my hips pounding down as if I meant to break her bones, shatter her pelvis for joyful spite, a smell around us as primal as sex but not from us, oh no, not from us at all. And her banshee voice, howling something and I was coming and I didn't care, I didn't care, I wouldn't stop and pounding and pounding in the lessening drain of my corroding orgasm and still that voice that was no voice at all and I bent my head impossibly back and saw our orbit, our slow decaying gyration above the Funhole, looked and saw as if in a mirror that Nakota's eyes had rolled back in her head and there was blood all over my mouth, all over her face, and the look on my face scared me so badly that I felt us fall, as if belief was all that held us; like Peter on the water I screamed, and Nakota in my arms unconscious, no help, a drag on my strength and perhaps it might be better, it might be easier for us all if I threw her down? Right, and I held her tighter, tighter, willing myself to block our fall with my body, stretched starfish-wide—measured in seconds, but it was that elongated time again, car-wreck time—and hit instead of darkness the floor beyond the Funhole, as if, disgusted with my weakness, my smallness, the Funhole had thrown us back.

Incredibly I was still inside her. It was hard to see, I was crying, trying to pull away but so drained that I managed only to slip partway out, and then I heard them: knocking, knocking, hoarse urgent call, Vanese, and Randy fainter, behind her, saying in that pushed-to-the-limits voice, "Because it *won't open*, that's why," and something indistinct from Malcolm, the tone—excitement, dismay—shared and amplified by his three stooges, his tinny Greek chorus.

"Help us," I said, as loudly as I could. "We're hurt."

"Nicholas," Vanese's voice, the way you talk to people trapped inside a burning car, "we can't get the door open. Did you lock the door?"

"No," I said. "The door doesn't lock, it—"

"We can't get it open," Vanese said again, and I realized she was crying. "How bad are you hurt? Should we go and get a—shut *up*!" sudden sharp hysteric cry, someone else's nervous startle and Malcolm's curse.

Boom, boom. Randy's thudding shoulder against the frame, boom, boom, and I pulled away from Nakota, unable to look too closely at her, crawled to the door, and with one hand turned the knob, Randy pratfall-tripping over me, falling to one knee in the smear of the floor. Vanese's voice, low: "Oh my sweet Jesus," she could say nothing but that, oh my sweet Jesus over and over again, and Malcolm's face, over her shoulder, greedy like a gawper at a public impaling, the three behind him wide-eyed human echoes and Randy bending to Nakota and saying, with the gentle voice of shock, "Nicholas, is she dead?"

"I don't know."

Randy said, after a moment, that her heart was still beating, she was breathing, yeah. "Put something on her," I said, weak resentment at the gawk of those faces, their avid blinkless eyes; my own damp nakedness meant less than nothing, but somehow they must not gape at hers.

Randy wrapped her in his jacket, lifted her as

Malcolm and Vanese helped me into my pants, steadied me for the interminable trip upstairs, and as we walked, our own little death march silent but for the whispered susurration from the three in the rear, Nakota all at once opened her eyes and said, slurred voice through a distinct and bloody grin, "Should've hadda camcorder."

Vanese went still, all over, and then, "You are *crazy*," pulling back, away from me, "you are all *crazy*," and suddenly she ran, almost stumbling down the stairs, she had no coat, she was out the door. I felt the new cold of the night rising around me, on my bare skin, and then we were at the flat, the trio simultaneously opening the door and obscuring our entrance, Malcolm helping me into a chair as Randy lay Nakota on the couchbed.

"What happened?" he said. "What the fuck *happened* in there?"

Nakota again, nothing short of death could shut her mouth: "Nicholas . . . lost it."

With admiration.

They left us, finally, Malcolm flanked by the stunned Malcolmettes—seeing was, apparently, believing—and Randy carrying Vanese's coat. "You gonna be all right, man?" looking at us both, stupid survivors, tired maybe of patching us up, or watching us patch each other. Maybe just tired.

"We're fine," Nakota said authoritatively. "We'll be fine." Then, "Randy—did you see it?"

I thought she meant the spectacle, wondered how in hell even she could be so brutal, then saw his slow nod.

"It's slag," he said. "Fuckin' slag." And was gone.

Feral-bright eyes, poking me in the ribs. "We melted steel," she said. "Both of us. We melted steel."

I had never seen anyone look so smug. Torn lips—which accounted, thank God, for most of the blood, though her mouth was going to look pretty weird from now on—and loose teeth, raccoon bruises around both eyes, glittering eyes because she was one happy girl, our Nakota, our crazy Shrike, maybe Shrike was a better name for her after all.

"I think we should always have sex there," she said.

"I think you're a goddamned lunatic." I rubbed my eyes, sore left-hand fingers, I hadn't looked at my right hand—wrapped now in the last clean towel in the house—and I wasn't about to. "Nakota, I hurt you. I could've hurt you more, maybe, God. I don't even want to think about it, okay? I don't even want to go—"

Instantly angry, "Don't be such an asshole. This is what's supposed to happen, don't you know that? Don't you understand *anything*?"

"No," I said, in simple truth. "No I don't."

"Then shut up."

She fell asleep. I hurt too much in too many places, most internal, to join her, hut could not make myself do more than lie there in the dark.

Around me pure silence, no video, no voices, just the pale sporadic clatter of late traffic, Nakota's snore-breathing, soft rattling whistle from her injured mouth. Enough light to my eyes to see her, she looked like someone had worked on her with a pipe, and I began to cry, for her, because she was hurt, because I had hurt her. Because to her it didn't matter. Because it almost surely would happen again.

"Oh, God," in my throat, almost unheard but she heard it, half opened her eyes, and on that ledge of sleep I saw a gravity, the faintest breath of a genuine sweetness in the slow tired blink of her eyes, of the sore smile she gave me.

"Shut up," she said, and touched my elbow, meaning it for a squeeze. "Go to sleep."

And I cried harder, so hard and long that, childlike, I cried myself to sleep. And dreamed for once of a paradise that even I could reach, past darkness, a place where there was nothing left for my heart to carry. And I lay at rest there in paradise, and, looking up, saw distant and far above me a circle edged in black, and beyond that circle, like a living cloud, the quiet darkness of the empty storage room.

SEVEN

Well. Imagine for yourself the excitement, the speculation, the breathless phone calls that smelled strangely of a bent respect and constantly threaten to become drop-in marathons, even quiz festivals—they were such a curious bunch, the trio that Nakota, bright eyes and sagging lip, had maliciously christened the Three Dingbats. The only way I could keep them away from me was to threaten to bar them forever from Funhole proximity, taking shameless advantage of rights I did not have. But they didn't know that, which was good enough for me, though I also knew it wouldn't work for long.

Malcolm was a more difficult matter. I *had* promised to do the mask, and now was certainly the time to continue since I had rarely looked more like death. And I got him to stop playing the video, though only just. But what was almost worse, he insisted on going over and over the scene in the storage room, blood and sex and revelation, a puddle positive of melted steel; cold fingers patting my aching face through the chalky slap of plaster, he was doing the mask over, he had had new insights, he would share them all with me whether I liked it or not. Nakota could at least find periodic escape in the musty comatose serenity of Club 22, but for me it was nothing but Malcolm, and his theories, and the nervous blurt of the ringing phone bringing questions and questions, the endless loop of speculation that if not meant so seriously would have been hilarious. In a pitiful way.

"They're your friends," I said to Malcolm. "You talk to them."

He shrugged. "They want to talk to you, Nick." Offhand smile of petty malice, scraping tool tapping lightly against the table's crooked lip, crooked as his own, as warped as his enjoyment of the whole scenario: his pet puppies surrounding someone who doesn't like dogs.

Exhausted by their idiocy, their stupid unending phone calls, by the specter of our little merry band grown insidiously larger, the exponential creep of a process whose end I not only could not predict but did not want to understand, I took the predictable way out. I told them they could visit but that was *all*, if they took even one step toward the storage room that was it, they were gone. They agreed with a haste that was suspicious even to me, and I fool easy.

Throughout the day's work I speculated on that call.

"What the fuck," I said to Malcolm.

"Don't move your lips! For God's sake, how many times do I have to tell you not to move while the plaster's drying," fussing like a nurse in the violent ward, so obsessively close in his inspection that if I looked, and I could hardly help it, I could see the miniature veins in his eyes, red as a dingbat's lab coat. When I was again successfully immobilized, he slouched back across the room, to sit smoking a succession of his horrible cigarettes while I sat straight-backed as a mummy, the usual unbearable itch begun in the small of my back, waiting for the plaster to dry.

"The whole thing blew them away," he said.

Too bad not for real, huh? Although this was not true, or not entirely; I had nothing personal against the Dingbats, I just wanted them to go away. Taking Malcolm with them. Neither of which was even remotely probable anymore.

"I mean it really blew them away." Long expansive puff; how, I thought, can he smoke those things without puking? Even Nakota couldn't take the smell, which lay all over the flat now like a base coat of cancer. "They can't stop talking about it."

Yes, I noticed, but to say it wasn't worth his inevitable squawk about the plaster, so I didn't. Now my hand was throbbing, too, in a more-than-usual way, and I rubbed it, slow, against my thigh in an empty search for comfort, wishing it wasn't so cold in the flat, wishing Nakota was there, wishing I was alone. By the time he freed me from the plaster I was so jittery with irritation the very swish of his hair was enough to make me want to stuff him headfirst down the Funhole without so much as a cheery farewell, and of course it was just then that the door opened to reveal the grinning triumvirate of Dingbats, all of them, God help us, wearing sunglasses. In the snow.

First of all they wanted to watch the video, and when, yelling from the bathroom where I sloppily scrubbed my face (the only pleasure I was likely to have all day), I told them no, they said they wanted to "interview" me about my "feelings."

Oh right. Even for them this was going too far, what next, a documentary? "The only feelings I have right now," I said, slamming out of the bathroom, my stiff jaw still outlined in a sticky ribbon of mingled Vaseline and plaster residue, "you don't want to know about. And what the hell do you mean, interview me? Interview me for what? Your personal archives? Your diaries? What?" Nobody answered. I could feel in my chest a pleasant bubble of rage, freely mingled with self-pity and an overriding regret that Nakota was not home to chew them the new assholes they deserved, side by side with the drier knowledge that she would far more likely egg them on.

"Either you weren't paying attention, the other day," I said, "or you're stupid, and I would hate to think anybody could be that stupid. Even friends of yours," to Malcolm, who froze in the act of lighting another cigarette to give me a look less piqued than surprised, as if one of the drying floor-bound blobs of plaster had spitefully bitten his toe, and he their benign creator; fathom for yourself the sheer ingratitude.

"This is not a game," I said. My hand on the refrigerator door, so angry I could barely remember what the hell I was doing there. When in doubt, get a beer. It can't help, but what can? "This is not some fucking art-school field trip, this is the weirdest motherfucking thing you will ever see and if you tell so much as one single person about it, if you even tell them where this *building* is," and, voice risen, I had absolutely no idea how to follow that one up, I had had no prior experience in making threats that were meant to be taken seriously, so I slammed the refrigerator door as hard as I could, sending a cracked and empty juice jar and a flutter of outdated coupons to the dust-gummed floor below.

Silence. "Don't make me tell you again," I said, and marched back to the bathroom before my traitor face could display the lunatic bray of laughter fighting to blow free. As I closed the door and jammed both faucets to on, a pure continuation of silence, I thought: So of course the first thing they do is run downstairs, right? Which made me want to laugh even harder.

But they were still there when I reappeared, talking quietly among themselves, only Malcolm aloof as he sat cross-legged on the floor, trying to scrape the plaster dust from under his nails; he had nails like a goat's. No one looked at me. In the face of such excessive casualness I became, true to form, more nervous, tripped on my way to the stereo, almost mashing Malcolm's black-booted foot.

"Watch it," and I shrugged, turning on something, loud. My beer was almost gone. Fancy that. To say something I asked the Incubus woman about music, who did she like to listen to. The answer was, as I expected, neatly suffocated by a crash course in modern music theory, which is to say heavy on the bullshit, but I did find out her name. Doris. She was Doris, and the other one was Ashlee, and the guy was Dave.

None of them drank beer, which figured, but they were at least willing to sit and watch me do it. As my slump grew more pronounced Doris's eyes brightened, the gestures of her chapped hands became more animated—she was one of those people who love to be told they can't talk without their hands—and Ashlee laughed and Dave was even moved to crack a joke, something about the superrealists who froze to death when they went to the drive-in to see CLOSED FOR WINTER. Imagine! Levity. Malcolm's silent sulk blossomed at last into open disgust as the hours passed and no one asked his opinion, studied the mask, or even commented on the new direction it was taking, a sharp spiral downward if anyone was interested in my opinion which they doubtless were not. Unless of course I wanted to talk about the Funhole.

Which I didn't. Nor would I allow them to, giving them the brick wall stare when they tried (and they did try, especially Doris, she was a regular Nakota when it came to taking no for an answer). I caught them peeking, swift and blind and sneaky, at my bandaged hand, and wondered if they guessed what painful shiny rot lay beneath, wondered if they caught, as I did, its mushy scent on the smoke-dry air, and if they did what images it planted, what dark romantic horseshit they conjured from parched imagination's empty soil. Because no matter what they thought they knew, I knew they had never seen anything like it. And never would, if I could at all prevent it.

From floor to chair, to bathroom, to refrigerator, letting the door bang with a cold moue of distaste: finally Malcolm's aggravation overcame him. "I'm taking off," he said, and with a stare long enough only to show his consuming displeasure with us all took his premature leave, pointedly not slamming the door. His cigarettes lay forgotten on the floor where he had first been sitting, and it took me just a moment to toss them gleefully overhand into the trash.

"I hope they were expensive," I said, stopping on my way back to get another beer, reflecting as I did how truly bad my hand smelled tonight, was it getting worse or was I growing more sensitive. Ashlee said something to Doris, who shook her head, brisk positive motion, shimmy of ragged hair.

"How come," sitting back down, my unsteady gaze rolling from one to another, "you didn't go with him?"

Dave shrugged.

Ashlee shrugged too and looked away, and Doris, the eternal spokesperson, for once had little to say. It was about then when my drunken boredom overtook me, even being persecuted by the Funhole in one of its less indulgent modes was more entertaining than this. I flopped to my feet and told them it was time to go. At first they didn't believe me, but I was insistent.

"If you hurry," I said, "you can still catch up with Malcolm," oh they were a fickle bunch of fucks, I thought, showing them the door, just drunk enough to find it funny. Which Nakota, when she came home, emphatically did not.

"Oh great," fast and vicious stripdown, tearing at her uniform where it stalled at wrists and neckline, whipping the empty clothes at me. A button struck me softly in the eye. "That's just what we need: a fucking bunch of yahoo dingbats coming to sit at your feet. Are you that desperate for company? Isn't Malcolm enough for you?"

"Get off my ass," I said, but mildly, still anesthetized and anxious to stay that way. The stink of my hand had metamorphosed into a warm aching smell inexplicably like dirt, soil, the ground outside, an unexpectedly homespun odor that was adding to my idiot sense of wellbeing, perhaps even a contributing factor in my small but proud erection, which I waggled now at Nakota in an attempt to turn her attention.

"Put that stupid thing away," she said, lighting a cigarette, mean and naked on the edge of the bed. Why was it that no matter how cold it became in the flat, she never shivered, never showed any visible sign of discomfort? "The thing to do," dismissing for the moment both my words and her anger, "is get the camcorder again, and make another video so—"

"I am not making another video," I said, alarmed. "I'd like to trash the one we have."

"I wouldn't," she said, eyes bright with warning, two meanings for the price of one. "If you weren't so chickenshit," blowing smoke, "*and* drunk, you would realize that—"

"Drunk's got nothing to do with it," I said, pushing up on my elbows, soft wince as my sick hand brushed the bed. "You don't—"

"—*another* one, so we can *compare* them," louder than she needed to, angry at my uncharacteristic interruptions, I was getting out of my place again, clown prince of the Funhole and forget that I had my own agenda, forget that I was, according even to her own theory, in some bad way an engine to keep the drive. I was supposed to be bait, and catalyst and straight man, to dispose if necessary of worshipful stray lunatics, and oh yeah, empty the ashtrays, too.

She was still talking. "—if any changes have taken place, then we'll have documentation." Crushing out the cigarette. Swift swallow of mineral water, as flat and unappetizing as the smell of her body as she leaned across me to set down the glass. "Even you should see the sense in that."

"You sound like them," settling back to cradle my hand beside me, silent dirty drip of fluid onto the already-soiled sheets, what did I care. "They wanted to interview me today."

"Interview you?" and she laughed, reaching for the blanket to wrap herself in, cold cocoon for the insect queen, the reader of buggy runes. What had she done with them, those twisted little bodies? And the mouse, whatever had become of it? "What're they going to do, start a fan club?"

"Funhole Fan Club," I said, made faintly nauseated by the change in odor from my hand, from the color of the sheets where the fluid lay discreetly pooled; I moved away, a bare small inch. Outside traffic was exceptionally loud. I lay listening to it as Nakota fell to her own brand of rest, to dreams gashed with smelly wonders, peopled with the strengths of her delusions, what were her new ones going to lead us to? Another camcorder my ass, though in morning's reality there would most likely be very little I could do about it, there never was, was there? Never had one been so neck-deep in shit and so helpless to reach the flusher. If only I could believe that none of any of this was my business. Or my fault.

Doris had a camcorder.

Of course. And of course Nakota found that out the next day, Day Two, my happy trio over early with McDonald's coffee and dry muffins, and immediately the pair of them perched knees to knees, chummily on the couch while Dave and Ashlee sat sketching on napkins with Malcolm's expensive drawing pencils, pictures of what they thought might be in the Funhole. And *giggling* over it, God. *Romper Room* for demonics. I was all out of bandages so in dull desperation I sat trying to wind half a T-shirt around my hand after stuffing toilet paper in the hole itself, a process as uselessly messy as the hole itself, too, if you wanted to get philosophical about it, if you wanted to think at all.

"Let me help," Ashlee said to me.

"Not a chance," through my teeth as I strained to hear what Nakota was saying to Doris, what was giving her that bright-eyed grin.

"—back around noon," Doris said. "He said he had some stuff to pick up, you know," hands shaping a face in the air, "for the mask."

"We could go there right now then," Nakota standing with quick energetic grace, pocketing my keys since her car wasn't running. "At least start on it today, before I have to go to work."

"Start what?" although I knew, it was the fucking video, she just couldn't wait to mix whatever brew she'd been scheming on last night, her documentation, a travelogue of the indescribable maybe but maybe just a bigger fucking mess for us all and in particular me, why had I ever left that storage room, why had I even bothered to come out? My clearheaded plan had been just another self-deception.

"Start what," I said, and stood, still and shaking, to block her exit: an unheard-of defiance, so surprising that she laughed, as the others sat watchful, avid as birds, Doris arrested in the act of standing, human tableau of indecision.

"Get out of my way, Nicholas," with no more than usual malice, but when I refused, a feral smile as she pushed at me, sharp fist in my shoulder, hard enough to show she meant business, and I pushed back, hard enough to say that I did too. She stared at me the way you stare at Fido when he growls at you over the table scraps, and then without preamble hit me, a brisk and painful punch. Ducking into the blow I reached for her, grabbed hair and shoulders and shoved her hard against the door, held her there and said so only she could hear, "Don't do this, you hear me? Don't do this."

"You are so—" she began, then shook her head, shook off the notion of actually explaining to me my own stupidity, her gesture indicating the inherent waste of time in such an occupation. "You're willing to go on the same way forever, aren't you? Just going in there and taking whatever you get, hands out, gimme gimme gimme like a fucking two-bit beggar. That's your whole style," glancing around as if to indict me by my own squalid helplessness, so virulently displayed in the sorry way I lived. "That's you. But it's not me, and I'm not going to waste my time trying to convince you of what an asshole you are, what a cowardly piece of shit not to take what's being offered, what's being practically thrown in your face. So if you really want to stop me," blue-white incredible smile, daring me, daring me, "then I suggest you kick my ass. Otherwise, get the *fuck* out of my way."

Who blinked? Who do you think, head down, stepping back, my hands dropping reluctant from her shoulders, trembling up and down my arms with anger unused, the dash of adrenaline useless in my blood. "Well come on," impatiently to Doris, who leaped up, passed me without a look, maybe Nakota would be her new mentor now. They didn't close the door so I did, not embarrassed but oh, ashamed, for my weakness, my capacity for defeat, my endless versatility in displaying both. When I got around to looking at them, Ashlee and Dave were pointedly not looking at me. One of the few things, perhaps, they were good for, but now I was in no mood.

"Go on," I said, "why don't you go with them?" and with no more invitation they stood, leaving Styrofoam cups, a crumpled bag, their silly scrawled drawings, and Malcolm, his voice as he passed Nakota and Doris in the hall, his miffed surprise as Dave and Ashlee hurried past with artificial smiles. "What the hell," he said to me, over-shoulder glare and bag in hand, his hair in some new complicated braid, "was all that about?"

I shook my head, shrugged, my two most convincing motions. For once I looked forward to the ritual of the plaster, the cold sealing of my mouth. Malcolm was especially rude, especially when he saw the wasted drawing paper, but even that I welcomed, just deserts, proper punishing scorn for the weakling I was: about that Nakota was essentially right, but about everything else so wrong, immutably mistaken in profound and ominous ways that only I, it seemed, could predict: perhaps it takes a coward to see where the danger really is.

By the time they got back Malcolm's irritability had trebled, due to some malfunction of material and an unfortunate incident involving half a cup of coffee, and I awash in my own jittering dread making matters worse by twitching every time I heard a sound in the hall. The four of them walked in together, Nakota of course in the lead, the camcorder bag jaunty in her hand, expert sneer of one-upmanship as she breezed past Malcolm to light up one of his cigarettes.

"You look like the cat that just ate shit," he said, and she laughed.

"Looks like you're making a mess," glancing around at the spillage, crusts of plaster, the broken faces of the two discarded masks. "I'm making a movie. Want to watch?"

"What the fuck is she talking about?" looking not at me, naturally, but at Doris, and in the same tone, "And where the fuck were you? I could've used some help here."

Doris shrugged. "We needed to get the camcorder. Nakota's going to—"

"What're you, her maid?"

"It's better than being yours," Nakota said, and winked at Doris.

"The camcorder was at my house," said Doris, somewhat aggrieved at his tone but too excited to care much, puppy-bright around the eyes, gestures going a mile a minute. "And we had to stop for tapes, too, we got a three-pack 'cause we're going to—"

Abruptly Malcolm pushed away the kitchen chair he leaned on, shoved it so it skittered, a motion that (as we all knew from the movies) signified a man at the end of his patience. "I don't know what stupid games you're playing, what kind of shit," sparing a glare for Nakota, who ignored him as she continued to smoke his cigarette, "she talked you into, but I am working on an important piece here, I am *trying* to *create* something here that is a little more enduring than some fucking two-bit home movie and I—"

"Oh *roach*," Nakota said, "shut up."

It was a gift with her, the ability to throw just the wrong switches at just the wrong times. Malcolm's face swept red, his overbite fairly bristled with rage as, Doris in the lead, the other three took prudent steps to put themselves at the periphery of the action, while Nakota stood smirking as usual, the center of the blossoming storm, tapping one slim-handled sculpting tool against her skinny thigh as Malcolm, braid swinging, launched into his eruption.

Still faintly plaster-dappled, I rose unnoticed in the general tension, slowly circling back around the kitchen table and quietly out the door, closing click soft behind me and I ran like a bastard, hurry hurry hurry on the stairs and into the storage room, shut the door with a slam and my back to it, saying to myself, Think, think, she'll be up here any minute, what can you do? What

and whack, whack, her insistent fist already at the door, oh God is there to be no time of grace at all? No. No. "Nakota," I said, positioning myself in as braced a stance as possible, why wasn't there a lock on this fucking door, "go away."

Even I could hear how lame I sounded; she didn't even bother to laugh, just used Dave to slam open the door, sending me into a balanceless spin across the floor, clumsy polka that left me sprawled on one knee as the four of them trooped in, Malcolm apparently too proud to join the fun. Nakota grinning, the camcorder poised in her arms like a favored pet, the others rubbernecking, awed no doubt by the sheer dusty normalcy of it all, all until you got to the hole in the floor of course, you're not from around here, are you?

"Go away," I said again, my hand begun a threatening throb, the Funhole behind me as ominously still, like the calm surface of a midnight lake just before the heralding ripples of the monster. "This is wrong, and worse than that, it's *stupid*, look how much trouble we had the last time we—"

and a thought like a sledgehammer: You should have stayed upstairs, asshole, she says it doesn't work without you why the *hell* did you tear ass to get in here oh you stupid fuck

and Nakota's snarl, "Get out of my fucking way!" as the record light went on, idiot glow of the LED, and she advanced on me like an army, her own small cadre of troops almost too excited now as she backed me to the hole itself, an almost inaudibly deep grumble begun that tremored the floor beneath me, oh Nakota am I going to have to hurt you to stop you? Again? I can't I

and without thinking I grabbed her, left hand a fist in her hair, clenching right hand, hole hand, over the maw of the camera, you want to take a picture of a hole well I got a hole for you take a picture of *this*, coating the lens with the drift and glitter of my slime, the juicy scum that incredibly began to bubble as it touched the surface of the lens, devoured the hood in swift corrosion, a mobile cancer and still my hand in her hair, grinding, twisting, it had to hurt and at that moment I didn't give a shit, it was her own fucking fault *her* fault not mine. Not mine. And still the creeping burn, destroying the body of the camcorder itself, eating away as far as the strap and the useless box dropping now, falling to the floor, a hollow sound as it struck and with one swift thoughtless motion I kicked it down the Funhole, and only then pushed Nakota down, and away.

"There," I said. Wet all over. Sweat. Maybe piss, too, for all I knew, and shivering in the chill aftermath of anger, Nakota rising furious before me, toxic genie from some unimaginable lamp, snake from a basket: "Oh you stupid motherfucking piece of *shit*—"

And she hit me, very hard, I was expecting it and it didn't hurt, really, very much at all, although the force of it jerked my head back, silly drunken wobble on my aching neck, and the ooze of my hand, no longer napalm, down to a timid trickle. Arm drawn back to do it again, perhaps many times, and Doris, incredibly, catching hold of that arm, saying, "Don't. Don't, Nakota."

Looking, as she said it, at me, the same gaze from Dave and Ashlee, a look far worse than any tantrum of Nakota's could ever be: it was bubbling awe, it was nervousness; it was fear. I turned my head away, Nakota, ugly, saying "I'll just get another one, Nicholas," and Doris mumbling something, words that had the effect of an eyedropper on a greasefire, nothing but pops and sizzles and still beneath my feet that earthquake jiggle, like something coming from far, far away.

"Just get out of here, okay?" over my shoulder and I turned back enough to see them staring at me, see Doris and Dave taking Nakota's arms and walking her out of the room, Ashlee the last to go, wide eyes gleaming like roadkill's in the instant before the car. And a subterranean undulation as the door swung gently to, I lay beside the Funhole and felt that murmur in the flesh of the floor, felt the shadowless weight of Randy's twisted ladder lying close beside in an attitude of commiseration as inescapable as my thoughts. I always made it worse, in all my simple strategies, my convoluted acts, invariably I always made it worse.

Why was that?

Why do birds fly?

Why does metal conduct electricity?

Why does wet stinky smelly shit come splattering out of my hand? Why, it's nature, isn't it; isn't it *just*.

I didn't come out of the storage room for a day, almost two, lying guiltily slack, fallow if you will. On reemergence the hall was empty, cold with a damp chill that passed the skin to settle leechlike in the bones. Upstairs, gripping the banister like a ninety-year-old arthritic, creeping into the flat like a burglar, the door closed but unlocked, good thing I had nothing anyone wanted. No: not right: half-slumped at the kitchen table, open beer and chewing bread smeared with ancient salsa, Randy. Smiling a little when I entered, gesturing with the bread.

"Sorry, man, didn't mean to help myself, it's just I been waiting so long."

"Don't worry about it." One-handed palm of cold beer can, doubling my shivers going down but I drank, two swallows, four, half the can gone into the grind of my empty stomach and the pleasing small luxury of a solid belch. Looking around I saw full ashtrays, a rectangle of newspaper, Malcolm's tidied tools, the mask itself nowhere to be seen. "Where is everybody?" I said, false nonchalance, fingers as cold as the can they held.

"Well. That takes some telling," but he smiled as he said it and some of the stick went out of my spine. "I wasn't here for part one, but I guess Shrike blew some kind of gasket when you wouldn't let her make her video—"

"It's Doris who should be pissed," I said. Got another beer. "It was her camcorder."

"Yeah. Anyway Shrike was busy throwing her fit when I got here and Doris says, Doris's the one who kind of looks like Malcolm, right? Right. So Doris says, Cool off, Nicholas is really onto something important here and it won't do any good to piss him off, he's the only one who knows, he has the answers blah blah blah, all this shit like you're some kind of guru, you know?"

That roadkill look; "I know."

"So Shrike says, everybody fuck off, I'll do it myself. And Doris and those other two assholes—"

"Dingbats."

"Dingbats, right," emphatic nod, "They all start arguing and Malcolm just blows up and says, You're all crazy and I'm out of here. And he takes his mask and goes home. Or somewhere. And nobody goes with him, everybody just sits around waiting for you to come back—"

"Nakota too?"

Headshake. "She took the video, though."

Ah, *God*. The fucking video, I had forgotten. My carelessness, how vengefully would it come home to roost? Stop it, I thought. Stop making things worse than they are. "What about everybody else?"

"Out to eat. Out to *lunch*," shaking his head, "they're out to lunch all right. Is there any more of those beers?"

We drank them all up, but, drunk, my worry undimmed, I spun my silent fantasies of what Nakota might be doing with that video, *The Funhole Part One*, what remorseless mischief she might be making and me unable to fathom, much less put a stop to it. And Randy putting on some extremely loud thrash music. And the beer going down. And the dingbats, coming back. Whooping in the hall, some weird Chilean wine, two bottles apiece, apparently we were all going to have a party.

They approved the music, as boisterously approved Randy, who did not return the favor or even comments directed at him, saying once to me, under cover of their chatter back and forth, their theories too silly to remember past the second spoken, "Guess you're their Malcolm now."

Dull negating headshake, but we both knew he was right. It showed in their eager deference: my choice of music, my choice of chair, my choice opinions, at this point unexpressed beyond a few dispirited grunts; respectful their offers, even, to get me another beer. It was not so much ridiculous as scary, it got to me after only a very little while, and Randy too: he left and left me there, stranded in my growing island of pained drunken silence and beer-can armor, and still the gnaw, Nakota, where are you? Destructive force with a chip on her shoulder. You left her with the video before, I argued, nothing happened, nothing will happen now. Nothing bad will—

And the door, when had it opened, who could hear in that caldron of noise, and she, in night-damp Club 22-wear, my relief at her presence completely evaporated by the look in her eyes. The others, Medusa-like she scared them silent. Ignoring them, her gaze on me, one hand closing the door, the other holding the black plastic of the video.

"You win again, fuckface," and she skimmed the video at me, hard square Frisbee with amazing force and it struck me so near the eye, my warding hand useless and the sudden bright plop of fluid onto my skin, circular jelly mixed with the dimmer color of my blood. Someone turned the music down; Ashlee offered, small voice, to get me something to wipe off with.

"Get out," Nakota snarled, at her, at all of them, not bothering to look as she lit a cigarette and threw the lighter at me too. It missed. They stood, I felt their stares, and wearily I said, "Go on, go home," like a cop at the scene of some exceptionally lurid crime, nothing to see anymore, folks, move along. "Go on," louder, and as if shaken from their shock they moved, herding out the door, careful to keep their distance from Nakota as they might skirt a living fire.

"Quite the fans you have there," advancing on me, newly furious that my suggestion had worked where her order had not, "quite the little groupies. Did you *know* it wouldn't take?"

Already exhausted by her anger, the beer roiling flat and gassy in my timid gut, "Take what?"

"The *video*, you asshole. Did you know it wouldn't take?" and without so much as a breath, "You don't even know what I'm talking about, do you? I tried to copy it," and a hissy little laugh, enjoying despite herself the expression on my face, I'm sure it was unique.

"I don't know," blowing smoke at the blood on my skin, "why I never thought of it before. What if you played it ten times, at the *same* time, ten tapes going at once. Would it be clearer? The paths, I mean, the arrangement of the—" and suddenly swerving that train of thought, remembering whom she was talking to: "But it didn't *work*."

I tried, stupid backbrain reflex, to help. "Maybe the tape was no good, the one you used. Maybe the—"

"Maybe it won't work even if I tried it on a *million* tapes, maybe it can't work," cigarette up and down in her mouth, little black arrow now indicating eyes so venomous with knowledge denied that I helplessly turned my gaze away. "*I* think there's something in it that resists being copied. And if I really thought you knew what that was, I'd put this out"—pointing the cigarette at me— "in that," nodding at my right hand which still bled its own brand of plasma, slimy on the tabletop, "until you told me."

"I don't know shit about what works and what doesn't, or why, and I don't give a shit either," and it was true. I was just so tired. I was going back in there tomorrow, going into storage if you will (and even if you won't I will, I almost have to at this stage of the game) and as for her paths, I was less uninterested than blessedly unaware and determined to stay that way, I wanted nothing of her theories to cumber me as I lay like a snake on my shivering belly, staring into the dark of a negativity that stood for nothing, nothing we could know. Her most trenchant speculations were less than the guesses of a fool, as cogent as Malcolm's for that matter and as meaningless. I knew that this was so as I knew the Funhole was a process, as I was convinced that my heart beat and my body used air, having no personal explanation for any of those processes beyond the cool fact of their existence, beyond saying This is the way things are. Which is almost certainly why she hated me, then more than usual: for the utter depth of my acceptance, my, to her, lackadaisical acquiescence to conditions she was convinced could and must be altered: as if a prehistoric Nakota crouched rubbing wet sticks together, furious with Neanderthal me for not helping her discover why she couldn't make fire.

"I think," I said, very slowly, my mouth rubbery, now, as the rest of me, from the beer, the two-day lack of food, the churning of worry like liquid salt in my stomach, "I think I'm just gonna go to bed."

She said nothing at first, a circumstance so remarkable that I almost remarked on it, feeling her watch my shuffle to the bathroom and even back without a word. Sitting on the edge of the bed to peel down my socks, my cruddy jeans, and she a cold tableau, finally saying as she turned away, "I never expected any help from you, anyway; you're incapable. Just keep your little groupies out of my way."

"They're not my groupies," I muttered, slumping back to a sleep as restless and impure as any I had ever suffered, waking time and again to her poker-backed priestess stance, there in the glow of the TV. In the light of the uncopied video. And I turned my head away, into the minor crevice of the pillow, and tried to think nothing at all.

EIGHT

Though I played no razzle-dazzle, gave them nothing whatsoever to feed on, still they dogged me, my little groupies, my animate source of irritation: to Nakota, to whom their bumbling attempts to stick up for, and worse yet listen to, me were evidence of almost blasphemous defiance, earning them a high spot on her shit list when she bothered to notice them at all; to Malcolm, who also considered them traitors, this attitude of course strengthening his axis with Nakota; to Randy, who uncharacteristically refused to find any humor whatsoever in their duh-huh style, insisting instead that I should get rid of them ("How?" I said, and he, unable to recommend to weakling me his usual no-nonsense method of choice—the bum's rush—ending frustrated and irritated, then, with me as well); only Vanese could stand them, and she only marginally—they were also a kind of collective symbol to our little band, their presence become to each the vindication of a particular theory, one to a customer please, no pushing. Nakota thought they were the walking indictment of my lame-ass methods in dealing with the Funhole, conclusively proving that anyone who swallowed my theories; which were of course practically nil, ought to be given a Drano chaser: Malcolm scorned them as cheap-thrill seekers when he had cherished for them a more exalted destiny, that of professional art fuck, although naturally he used a different term. Randy thought they were pretentious assholes, which they were, who should never have been trusted with such a mystery as the Funhole. Vanese thought they were assholes, too, in themselves basically harmless but also a harbinger of worse to come, the front row of a crowd whose control would not be possible.

She told me this the afternoon after Nakota's video-slinging event, while the flat was pleasantly empty but for us, me with a plastic sandwich bag full of ice cubes pressed, at her insistence, to the swollen cut above my twitchy eye. "That girl is some kind of hard-nosed bitch," Vanese said, without admiration. "What she needs is somebody to take her down a peg or two. Or twenty-two."

"Sorry, wrong number."

"What're you going to do, Nicholas?"

"About what?"

She sighed, a sad little sound that made more melancholy the backdrop of the sullen afternoon, dusty shadows lying in flat oblong planes, making of the whole room a complicated rebus of exhaustion and want. It even depressed me, and I was used to it. "Oh, Nicholas," that older-sister face again. "You're supposed to be in charge."

That surprised a laugh from me; I shook my head. "No way. No *way*. If anyone's in charge around here it's the Funhole."

"That's just what I mean. The Funhole, shit, that's no person, that's not even hardly a thing." Strong stirring motions in the sluggish goo of her convenience-store coffee. "Somebody has to be in charge, and it picked you, didn't it?"

Again, "No way," uneasy with the very idea, more uneasy still as she nodded to my newly rebandaged hand, courtesy herself, saying with that nod, Well isn't that the proof? Isn't it? "No," I said. "I'm just the first asshole to stick his hand down there, that's all."

"You really think so?" A pause, what was she thinking that needed careful phrasing to speak aloud? "Shrike, Nakota, she says you're the one who makes things happen. You think she could've melted that camera? Think any one of us could have—"

"I don't want to talk about it," I said, reaching balanceless from where I sat for the refrigerator door, bobbling in my seat, and I almost fell; could any clown such as me be in any kind of charge, strange groundskeeper for the gateways and the paths as Nakota kept insisting on calling her revelations, in charge of things I could barely comprehend, let alone understand? The sun slipped another notch, the shadows uglier in their depthless length. Bleakly, "There's no more beer."

"That's all you need—put that ice back on your head."

"Be my mother, Vanese?"

She smiled, a little. "You just better be a little careful, you hear me, Nicholas? Especially now, with your three new friends. I keep telling Randy, and I tell you, they're the shape of things to come."

"Then the shape must be a question mark."

I wanted to make her laugh, wanted to hear it, but her smile was too small; pouring out the sludgy coffee, picking up her key chain: heavy fake-gold heart shape chunky with keys, beside it some kind of tiny dangling locket, Randy's picture probably inside. "Is Randy coming tonight?" but she shook her head, he was tired; he had been snappish lately, neglecting his own work to come dally at this darker shrine.

"He needs some time off," over her shoulder as I followed her down the hall. "You ask me, you could stand some, too. Little rest makes a lot of difference."

"I bet it does."

Pausing there a moment, long intake of breath to ask a careful question: "Do you know—what does 'transcursion' mean?"

I shrugged. "Never heard of it."

"Me neither," gentle unconscious gnaw of lip, "but they were talking about it, before. I heard Shrike, Nakota say it once or twice. I just wondered if you knew."

"Never heard of it."

Famous last words.

Still Malcolm's tools lay unused, still he kept minimal contact with me; hadn't even been over to watch the video—actually a moot occupation, I hadn't seen it myself in weeks and in fact it wasn't even there to be seen: Nakota presumably carrying it around with her, sleeping with it at night (but not with me); while still nominally in residence she too was unusually scarce, though she always managed to be around on the occasions when I found myself beside the Funhole, greedy for the revelations she was sure she could interpret, hungry to walk at least mentally the paths she kept insisting lay spread before us, before her, like some dark garden. Garden of evil. She read a lot of Ben Hecht. Malcolm did too, or said he did, privately I thought he never got further than the tabletalk equivalent of Cliff's notes but what did I know, maybe he was a closet scholar. Yeah, like Nakota was a closet nun.

Maybe they watched the video together; they'd done that before, hadn't they. Maybe the video was, now, a tool for them, and more, perhaps the third component in a ménage à trois, she and Malcolm twisting, sweaty and boneless, in the leering glow of its looped images. Of course that would bother me, but not for the usual reasons, Nakota's idea of faithfulness was remembering my telephone number and anyway there was nothing, from her point of view, to be faithful to: I was the one who loved, not she. Worth worry, though, was the wonder of what she was really up to; there was no sense asking her, nor Malcolm, neither were likely to tell me if the flat was on fire.

Working on the theory that even a broken clock is right twice a day, I asked Doris et al if they knew what Malcolm was doing, if they thought he was coming back to finish the mask or at least get his crummy tools.

"Is he working on something new?" I asked, sitting before them, hands loose in my lap, faint sounds from the flat above us, somebody fighting, slow and dreary repetition of shopworn curses and sighs. "Some new project or something?"

Shrugs, blank looks, their natural habitat. Ashlee picked a hangnail with a surgeon's precision. "I don't know," Dave said. "Last I heard, he was still working on the mask of your face."

"We don't see that much of Malcolm anymore," said Doris.

"Why not?"

No one answered me. I asked again, more crossly, for God's sake even they must have reasons for their actions: "Why not?"

Back and forth, a look passed like a dead fish, you tell him. No, *you* tell him. Finally Doris said, "We don't share theories with him anymore."

Share theories. I'd've had more luck asking the Funhole. I opened my mouth to say I don't know what the hell you're talking about, but Ashlee spoke up, a subdued tone, frown line between her eyebrows: "It's those people, you know? Nakota's friends. I don't like them."

Nakota's friends. Is there a word for the feeling that trickled down my spine? "What friends?"

"*You* know," reprovingly, but with a hint of unease, perhaps I did not know, perhaps she would have to actually tell me. Looking for help to Doris and Dave and my voice rising, I couldn't help it, "*What* friends, for fuck's sake? What're you talking about?"

"Well," Doris, nervous in a new way, swift looks between the three of them but never at me, "it's some of the people who hang out at the Incubus. They're not interested in Art, you know," including without conscious thought that obligatory capital A, as I sat kneading my bad hand against my good one, a warm foreboding, Ashlee picking her hangnail a mile a minute. "They just want to, to—"

"They want to be on the fringe," Dave said, from his useless stance at the refrigerator, searching for wine that wasn't there. "They want stuff that's, you know. That's out there."

"And Nakota told them about the Funhole?" Any other time I might have laughed at the squeak of my voice, a cartoon character confronting the inevitable mortality of the brick wall, the canyon floor, the OFF switch on the TV. "She told them?"

"I think," Ashlee, very slowly, looking all around her for support, "she showed them the video."

"It makes a very powerful statement," said Doris, with a solemnity that roused in me the immediate urge to strangle her, Nakota, myself. Everyone. A greasy tingling in the hole of my hand, crushing it hard against the sloped bone of my kneecap, over and over and thinking, thinking, staring at nothing until in sudden pause I looked up to see the three of them, staring at me with such childish woebegone anxiety that I felt a mingled rage and tired—what? Pity? Sympathy? They were just dingbats, after all, the minor-league version of what they decried, looking for the small thrill, the neatly boxed excitement. The Funhole Gift Set, prewrapped.

"Go home," I said, "go away for a while. All right? I just want to be by myself for a little bit. All right?"

And their nods, more eager to be gone than they wanted me to see, jackets and smiles and they would call, yes, maybe they could come back later? Maybe we could all talk? Yes, yes, nodding at them, don't let the door hit you in the back. Nearly sprinting for the phone.

Randy wasn't home, but Vanese was, and in her silence, created by my anxious questions, I knew she knew what Doris and the others were talking about; I leaned my forehead against the wall, I closed my eyes to await the answer.

"Bunch of assholes from the gallery," she said, "they're always up for some weirdness, the bigger the better. They'd just eat that video *up*." Stringent disgust, I could picture the look on her face and felt no reassurance, it was as bad as I feared. The floor, falling beneath me. Things are never so bad they can't get worse. Especially when Nakota is around, especially when she's mad.

"That fucking bitch," she said. "Just doesn't care, does she?"

"No," I said. "I don't think she does."

After I hung up, I stayed standing, trying harder and harder to think but finding a mournful fatalism every way I turned, there was no way out. I knew what she was doing, now, and no doubt Malcolm was in on it, both of them pissed at my groupies, as they called them, at the *fact* of my groupies, at anyone—what had Doris said, yeah, sharing theories with me. Treating me as more than a barely necessary appliance, the crank that makes the magic box run. No camcorder, I had ruined that for her, no new video for you, Nakota. No copying the old one either, she maybe blamed that on me, too. And Malcolm beside her, to nurture her spite with the spurts and gushings of his own, withholding his mask from me, from his traitorous disciples, why hadn't I seen any of this coming? Was I always doomed to be the fucking dupe, the one who never knew what was going on? Stumbling around, waiting for the anvil to fall on my head. No wonder I had a hole in my hand.

The fight above my head was still going on, the kind of circular bitching that reaches a certain level and then goes nowhere in particular but round and round. I turned on no lights, got a beer in the dark and crept to bed, lay like a troubled fetus in the soiled swirl of blanket and sheet. No Funhole for me tonight, my hand at this decision racked with a sudden petulant throb, my own petulance rising with a brief but telling urge to cut the motherfucker off, how's that for downing a lifeline, cutting off communication one might say. Call me Lefty. Maybe I could just—

Talking. Not above me. In the hall.

A questioning tone, some guy, something, and then Nakota unmistakable: "He's not here." Someone else, and her scornful answer: "Because it doesn't *work* without him, dipshit." More talk. As slowly as my breath was fast I set the beer down, careful, careful, pulled the covers up so there was only a dark half circle, breathing space, tried to look like a messy bed. They were still talking but I couldn't hear, pulling up the covers had made it worse. What to do. Maybe I could play turtle, put my head out enough to hear and then if the door—

Which it did, and the light too at once and my clumsiness betrayed me, Nakota in instant triumph seeing the whorl of blanket f or what it was and saying, "There he is," and me raising my head, reluctant and half-blind, blinking at *her* groupies.

Whom I saw at once were more trouble than I felt up to handling: six or seven of them, hunching shoulders, big jackets, hands impatient in pockets and eyes like tracer gazes going all around the room, all of them stupider, meaner, wilder, more prone to that special brand of idiocy which most often turns into wreckage, spillage; blood. They smelled blood, all right, or maybe worse that more esoteric fluid that dribbled from me now, in a brightly vindictive stream that soaked the pillowcase and turned the sheet to clotted silver, a party color is it, well let's start the party now. When in doubt, attack, right? And I was nothing if not always in doubt. About something.

But not Nakota, who, I saw and plainly, relished this role as field marshal, why not, it was the kind of situation she was born to not only milk but throttle till it was as juiceless as a skull in the desert. Head back and hips like rim shots as she walked over to the bed, sat chummily beside me and said, brisk elbow and dry grin, "So. What happened to your little friends?"

"They got a life," I said, as shittily as I could muster, which wasn't much but it might fake out her buddies who now stood like half-domesticated slaves in the center of the room, waiting for her to say something, to tell them what to do. "What's all this?" gesturing openly with my leaky hand. "Malcolm's friends?"

It didn't piss her off, as I had lamely hoped, or fool her for a minute. We both knew who they belonged to, and never mind that Malcolm's charisma quotient had always been at least a quart low, that he couldn't assemble an army at gunpoint. But let's just remember, shall we, let's make sure we don't forget that he'll be more than happy to hoard what Nakota collected, her cadre of dissatisfied jerks masquerading as the cheapest kind of mystics, fun junkies out gunning for the biggest fun of all; he'll be more than ready to use whatever weapon, however blunt, they constitute, to serve whatever banal and horrible concept he—and worse, she—thought "best." And of course we also know who it's best *for*.

"We're going to watch the video now," Nakota said. "Join us."

"I was sleeping," I said, and she shook her head. "No you weren't, you fucking liar. If you don't want to watch with us, then get the hell out."

You wish, I thought, that sudden concealed sparkle a clue as subtle as an ax. I know what you want me to do, I told her with my eyes. And I won't. No, I won't.

And I didn't. Instead I lay tense, faking nonchalance as I observed Nakota's sorry fucks sprawled slack-jawed before the TV, watching the video, the video, the video until I wanted to jump up and run out of the room, which was probably part of the point. Maybe all of it, though I wasn't vain enough to think so, and anyway Nakota was famous for her crisscross motives, occasionally reaching heights so dizzyingly Byzantine that even she couldn't say with certainty what the real reason was.

See her now, hair pulled into some weird new topknot, big fat coat that she no doubt had appropriated from one of her followers, knees bent and dirty shoes up on the edge of the couch. See the hinty smile that whispers of plot, see the glaze of her eyeballs as she watches a scene she's seen a zillion times and more but she doesn't care because it's not really what she's seeing, oh no, there's quite a different movie playing in the cold zone between object and inner vision. And so absorbed myself I didn't notice the new mimicking smirk till it was right in my face, build like a decadent soccer player and blue eyes lined thick like Cleopatra, a smell from the big jacket like cigarettes and too sweet after-shave. A chummy lean, like we were pals.

"She says," said the face before me, indicating with a nod Nakota, "that you can start that hole up."

That hole. "You believe everything she tells you?"

"Only when she's right." Smirk magnified by closeness, something gummy in the corners of the mouth. "She's been right all along."

"So far."

"Yeah. So far."

Sudden and startling, a yell from upstairs, the fight invigorated and louder now than the TV, not that there was much of a sound track but the mutters and grunts of the watchers, most of whom turned now to Nakota, interrogatory stares and she said, "It's the people upstairs" like they were too stupid to figure this out for themselves but in fact they must have been if they needed her to interpret two people screaming "Fuck you" at each other.

"You know Malcolm?" said my new friend, reaching into his jacket to pull out a pack of Kools. I nodded, and he did too, as if this was just what he'd expected. "I saw the mask," he added, and smirked again, seemed about to comment further when a truly banshee-quality groan from above and Nakota, looking at me, said, "Do something about that."

I was about to suggest an alternative plan, involving a painfully novel sex act she might perform either alone or with her followers, when I saw one of them leave his comfy position on the floor, out the door and his purposeful feet in the hall, and I thought: Oh. I see, and even if I hadn't Nakota's gratuitous smile crystallized the notion: she was showing off. And a tiny chill as wet as a trickle of blood shivered through me, raising my skin to pebbles of gooseflesh, I pulled the dirty blankets closer and the guy beside me said, "You cold or something?"

"It's just my leprosy," I said, making the mistake of using my bad hand to adjust the blankets, that jumbled flood of silver leaking firm and shiny across my wrist, across the bedclothes. My earlier bravado evaporated, I tried to hide the mess but no, he was staring at it with a genuinely blank look, as if I had just farted out a cloud of ducklings, or began coughing up hundred-dollar bills.

With my other hand I swept the covers back up, now you see it now you don't as victorious footsteps and Nakota's errand boy back, smiling proudly: "I told them to shut the fuck up," and the others grinning in return and Nakota not grinning at all, just the smallest fold of a smile, pointed at me like the casual tip of a knife. I nodded—touché—maybe she would be satisfied with that particular hoop, maybe we wouldn't need to see another proof of what she could make them do.

They were still there when I fell asleep, uneasy at sleeping in that company but unable finally to outwait them. The last thing I remember hearing was Nakota telling them about the jarful of bugs, so very long ago, strange den mother and her troop of devil scouts around the flickering cathode fire.

Even in sleep the cold pursued me, a bloodless feel to lips and fingers as if I lay drained, vampire's snack, unremembered suicide attempt. In my dreams my hand was a key, a literal key to the storage-room door, and on my breathless chest like an animate gargoyle the guy who had sat on the bed, sawing with a grainy back-and-forth verve at my ramrod wrist and behind him, lips pursed in silent glee, Nakota was busily nodding him on, an empty pickle jar in hand to catch the jiggering spray.

"That's right," she was saying, "that's right," and I woke, a loud startled "Huh!" of sound and the flat was full of drizzly day, it was morning, maybe even afternoon. The blankets were twisted, tight and uncomfortable, around my waist, my wet right hand lay clenched against my sweaty face, and two of them, one the bed-sitter, were sitting at the kitchen table. Waiting for me.

Trying to ignore them, I stumbled up, across to the bathroom, washed with one ear wearily cocked, what were they doing? Back out to get a beer, it was going to be that kind of day, I resumed my cocoon as the bed-sitter said, "Those people upstairs are real assholes."

No reply from me. It was not a statement I could legitimately argue with, but then again he was in no position to call names. They glanced together at me in my silence, and tried again.

"Nakota says you fucked up the video. Copying it."

I shrugged, the sudden rapid polka of an eyelid tic starting up, idiotic flutter and I rubbed at my eye, pressed the cold can against it to make it stop. The whole flat stunk like the inside of a bar, that dry generic reek of alcohol and smoke. Maybe they'd had a party, while I'd slept my nightmare sleep, maybe Nakota had been the entertainment. Maybe I had, for all I knew.

"She says you don't know about the paths."

"I don't care, either." The beer tasted very bad.

"She says," said the other one, his voice a glottal mumble like he was talking through a tasty mouthful of snot, "you don't *believe* about the paths."

Oh, God. "I'll tell you what I believe," I said, with venom born of a restless night, a sorry ache in my head, a sorrier one in my hand that even now began to burble and spit, fat slow silver bubbles and I said it again, "I'll tell you what I believe. That nobody knows anything about anything more complicated than breathing in and out, and *especially* not about that fucking Funhole down there, and that includes Nakota, that practically *defines* Nakota, am I going too fast for you or what?" and I hurled the beer so it barely missed the TV, one of my rare displays of temper but it pissed me off, it truly did, to wake after such a night to find the palace guard, armed with stupidity and questions, it was worse than having Malcolm there. I had my mouth open to continue in this vein and deeper when knock-knock, who's there, sudden anxious fantasy of the irate neighbor from upstairs but no, almost worse: the Dingbats, all three, smiles turning to sudden worry as they saw the other two, the blurt of fresh beer stain on the wall, smelled the ozone of tension and tried to simultaneously discern and assess their effect on whatever was happening fast enough to stop if that was necessary.

All in all they were deeply confused and showed it, so openly that I felt a vast wave of irritable pity, and on that wave threw down the blankets saying "Wait a minute," and dressed, fast sloppy toilette and grabbed up my jacket, herding them before me out the door. In the dull arctic slush outside I stood, eye ticcing as I zipped the jacket, and told them I wanted to go out for breakfast.

"It's almost dinner time," said Ashlee timidly. "Not for me." Doris drove, the four of us squashed into her squatty little Honda, her stick-shift style particularly vigorous and unpleasant, my headache worsening with each slam from first to second, second to third. She cranked the heater till the windows fogged, till I could smell the distinct degree of each passenger's state of cleanliness, most of all unfortunately my own. Of course at the restaurant we got stuck with a booth; once again I ended up next to Doris, the grit of her eyelashes, the fudgy smell of her perfume.

Blew on her tea, splashing it on my hand in its stained washcloth shroud, and chattering drone, long spiel about various methods that might be used to accurately document the Funhole, it was after all a paranormal site, there were ways: temperature readings maybe, in the storage room and the room below, maybe an interview of each of us (a nod almost painfully meaningful, meaningfully at me) describing our reactions to, and theories concerning, the mystery; perhaps a thorough medical investigation of my hand? Ignoring this for the absurdity it was, I stared at my chili corn dog with loathing, Dave had talked me into it against my will and for once better judgment; it looked like something the Funhole might have coughed up.

"Obviously it's not a *natural* phenomenon," said Doris, clearing her throat, Ashlee a moment later in identical nervous echo. "I mean, there's this *hole* in the floor, but nothing's underneath it, it doesn't *go* anywhere. I mean that's what they'd say. Researchers. But we could document the things we do know, we could investigate—"

"Like tapes, you mean?" Tactless Ashlee, and Doris's bright scowl of displeasure, no not tapes, but "You'd almost have to use some kind of video methodology that—Nicholas, what's wrong?"

I shook my head. Dave said something about science and mysticism don't mix and Doris said something back and it went round, pre-doomed attempt to classify the unspeakable, me turning my chili corn dog in small loathing circles to mimic, maybe, their talk.

After a while I noticed them noticing my glazed mourning, my lack of appetite, Doris in clumsy delicacy asking if "something" had happened, Twenty Questions, Oblique Edition with the three of them perched bright as birds until to shut them up I gave a clenched abridged history of the night before, just enough to give them the drift. And with luck the idea that perhaps for now my flat was not the place to be. By the time I finished they were done eating; I gave my plate one last resentful glance, pushed tardy out of the booth, no longer even nominally hungry but definitely sick. Sick around the edges.

The drive home, head leaning against the sticky passenger-side window, eyes closed. Would Mr. Bed & Friend still be there? Nakota? Complete with an army of blank-eyed vicious morons in big fat jackets with big fat notions force-fed them by that queen of misdirection, who was using them all as surely as she had once used the bugs in the jar, the terrified mouse at the end of a string? She would dangle them just as cold-bloodedly, and part of me said: So let her. Who gives a fuck.

I made them stop for beer. I even let them pay for it. What the hell. If I had to be a fucking guru, I should get some kind of privileges from it, shouldn't I? And even if I shouldn't, who cares? Who cares.

First up the stairs, slow breathless chug, hoo boy was I getting out of shape. As I passed the second floor, my entourage still unfortunately in tow (good job scaring them off, Nicholas old man) I was surprised by a wash of, what? Nostalgia? Oh *God*. Homesick for the Funhole. Maybe I deserved whatever I got, whatever that turned out to be. Still it was true, and never mind my posturing disgust, it was worse, and less, than a gesture. No matter what sort of place it was—dark stinks and dancing slag and undisguised a lure so monumental that it need only make its promises in fluids and in blinks—it was, beyond denial, the place for me. Oh, God.

The flat was silent, which cheered me momentarily, if I could just get rid of the Dingbats maybe I could get drunk and fall asleep, the day was shot anyway, wasn't it? But no sooner had I turned the key than the footsteps of the three heard vaguely from behind turned out to in elude a fourth. An unwelcome fourth, judging from the silence and I turned to see, who else, scary shorn head and a smile even uglier than before but in a new way: Malcolm. With a box under his arm.

"Look who's here," he said, as if this were his apartment and we some vulgar interloping peddlers, maybe come to sell candy or magazine subscriptions. "I thought you'd've taken a swan dive by now."

"Out the window," I asked, pushing the open door, "or down the hole?" I took the beer from Dave's arms, opened one right there. Malcolm stood to face me, cradling his damnable box and it didn't take a rocket scientist to figure out what was inside. He saw me looking and smiled.

"I finished it without you," he said. "I didn't need you after all."

"Congratulations."

"I'm gonna put it up tonight, when Nakota gets home."

"Who gives a fuck?" My trio fidgeted silently in place, Doris the first of the wedge, the other two slightly behind. The flat looked exactly as I had left it, cold and messy and unappetizing, my fading prints and magazine cutouts like some set designer's idea of badly simulated bohemia, flophouse chic. All it really needed was Nakota and her bunch for it to be truly hell. "Quite frankly, Malcolm, I don't care if you hang it around your neck," and out came a satisfying belch, big and round, "as long as you leave me out of it."

As if on cue, bang the door and Nakota, Mr. Bed, and three others, all but she smelling very much like Club 22, she was dressed in her barmaid black but I didn't think she would be working tonight. Not serving drinks, anyway. She took one look at Malcolm's proudly held box and said, "Done, I see," with the utmost boredom, not even malicious, not really, just an obvious trigger and she pulled it, almost out of force of habit.

"Wait till you see it," he said, but she had already turned away, speaking to Mr. Bed in some incomprehensible private slang, again I heard the word "transcursion" and wondered if I ought to ask. One of Nakota's geeks reached for one of my beers and I grabbed his wrist, hard, though he outweighed me by a good twenty pounds, and said, "Put it back, fuckface."

Nakota laughed. "Bad mood?"

"Eat shit, you," and instantly her trio turned on me, and with a sad and astonishing courage, mine on hers: Dave, nervous and too loud, "Just be a little easy, all right?" and Mr. Bed's contemptuous smile and Malcolm's snort of disgust at the whole circus, for once I agreed with him, a circumstance so bizarre that in pained confusion I set aside my beer and rubbed hard at my head, dislodging as I did so the clumsy bandage and now, for all to see, the silver leak, sick glossy shine on my skin like mother-of-pearl, like the flesh of the drowned and I snarled "What the fuck's everybody looking at?" and took up my beer again, sulked my way back to bed, and Nakota's breezy nod, agreeing: "Really, what's the big deal? You've all seen freaks before."

Dingbats glaring at idiots glaring back, Malcolm clutching his box, Nakota across the room giving me the look I hated most, and the phone rang: Vanese, asking, Is Randy there yet? Just the element I wanted added to this mix, just the man I wanted to see. Rub, rub, at my head, my brain swollen from thoughts too big, it had all gotten too big. What began as me and Nakota, me and my erstwhile beloved speculating on a bleak tantalizing chimera, had become people (who of course in their turn became factions, with competing theories and competing wants), and masks, and Randy's moving sculpture, become too big for me because I was after all just a small guy, just a little man; just big enough to fit morsel-like down the Funhole. Nowhere to hide but the storage room, nowhere to go but up. Or down. Let the games begin? Not so much, I thought, no longer bothering to hide the gulping dribble from my hand, that I minded putting on a show. I just didn't want to put it on for *them*.

Mr. Bed seemed now to be reading my sorry mind as, turning to Nakota with a backhand glance at me, asked sotto voce when the hell's the action, you promised, remember?

And Ashlee, of all people, loud and tremulous in the center of the room, looking at me, *to* me, "Nothing happens without Nicholas. Nothing *can* happen without him, so you just better stay out of his shit, all right?" and the three of them, my dingbats (and when, a cold snide voice blossomed to ask inside that three-story brain of mine, just *when* did they become *your* dingbats, when did you become some cheapshit stand-in god?), turned to me with an identical look between them, three faces with one emotion, and the naked responsibility I saw there making me almost frantic for escape but when you put the key in the lock, when you crank up the magic box, why then what happens? And who, who, I ask you, is ultimately responsible?

Frozen in my private sick tableau, half conscious of the merry fluid, brisk and faintly odoriferous, looking past its snail-trail glimmer to the twist of Malcolm's face as he said, unnecessarily loud, "I'm going to do what I carne here to do. You can come with me, or fuck off, or whatever you want."

And he marched out like a marine, Nakota's yahoos half-inclined to follow at once, as if, mindless as radar, they must track any kind of movement, my—the others, Doris and Ashlee and Dave, looking to me. Me looking away, to meet the warm shock of Nakota's gaze, very close, how had she managed to get so close? In her voice a thrumming sound, was it really her voice? The phone rang again.

"Coming?" she said, leaning even closer to brush her speaking lips against my skin and for me a grateful shiver, it had been such a long time since she had deliberately touched me. She kissed my cheek, an action at heart so brutally calculated that I should have been sickened by its falseness, but how could I be when it was so essentially Nakota?

Quietly, "It's your show," another calculation and I knew that, too.

"Go if you want to," I said. "Just leave me alone."

A venomous smile, I was balking her again. "You might be surprised," she said, even more quietly. "You might be sorry, too."

I closed my eyes. "I'm already sorry."

"Tell me about it," and gone, not even bothering to close the door behind her. The thrumming I had heard before, thought it the under-pinning of her voice, some fault of my hearing, showed itself to be neither; Funhole music; of course. Of course. Lassie come home. I put my hands to my head, fingers in my ears like a stubborn child, looked up to see Doris bent, hand aborted in a gesture, peering into my face. I took my fingers away from my ears, the better to listen to what I didn't want to hear.

"Are you going to let them do this?"

"I'm not letting anyone do anything," I said, very very tired. "I'm just staying the hell out of the way," and then cold air and Randy, through the open door.

"Funny customers," he said at once, getting himself a beer and one for me, at least you could always trust Randy to do the right thing. Ignoring Doris, who joined the worried cluster of Ashlee and Dave, he sat beside me, saying again as he handed me the beer, "Funny customers. Shrike's bunch, you know, they're big-time fuckups, I don't know if you want them anywhere near that room."

"I don't see any way of stopping them."

"I'll see what I can do," abrupt and out the door, my trusty right-hand man. Good thing for him he wasn't. I put my right hand to my head and sure enough, the thrum echoed there as well, remote speaker, broadcasting live. As live as it gets. Above that sound I could hear noises from downstairs, noises too from above, neighbors. Bitching. But not at each other. I caught the words "punker assholes" and thought, Uh-oh.

Doris asked, "Should we go, too?" and at a loss I shrugged, my usual cheap response to any situation. They took counsel together and with an over-the-shoulder glance, the three of them weirdly like swivel-necked dime-store toys, left. And left the door open.

Hallway cold and I pulled the blanket up around my neck, cementing the seal with the glue from my hand, and closed my eyes. A calmness I had not felt for days, weeks, drifted warmly over me; I felt almost good. Must be the solitude, certainly a rare commodity these days.

The thrum became a lullaby, God knew I needed rest. Not just sleep but rest, a breathing space, a place in which to forget. From upstairs I heard a shout, again, but this time I felt no warning pinch, felt nothing too, at some garbled groan from below. They said it didn't work without me? Very well, I was doing my part, I was doing nothing. The role I was born to play. More yells, and in the ringing echo of their wake I felt myself slipping off to sleep, what a lovely pleasant thing to happen, what a fine idea. Warm, under the covers, and my hand smelled so *good.* Good enough, in fact, to eat.

"Nicholas!"

Fuck. "What is it?" opening one cross eye, how had I gone so deep so fast? Exhausted, that's what it was, and always somebody to wake me when I wanted it least. In this case Doris, bug-eyed, hands a mile a minute, "Hurry!"

"What?"

"They're all yelling, Randy and Malcolm are pushing each other, Malcolm's got that mask nailed up and everybody's going *weird,* they—"

"I don't care if they kill each other," which at that moment was absolutely true, all I wanted was the benediction of unconsciousness through the good offices of sleep, it did not occur to me to wonder why I was so easily able to sleep at a moment when I should have been scared shitless. Yes, a small part of my brain said, professor-bright and pointer in hand, why is that? And that was what frightened me, finally, scared me awake and Doris taking instant advantage of my renewed consciousness grabbed my arm to haul me upright, it must have been like dragging a dead man, a big wobbly sack.

Out the door and from the stairwell I could hear it, Randy yelling, "Let go of me, motherfucker!" and Malcolm's screech: "Don't *touch* it! Don't *touch* it!" and Doris in desperation at my inadequate speed pushed me, hands in the back and I stumbled, I wasn't going fast enough, I almost fell.

Hands on the newel post, swinging around like a child does in play, an actor in a movie and I saw a babble of motion, heard a sonorous tone that seemed to be emanating from somewhere close by the storage-room door, where Randy tussled now with Mr. Bed, another of Nakota's goons pushing Malcolm who was yelping like a pig and somebody's *head* above the door. Hey, I thought, that's my head.

Plaster white and blind-eyed, frozen face not in peace but in ice, the coldest place of all. The mask.

From which the sound issued. Twin to the sound of my hand. Twin to the sound of the Funhole, so loud it seemed from behind the door and a pull like gravity, I pushed without effort through the crowd, Malcolm's yell directly in my ear, Nakota at my elbow, the others lost in swirling babble, the Brownian motion of a hopelessly unchoreographed fistfight, what the fuck were they fighting about anyway and someone, some guy I didn't recognize, the upstairs neighbor presumably, wild-eyed and bellowing "What the hell is going on!" with such enraged and poignant confusion that at another time I might have felt sorry enough to explain.

But not now. Nakota hanging on me like the leech she was, I could feel the pant of her excited breath, and again without effort I pushed her away, shook her off, pushed in the door and a great vast scream of heat, like throwing open the door to a blast furnace, like Shadrach in

the fire I advanced, careless, welcome, I could dance like Vulcan in a
cindering flame, I could dance with Randy's sculptures and one advanced
upon me now, its metal limbs flung wide in fractured greeting, where
had I been for so long? The leak of my hand gleamed, I understood the
motif of silver now. Pressing my hand to the melting metal, a hissing
sizzle like the boil of steam, but this steam was molten, this steam was
iron. Fusing me to the metal. Pulling me like a magnet to the Funhole
where the heat burned so delirious that I thought it would burn me
alive, the ancient suns rising about me like a mantle, my arms reaching
to embrace the fire as they embraced the sculpture's living metal and
through the burn an echo, the bubbling thrum, thrice loud: the mask.
My hand. The Funhole.

Me, myself, and I.

And I giggled at the joke, so *warm,* my sweat like metal and my pupils
scorched wide and at once the sculpture's grasp fell from me, and sorry,
I turned to see figures, bodies, walking toward me, weak silhouettes
against the pallor of the hallway, and I said, "Who goes there?" and
in the speaking saw at once the unmistakable scarecrow tilt: Nakota.

With three, four others, and maybe Randy back behind, it was hard
to see. I thought I heard myself say, "Stay out!" though I didn't feel
the words in my throat, of course it was so hot in there it was hard to
feel anything but. I waited until Nakota was very dose indeed before
I pushed my face to where it seemed hers was, through the shimmer,
through the sweat, and said as loudly as I could, "Get the fuck out of
here, and take them with you."

Though of course she didn't listen, maybe even couldn't hear me
through the howl of the heat; whatever, she pressed on, pushed forward,
pushed in miscalculated impatience against me. And for her trouble
got a burn. Hissing back just like a cat, a snake, holding her forearm
away from her body and as two backed from the fray another body
passing hers, oh here's a real brave dickhead, here's a real toothsome
treat. That one I saw with warm amazement was trying to get around
me, was actually trying for the Funhole itself, and I said, "Oh no you
don't" and I grabbed, I burned, I didn't really want to but truth be told
I didn't care, really, and really it was something to see my hand sink

into his skin, into meat, like a brand, a mark forever, he screamed—I heard it clearly, even through the ever-building thrum, the sound of a monstrous engine running hot—and Nakota chose that moment for her end-around. Sneaky bitch. Backhand, didn't think I had it in me, did you? Did you? And more, a bigger crowd crowding in the doorway, my vision snapping finally clear through the heat shimmer and I saw them all, too many, I could hear. Randy yelling and I yelled back, he didn't hear me so I did it again, "GET THEM OUT OF HERE!" and the neighbor guy and one of my, one of the Dingbats running presumably for cover, and in the room the marked man, Mr. Barbecue between the other two who had come in with Nakota but it seemed were more than ready to leave without her. Shitheels. "Take her with you," I said, and it was somewhat comical to see them drop their buddy in her favor, I had to laugh. I had to. And them gone, and the door thankfully closed. And me all alone.

With the heat. And the burn.

NINE

And the cold inevitable of the morning after.

On my back in the breathing silence, Cinderella, ha-ha, after the ball, my right hand scorched a porky pink and all of me sore with the ache of extreme muscular exertion, I had done some work last night, yes. Dancing with the sculptures. Burning people. Hurting people. Proud of yourself?

But what else—turning, groaning, to find my pisspot, seeing on the floor the charcoal skidmarks, the whole room stank of burning—what else could I have done? I had to stop them. I couldn't let them go down the Funhole, no matter what. What else could I have done?

Well, said my brain. For starts you could have stayed upstairs. Since it won't work without you.

Oh what a trick. And see how easily I had fallen for it, stumbled into it like a practiced buffoon. Br'er Funhole; no wonder it wanted me in charge. Please don't stay behind, you'll miss the fun, and after all you're the main event! Lured to sleep and then let to wake, Doris bearing the backhand tidings meant to get me down there so the show could really start. Put up the mask, Malcolm, nail it up for everyone to see, make a big production of it, let's get the neighbors in on this. Stir the pot, Nakota, mix it up with all your mysticism and that special selfishness that can barely recognize the existence of others, let alone their safety; stir it up good and bubbly, and don't forget to add your goons. Try to help, Randy, what can't be helped. And you, Doris, you get the supporting role, you get to animate the human corpse, you get to play Funhole messenger.

And in the end, the eternal Why me, but after all why ask. No answer, and maybe I wouldn't have understood one if I got it, maybe I didn't have the necessary smarts, maybe they'd been sizzled out of me the night before in the dreadful burning flash of what almost happened, and bad enough what had: Nakota hurt again, her stupid sidekick too (how bad?), and the neighbor, maybe more, seeing, what would he tell of what he'd watched, who would he tell? One big enormous botch, even orchestrated it could not possibly have been handled more clumsily, what next, a news crew? Live from the Funhole? Even now there was no guessing how bad things really were, or how much worse they might become. All I could do now was try to repair the damage, if possible, with what little I had. Or was.

What I did have, though, what I did understand, was responsibility. Yes, of course, it was the naughty Funhole back of everything, but who got the blame: the box? Or Pandora?

Fumbling at the door, out into the hall after a careful peek, no one there. Punishing cold. My feet were bare, I didn't remember taking off my shoes. The mask stared down at me in pale indifference, and I felt insulted, somehow, being mocked by my own face; I reached to tear it down but my arms were too short, my need for haste too great. It was a good likeness, as they say, and with its eyes closed it achieved a sort of blank serenity: a sorry peace, but then again that was more or less me; in the end he had done a good job. Malcolm's major work: my face. That ought to piss him off.

If I hurried, I thought, washing up in the empty flat, water sluicing down my aching arms, ignoring the ugly whiff of burn that lingered there as well, if I was quick, if it wasn't snowing—it was—well still I should be able to get back before anyone else; it was still early, not even ten. Pandora could not correct her original error, but I bet she didn't go around opening boxes anymore. Or leaving them loose for others to open with curious fingers more ignorant than hers.

So. It was a good lock. Expensive. Not a combination lock, I could just imagine myself trying to remember three numbers—in order—in a crisis, but a padlock, the kind they show being shot with a gun and still it doesn't open. Nakota didn't have a gun but she knew where to get one, and I had to be sure.

The salesperson thought I was weird, counting out quarters with my bandaged hand and my two-dollar limp, but since this was not a new experience I gave her my looniest grin.

"It's for my cage," I told her.

She was studiously smiling, her face pointed away from my face. "I hope it works," she said.

Bag in hand, left hand, my right held beside my body like some useless club and it certainly was. Thinking as I slogged through the parking lot, Well, this is kind of a bitch since Vanese was both the only one I could trust and the one most likely to oppose me, but I had to try. Driving slowly, maybe the last snow of the year, clogging the streets and re-eroding the dubious skills of drivers who'd had a week of dry weather to forget. Crazy or not, at least I could always drive.

Vanese answered the door and lost whatever smile she might have conjured; still she didn't look technically pissed. "Come in, I suppose," she said, and that made me smile.

"Well, at least I know where I stand."

The apartment was larger than mine, which was no feat, but there was a borne look to it that my place would never have. Randy's art was everywhere, some pretty nice pieces, there were snapshots of the two of them, of friends, there was a bunch of dried stalks and leaves in a big ceramic pot. Beat-up friendly furniture. All the amenities missing back home at the flophouse of the damned.

She nodded back at what I guessed was the kitchen. "I was frying some sausage," she said.

"You want some?"

"Yes," I lied, followed her to a square little box of fake red brick and a grease-brown galaxy of refrigerator magnets in the dubious shapes of fruit. She nodded me toward a cupboard. "Cups there, coffee there. Milk in the fridge if you want it."

I didn't. Smooth fingers on a knife, chopping peppers. She had on some bright green do-rag or headscarf or something, a Cleveland Browns T-shirt. Dumping the peppers into the pan, bright sizzling flash. "I heard all about last night," she said. "I'm real glad I wasn't there." No smile, severely stirred the peppers, hands efficient with auger. "I wish Randy hadn't been there either."

"So what do I want."

"Right."

"Well, first of all I'm sorry—" but she wasn't buying that shit, not for a minute.

"I know," she said. "It wasn't your fault. And that is your fault. You're supposed to be in control here, Nicholas." I didn't say anything. "You're the one who started this, or the both of you did, whatever. But she's crazier than a shithouse rat, crazier than you even, Randy told me what she did last night. She doesn't give a tin shit if people get hurt. If they get killed. That guy's arm is fucked *up*, you hear me?"

Again I said nothing, but a sick circle opened in my chest, a heavy feeling like the worst of blame. I wanted to know how bad he was hurt but had no courage to ask. Instead I cast down my gaze, drank coffee through dry lips.

"You think she cares about that guy? About anybody? *Shit.* There's no trusting her at all."

"I know that." I tapped the bag. "That's what this is for."

She dumped the sausage and peppers on plates, ripped paper towels from a roll. "What is it, a choke chain?"

"Almost." I showed her the padlock, saw her face break into a smile of relief that discouraged me greatly, because she was happy for nothing and her disillusionment might cost me her help. But. "It's not what you think, Vanese. It's for locking me in."

"Oh great," and she threw her fork straight at my head, missed me, put both hands to her forehead the way my mother used to do. "God *damn* it, Nicholas! How can you be so stupid? That thing is going to *kill* you, you got that? Kill your ass! And you're going to lock yourself *in* with it?"

"Just listen to—"

"No, *you* listen! I've had about enough of this shit, I don't *need* this shit, you hear me? You hear me?" Her voice was getting higher as it got louder, I thought she might hit me or cry, sat waiting for either. Finally she sat down, stared at her plate, pushed at the chair as if she would go hunting her fork; I gave her mine.

A sigh as she took it, and she squeezed my hand; her fingers were cold. "I'm sorry for hollering," she said. "But all this is driving me crazy, and I don't know about the rest of you folks but I don't *like* to be crazy." She sighed again. "Eat your sausages, they're getting cold."

I finally got her promise—it took till the end of the sausages, wasn't easy, but I got it. "Today," I said, for maybe the tenth time. "Okay?"

"Yeah, okay. Today. Now, if you want," gathering up her plate and mine, taking them to the sink. Over the hot-water sound, "I have to ask you something, okay? Just one thing."

"Go ahead," already looking down, away, I knew what was coming.

"Why don't you," gesture with the ratty sponge, "just walk away? Let it go, let her fuck with it if she wants to."

"I can't, is all."

She kept looking at me. "Why not?"

Well? Why *don't* I? Because it doesn't want me to. Because I don't want to either. "I don't know," I lied, my face filling with simpleton heat, and she shook her head at me, slow pity, deep disgust.

"It's for her, isn't it? So she doesn't go in without you. So she doesn't," a pause, in vast wondering scorn at my stupidity, "hurt herself."

"Well no, not really," snagging the lie, wondering why it was, if it was, any worse than the truth, any less believable. "I just don't want, I mean I think it's better if I'm there, if—" Stop jabbering, you dumbshit, shut your red face.

Vanese shook her head. "Lord," she said, dried her hands, got her coat, and would say nothing else at all.

Once again the somber gather of supplies, a bigger load this time and Vanese's sudden question, "Not to be nosy, but where're you going to shit, Nicholas?"

"Down the Funhole," I said.

The mask spooked her. Adding to its menace was, perhaps, the fact that she had not seen it as it was now, nailed up in all its chilly splendor, chalk patina and ghostly eyes closed, the better to see what you're thinking, my dear. "Doesn't that thing give you the creeps?" she said, and then a dry chuckle, of course it didn't, of course I had seen worse. For that matter, so had she.

As she walked beneath it, to enter the storage room, I let my gaze drift up: Abandon Common Sense, etcetera. And in that pause I saw, I thought I saw, the features shift, the plaster bones and muscles glide into a new and frightful configuration, so unlike my own, and so familiar. The face from the video. The smiling face of nothing.

Smiling at me.

"Vanese," I said, soft as lost breath, "will you come and look at this?" *Did* you look at the mask? See it? And again the change, shift backward, into neutral if you will: my own face, white-skinned and silent, giving nothing away.

"I don't want to look at it," she said, from inside the storage room. "I just want to get out of here. This place is *cold*."

An ether smell.

"How can you stand it?" stepping unwittingly closer, rubbing her arms as she looked around. "I mean how—"

And Randy's other sculpture, *Dead Head* or whatever he called it, tiny sinuosity, did it move or not? Did it move toward her? "Vanese," I said, "I think you better go."

"Well. Okay. You got everything you need?"

"Yeah. Everything."

It was definitely moving. I saw it moving, and heard as if some sneering sound track a giggling mutter from the ball, no one was out there, no one with throat enough to laugh, anyway, and anyway I don't get that joke. "Vanese," louder, "I think you should go right now. Just make sure you take the—"

The sculpture skull's mouth opened, little steel grin, and the rest of the half-melted metal leaped, emphatic thrust toward her, and grabbing the end of her coat, yanking her off balance and she shrieked, tiny little squeaky sound like a small and bad surprise, dead mouse in your shoe, dead bug in your cup. I grabbed her right arm with my right hand and dragged her, hard, away from the sculpture, it was burning a hole in her coat, a slender smoke like solder and the ether smell belched hard out of the Funhole and I shoved her against the door, yelling, "Get out of here!" And stood panting, listening to her breathless, listening to her snap the padlock on.

For long minutes I tried to talk to her, through the door, tried to ask if she was all right, but all I heard were murmurs, low-voiced mutters, and I yelled in scared frustration, "Vanese, speak up!" and heard in perfect mockery my own voice saying, "Vanese, speak up!" And the giggle, again, and I realized Vanese was long gone, she had left right after the lock was safely on. I took my place, then, arms folded, back against the door like a kid guarding a clubhouse.

"You don't take any chances at all, do you," I said. "You fuck. Do you."

The skull's mouth opened, perhaps the mask's mouth was flexing, too, but the voice came from the dark.

love you

I had known Nakota would be past furious, but as usual I underestimated her.

No screaming, no, she wouldn't waste her strength, but fighting, so it took Randy *and* Malcolm, with Dave a helpless observer giving me the blow-by-blow, to drag her away. Vanese came back with a tired report: "Dave's upstairs sitting on her."

"Good."

"Malcolm wants to put the video on."

"Tell Malcolm—no, tell Randy to break his fucking neck if he so much as touches that video, or even the TV, okay, Vanese?" Stupid absentee general giving orders through the door. I thought of Nakota, rigid with fury upstairs, frustrated hate like a laser frying a hole in the floor—no thank you, there're enough holes in here already, ha-ha—and made little speeches in my head, little noble declarations of my sterling intentions. When it was really selfishness. Diluted, yes, with worry for her, that was true, but that was selfish too: hurting her hurt me. What had she said? "Nicholas lost it." Yeah. And would lose it again, no doubt.

But now it didn't matter. Now I was safe. From Nakota, from her geeks, the Dingbats, everybody.

Head against the door, ah, a lovely quiet moment, alone with my empty head. A yawn so deep it reminded me of when I'd actually slept, last, a real sleep possible here on the lip of nightmares? Well. No doubt. Anything's possible, isn't it, when—

"Nicholas!"

Randy's voice. Tight.

"What?" sitting up, eyes open, heart starting up hard. "What's the matter?"

"It's Shrike, man, you don't know what she's doing, Vanese can't hold on to her—"

"Vanese shit, where the hell's Malcolm? Or Dave?"

"Malcolm left, Dave, I don't know where Dave is. I can't take her with me, I gotta go to work." Tighter still. "She wants to get a chain saw, she says she's going to shoot the lock off the door, she—"

"She can't, it's—"

And unmistakable, Nakota's witchy shriek from the stairwell, Randy gone and my scared yelling notwithstanding, that was the last I heard of any of them. I put my head in my hands.

A smell like roses, drenched and bewitching.

"It's not funny," I said.

My hand was itching, had been in all my talk with Randy, a horrible bubbly itch and I rubbed it viciously against the floor and felt a lump, something I absolutely did not want to see but I looked anyway: the smell, the rose made flesh. And blood. All over my arm.

"I said it's not *funny*," and I smashed my hand as hard as I could, like swinging a bat, against the door. It hurt so bad it was all I could think of for a long, long time, and that was good.

Not light in the room, but less dark. Scratching, like a mouse, close by my ear and I opened my eyes, my hand like a migraine still. Somebody saying my name.

"What." Oh my throat was dry. Left-handed I scrabbled for the bicycle bottle of water, drank a little, a lot. "What is it? Who's there?"

"It's me. Vanese." If that was really Vanese, then things were very bad. "How you doing?"

"Fine." I considered my hand. One of the fingers was definitely broken, or fractured, whatever. It was swollen like a cartoon hand, the hole in the center a cheerful carnival red. "I'm fine. Where's Nakota?"

"I don't know."

"What about you? Are you okay?"

Silence.

"Vanese, answer me."

The skull was mocking my words, moving its mouth in unison. "Vanese," I said again, and threw the water bottle at the skull. "Stop it, you shit! Vanese, please answer me."

"Nicholas?" A deep pause. "I don't think I want to come back here anymore."

"What happened? What—"

"She wrecked my car, Nicholas. Drove it right through my mother's garage." A slow sigh. "My mother got hysterical, Nicholas. She's just ..." Nothing. The skull winked at me. Something fluttered in the back of the room. "Randy said, I got to go to work. Take her somewhere. Anywhere. So I took her to my mother's, and she tried to steal my car. I got in it, and she, she just ran right *into* the garage, I thought she was going to drive right out the other side. She's crazy, Nicholas, I mean the girl is insane, something's broken in her head now." Another pause. "She hit her head. So did I."

"Is—are you all right?"

"She's fine," without bitterness, but without concern. For Nakota, or for me. "I'm fine too. The doctor gave me a couple shots, for pain, you know," which went a long way toward explaining that draggy Demerol voice, that emotionless drone. "But I have to get back to my mother's. At least," a slow funereal chuckle, "she left the car."

"Vanese?" Nothing.

"Vanese, are you still there? Vanese!" The skull rotated, a deliberate motion weirdly reminiscent of an old-time stripper. "Vanese!"

Very very quietly, through the crack of the door: "You better watch it, Nicholas."

Nothing else.

I waited. I waited a long time, long enough for the skull and its steel armature to come humping across the floor to me, lie at my feet like some hideous pet, in a grotesque excess of playfulness it even tried to nibble at my feet. I kicked it, hard, sent it rolling and it rolled right back and bit me, not hard but enough to make a point. I left it alone then, closing my eyes when it rolled onto its back, its whatever, to peer up at me. When I pissed I made sure the pot was close enough to splash it, but that was only an opportunity for it to mock me further, basking in the stream, a golden shower for a steel skull, it even sickened me and I thought I had gotten just about sick-proof. Apparently there were levels of unwitting perversion I had never even considered.

Nakota. Where was she. Wrecked cars and cracked heads and it was just the beginning because she was determined, oh my yes, she was the most determined person I had ever seen and I had very likely been worse than an asshole to think I could keep her out if she wanted in; what I had accomplished, in fact, was at best a delaying motion, at worst a challenge. And of course she had Malcolm. And her goons.

What was the saying? There were new goons born every minute, no silver spoons but hunger, instead, fed by boredom and nurtured by spite? Of course there were. And who held the map for Goon Mecca, who knew the way?

Who had the video.

I was sure of it. What I was most afraid of was what I most suspected: they were showing it. To other people. Recruiting. Nakota needed an army to get in? Very well, she would raise one up. She could do it, too.

But what else to do?

And from outside, the croon, small and faraway, "Poor Nicholas," the talking head, sweet like poison, the giggle beneath like an acid bubble floating, floating, ready to burst. I had a lot of time to call myself names. I used it all, more when I remembered that Vanese had the padlock key, then: who cares? I thought, watching the skull turn lazy circles around the Funhole like a race car desultorily lapping a track. Who really gives a shit. They'll get in or they won't, and nothing I do now is going to matter.

Because they're out there, and I'm in here.

The next voice I heard was Malcolm's.

"Hey, Nick," he said. "How d'you like the mask?"

I didn't answer. Hot, I felt very hot. I wondered if it were some effect of the Funhole's, or if I had a fever, or what. The whole room smelled very pleasant, as if someone had just given it a thorough cleaning. I shifted, wincing, against the door; even to think of moving my hand caused me pain. I turned my head to consider it, saw more flesh chewed away, and in the perfect center of the wound a gruesome little caricature of Malcolm, a clay Malcolm, gesturing and talking as the real one talked and gestured beyond the door.

"This is giving me a headache," I said.

"You're gonna have more than a headache pretty soon," Malcolm said. The clay Malcolm, or skin, or whatever he was, giggled in my hand. "Nakota's really mad at you."

"That would be a novelty. Why don't you go away, Malcolm, and leave me alone? You did your mask, that's all you really wanted, isn't it?"

"All I wanted at *first*," he corrected, and the head wrinkled its forehead, pursed its lips like some scab professor. "But there's much much more to all of this, right, Nick? *Much* more."

"You're right," I said. "And I'm keeping it all for myself."

Danger, inflammatory remark. He sure was easy to piss off, Malcolm, and since it was sort of fun and there was no longer any reason not to, I kept it up. "Yep," I said, snot-nosed cheerful, "a whole world of weirdness, Malcolm, you dumb motherfucker, and you'll never see any of it. There's enough going on in here to make fifty thousand masks, but none for you." I drank a little water. It tasted the way toilet water probably tastes, only not as cold.

"Wait till she gets here," he said, and the little Malcolm's face twisted up in a pink spiral, unrolled like fast forward to be Phantom of the Opera. Big deal.

"Don't threaten me with Nakota," I said. "I'm already scared of her," and abruptly weary of the game I clapped my hands together, ignoring the truly amazing pain this caused, gratified to see the little Malcolm squash flat and disappear, dwindling back into my flesh like scar tissue eroded by time.

The real Malcolm: no answer, no shitty retort, and for one cold moment I wondered if his silence had anything to do with my applause. Then: "Let's just forget about her, okay? You give me the key, Nick, and we can talk about it. Okay?"

"I don't think so."

"I'll tell you about the mask," he said, as if this was the rarest of treats. "It's—"

No."

"I bet you don't even have it, do you?" pissed off again; too bad; did he really imagine that two seconds' worth of transparent man-to-man bullshit would mean anything to me? "You probably gave it to that stupid bastard Randy, you—"

"I didn't give it to anybody."

"Then where is it?"

"I threw it down the Funhole."

A deep and complicated pause.

Then: "You're a liar, Nicholas."

Nakota's voice, and it gave me a chill, not because she was angry, not because she sounded crazy, or violent, or even particularly upset. Because she was happy. Why was she happy?

"You're right," I said. "I am a liar. I didn't throw the key down the Funhole, I stuck it up my ass. I stuck it up *Randy's* ass, Malcolm, how's that? What do you care anyway? You're not getting in and that's the end of it. When it's safe, safer, I'll—"

"You're no judge," Nakota said, calm and reasonable, what horrible shit was she up to, there where I couldn't see. "In fact you're not even worthy of what's happening to you. Saints and idiots, angels and children."

"Are you fucked up, or what?"

Malcolm, exasperated: "It's a quote, you dumbshit."

"What it means," Nakota said, and as she talked a stink blossomed, a smell like corrosion and waste, like the biggest garbage pile in the world decomposing all at once, "what it means *now* is that I should be in there, not you. Because I know what's going on. You stopped me from copying the video, Nicholas, but now I see that would never have worked, because it doesn't need to work. It doesn't matter."

I put my hand over my nose and mouth. It didn't help.

She kept going. "I know what all this means. I know about the gateways and the paths, I know that the Funhole's just an avenue to change. To transcursion."

I pulled my shirt off and wrapped it around my face like a bank robber's makeshift mask. She kept talking, on and on about transcursion, giving me first the dictionary definition—a passage beyond limits; extraordinary deviation—and then her own, infinitely more twisted interpretation: a change effected so deep, so fundamental, that when you emerged on the other end (if there was an other end, she wasn't sure and seemed content not to know; for now it was the trip that mattered) you would be yourself a process, an agent of the change, a branch office, say, of the Church of the Transcursion. And as her explanation continued, twisting and turning in upon itself and ranging into the wildest gibberish, not black holes but dark spots, not Funhole, in the end, but Fungod, the smell kept escalating, ranker and hotter and curling down my throat like a clotted rag and finally I screamed, "Shut up, just shut up! I'm suffocating in here!"

She stopped. The smell didn't go away but it didn't get any worse, either. No one said anything for a few minutes, then Malcolm: "The mask can talk, Nick."

Nakota, distant irritation: "His name is Nicholas, you asshole."

"I know it can talk, Malcolm. I can talk, too. Even you can talk, so it can't be that big of a deal, right?"

"It tells us things," Malcolm said, and Nakota's laugh, a dark humor: "Oh shut up. Nicholas doesn't want to know about those things, he might be scared. But he'll find out. He won't be able to avoid it."

Oh God, I thought. What things.

"Do you know what transcursion really means?" she said, laughing, she couldn't seem to stop laughing, and the mask joined in. My voice. My laugh. Dwindling to satisfied whispers, back and forth, and the movement of others outside, who was there? The burned guy? Was he there? Back for more? What others had she found for her stupid crusade, her blind sacrificial march the blood from which would somehow end up on my hands?

And I didn't want to know. And I wanted to open the door, find out, run away, was it my want at all or a reflection of Nakota's, was it some echo of self-preservation or a tricksy bit of Funhole business, this is all too much for me, I thought, this is all just too fucking much for me and I crawled over to the Funhole, my hand one greasy trail of pain and the smell gone overwhelming, I didn't care. No way out but down, right? No way out but farther in.

My right hand in as far as it could go, thrust in, jammed in, you want sexual metaphor, watch me, I'll fist-fuck the blackest hole of all. I was shivering, but the heat of my head was so intense it hurt, I felt sick like flu and sick from the smell and outside the voices getting louder, either it was a riot or my hearing was screwed up. Who cares. I'm in here, and I

love you

and my hand was *squeezed*, squeezed like caught in machinery, and I screamed, oh did I scream, my broken fractured finger bent and twisted and my other lesser bones twirled and blended in my flesh, and I thought as I screamed. This is what the bugs must have felt, as the sensation of swirling became that of suction, a deep and complex pressure, was it taking back what it had given or extracting from me what was mine, blood or slime, there was no getting away now, no, I would have to rip my arm off. Maybe it would do the favor for me, huh? Maybe it—

and the pain rose as I did, agony's levitation, drawn completely upright in an arrow line with tears running not down but up my face, dripping into my hair

"—don't—"

more; higher

oh help me

and still more to a point that, oh God, I had never imagined there could be so much pain in all the world, certainly not contained in the stupid simple vessel of my body, *my* body, and as I wondered why I was still alive my conscious eyes closed, taken by tunnel vision to a vanishing point, but though I couldn't see I could still *feel*, oh my yes, oh my God, wouldn't this ever *stop?*

It didn't.

But I did.

For a while at least.

Piss smell, and a pain in the small of my back. My thighs hurt, the creases at my crotch, an itchy pain that was so puny compared to what I had been feeling before I fainted, or passed out, whatever, it was barely worth noticing. I could see again. I could hear, too, although there wasn't much to listen to, no more yelling from the other side of the door.

No more voice from the Funhole.

Lying lover-close, almost atop it and my arm still sunk to the elbow, unwilling to test the theory of independent motion, luxuriating in the absence of excruciation: a man of simple pleasures, that's me. Eventually I would have to move, of course, if only to scratch that god-awful itch between my legs. I must have pissed myself in my pain, and now, best guess, I had diaper rash. I had to laugh at that, a little hoarse chuckle that ended with the beginnings of a retch, then a full-fledged heave and without thinking I sat up, assumed the position, head between knees as I coughed and choked in my dry nausea, nothing coming up.

When it was over I stayed slumped, arms balanced on my trembling knees, until I realized I had moved, my arm was free, and more amazingly free of pain.

Well, I thought. Do you really want to see this?

No.

Look quick and get it over with.

No.

I was afraid to wiggle my fingers, I was afraid I didn't have them anymore. I was afraid of what the hole, my hole, looked like now, after such intense communion, afraid, at last, not to look; nothing's worse than not knowing, right?

Right?

And that giggle, from outside, echoing in my ear like a tickling tongue. I looked.

And retched again, helpless rushing nausea of disgust, my mouth loose and dripping with saliva, and I looked again and couldn't stop, retching and I couldn't stop.

No palm at all, now. Nothing but hole, the fingers jutting impossible like the scared tines of a starfish, my wrist protruding beneath like some useless object left behind in an inappropriate spot. Shaking, all of me shaking, I turned my hand over; the back looked normal, as normal as it ever got. I turned it back again. Hole. Hand. Hole. Hand.

There would be no covering this with a bandage, no. No more hiding possible. The best I could ever hope for would be amputation, self-inflicted naturally, I'll cut the fucker off, that's what I'll do, I'll throw it down the Funhole, or maybe I'll tie a string to it and go *fishing*, talk about your catch of the day and I realized I was talking out loud, muttering, *smiling*, and a calm tiny part of me said Well, that's it, you're finally crazy. Congratulations. You've been ridden to the point where all you are is motion. Perpetually. And I stared at my hand, my hole hand, ha-ha, and flexed my fingers to watch them move, amazing, they look just like puppet fingers but where are the strings, hmm? Just where exactly are the strings to—

Boom, the door. Not a knock but a whack, the door itself shuddered and I opened my mouth and heard my voice, curiously distant, ominously dry: "Don't do that."

And at once the voice of the mask: "Do that," pretending to echo, malicious and cool. Voices, not so much answering as talking amongst themselves. Chiefest of course Nakota's, but somewhere in there, Randy.

So many questions, so little time. I put one hand to my mouth, rubbed it, tried to think what to ask first. "Who's there?" No doppelganger chorus; I can be grateful for the smallest of mercies; just watch me.

"All of us."

My hurting forehead against the wood of the door. Ask it succinctly, please: "How many is all?"

"You want me to count?"

Randy's tentative voice: "There's a few people out here, Nicholas." A pause. "Are you okay? You need anything?"

A hand transplant, for starters. Better yet a head transplant, if you can spare one, matter of fact just slide the mask under the door. We talk alike, we walk alike, sometimes we even—Randy was still talking, something about the mask and Malcolm was arguing and suddenly the sound of his voice, his stupid pompous voice, irritated the shit out of me and I said, "Shut up, Malcolm, or I'll come out there and I'll *hurt* you."

Silence.

Were they stupid enough to be scared of me? Of me? No one seemed to notice that there was still a big fat lock on the door, or if they did maybe thought I could surmount a detail like that, after all I had melted a camcorder once upon a time, who knew what I had up my sleeve? Besides of course my rapidly deteriorating hand. Another idea came to me: did they think it was me making the mask talk? With my new, improved Funhole superpowers? God *damn*, was everybody even crazier than me? Leave your love offerings at the door, folks, and don't forget, tomorrow is Virgin Day.

Laughing, soundless into my hand, my left hand, thank you, and I realized I had to sit down because I felt very weak, very much like falling onto my head. "Randy?"

"Yeah?"

"Is Vanese out there?"

"No." Dully, "I haven't, she hasn't been here in a long time, man."

"How long?"

Nakota: "You've been in there for a long time, Nicholas."

And how much of that spent unconscious? How much spent with my hand stuck down the Funhole, conduit for real, absorbing, oh God. She was still talking but I had stopped listening, I sat with my back against the door shaking my head, shaking my head until something she said caught my attention and I asked her to say it again.

"I said, we broke the lock off yesterday morning." A deep frustration just out of reach, bubbling like lava under the flat planes of her voice. "I wanted to try—"

"What she wanted," Randy, dry, "was to chainsaw down the door."

Malcolm, sullenly but with a certain oblique pride: "But the head said no."

"What head?"

Randy said tiredly, "He means the mask."

The mask said no. "Randy," I said, and heard the mask speaking in tandem, a purposely ghostly sound but I ignored it. "Randy, get Vanese. Get her to come here, I don't care what you have to do. Please," less entreaty than order, I didn't mean it that way, I'm sorry, please. "*Please*," I said, and the mask said crisply, "And everybody else, get the fuck out of here."

Shuffling sounds. People were moving. It was impossible to tell how many were out there by the sounds they made, and I couldn't count, I couldn't try, I didn't even know if I wanted to know anymore. Randy was promising something through the door but I didn't want to hear it, all I wanted in this world was to hear Vanese's voice, her comforting scolding older sister's voice explaining all to me, loaning the incredible belief, and if I was very very lucky she might say everything will be all right, Nicholas, you hear? Everything will be all right.

Silence finally in the hall, and I cried: big sloppy sobs, my chest shook, I was cold all over except the heat of my face and the heat of my tears, oh Jesus God I just want out of this but it's too late, isn't it? It's much too late, wiggling my puppet's fingers, staring at the little Funhole in my hand and wondering what might come out of it, one fine day, one fine exhausted moment when—

"Nicholas."

Nakota.

"Nicholas, let me in."

"Go away," I said, still crying. "Please, Nakota, please just go away."

"I can help you," she said, and she was probably right, if the help I wanted was to be trampled in her rush. "I'm the only one who knows."

Crying now so I could hardly talk, "Go *away*, Nakota, *please*."

And the booming sound again, radiant extreme frustration, rattling the knob and yelling you son of a bitch bastard cocksucking son of a bitch and "I'll never let you in," helpless on my knees, screaming at the door, "that's what all this is *about*, that's *why*—"

And her silence; and finally, her absence.

Vanese. Please, God, Vanese.

I must have slept, and deeply, because when I opened my eyes I felt suddenly not better but far more human, far more focused in simple sensations: ouch, my crotch hurts; I'm thirsty, I'm hungry, all of me is sore.

It was a relief, the plain tending to of bodily needs, not particularly dexterous but able: get the pants off, examination of the purpling rash, uh-huh. I had never seen diaper rash before in my life but it sure looked ugly. I poured a little water on it before I realized I was squandering, drank the water instead, the whole bottle. Then a paradoxical piss, and boy did it feel good, a plain piss, imagine. Eating, bare ass propped against the door, slowly because each bite was hard to swallow, Z-rations, mmm-mmm. Animal joys, can't beat 'em.

And another, keener joy: "Nicholas?" so close to the door she might have been speaking into my ear, my happy ear: "Vanese!"

"Yeah." She sounded exhausted. "What the hell's going on here, anyway?"

"I thought," struggling to swallow my food, "I thought you could tell me."

Silence. "Well, the lock's off the door." Then as I turned, swiveled against the door as if this would bring me closer to her, her anxious angry older sister's voice, "What's happening to *you*, Nicholas, they're saying all kinds of shit, they're—"

"I'll tell you," I said. "Then you tell me."

It was definitely a story, my version worse than halting but I got across to her, I think, the skeleton of it—feelings anyway, that much I knew from the sounds she made. Her version was, to me, far more interesting than my Man vs. Funhole routine, scarier too, but then I had a unique perspective, you might say an inside view.

She was gone for most of it, she said, but what she heard from Randy, on the way over, was nothing good. It started with Nakota's rabble of recruited idiots, Malcolm included, watching the video—

"I knew it." I sighed, no sense bemoaning the obvious, forget it, go on. "Where were you, anyway?"

"Where I was was at my mother's. Trying to get somebody to come fix her garage. Your girlfriend broke it."

"I know. You told me."

"I don't remember that."

"You had a lot on your mind."

Pumped up, then, all of them, giddy with whatever black shit they had swallowed, one toilet bowl to a customer please, following Nakota and lesser-light Malcolm. Trying to rip off the lock, the door, finally Randy arriving to scream at them—the one sight I was genuinely sorry I missed—and throw the words "manager" and "police" around.

"Did it work?"

"Not really. Not enough. The neighbors, I mean even here, people expect a little peace, right? They're getting restless."

"I bet." I felt like crying again, reached without thinking to rub the pain in my forehead, it hurts when I think too hard, and caught a sideways peek at my hand, my permanent badge of abnormality, of being kissed too hard by the dark; *love you*. Right.

"Anyway." Vanese, immensely tired of her story but determined to tell it. "They settled down a little, went back into your place—"

"*My* place? My *flat*?"

"Uh-huh." Yahoo Nation. Drinking out of my cups. They stayed there, still watching the video, listening to the gospel according to Nakota, getting cranked for another charge which ended when they finally got the lock off, despite Randy's dwindling objections, even he wasn't big enough to beat the shit out of a mob. Me listening and mournful, thinking, For once might would really have made right, but no, force majeure empty and weaponless before Nakota's geeks.

"Then what?"

"Then," very dry, "the door wouldn't open."

Slowly, glancing at the knob: "Nakota said—but there's no lock on this side. I mean, it doesn't lock."

"You mean it didn't lock before."

Oh boy. What now? As usual I had no clue, that ol' debbil psychic energy maybe, maybe something more complex, certainly over my sloping head. Nyah nyah Nicholas, now you can't get out even if you want to. Which roused in me a feeling of such delicate terror it was like walking across snapping ice, each step an incremental journey, farther from safety and the shore.

My hands trembled; I pressed them against my sides. "So now what?"

"You tell me," she said, and now there was sadness beneath the scold. "Randy said you wanted me here, and at first I thought, The key, he wants out. But you don't need the key anymore." A pause. "What do you need, Nicholas?"

"I don't know."

"What do you want?"

To come out, I might have said, but I felt bone-strong that this was no longer truly possible, even if I left the room forever, even if I could, I would never come out all the way. But. But.

I'm scared.

"I can't let her get in here, Vanese. It's bad enough with just me."

"Bad enough is right," a warm bitterness, I had the sensation of her face pressed close against the edge of the door. "Nicholas, I can't believe this shit, this is just *stupid*, you know what I'm saying?"

I didn't answer. There wasn't one, as far as I knew, or if there was, it was beyond me to give. Neither of us spoke. At last I said, "Vanese?"

"What?"

"I'm *scared*." Bubbles of spit on my cracking lips, bubbles of snot in my nostrils, and blubbering, groaning like a drunk, bare-assed and stupid on the floor, weeping so long at last I thought she had gone, tried to call her but could not seem to work my voice, no new manifestation, just simple soreness, simple dry pain. Standing, my aching knees giving friendly little knuckle-crack sounds, I went for more water, shuffling back, my dick banging softly as I sat.

Then her voice, still angry, wet now perhaps with her own tears; would she waste tears on me? "You bet you're scared. I'm scared too. Listen to me now: can you open that door?"

"I—" I coughed, cleared my throat. "I don't know."

"Well, try."

Nervous, I pulled on my pants again, wincing at their odor, the chafing pain, standing tense, poised on the balls of my feet for some great struggle. I put my hand to the door and pulled, hard.

Nothing. I waited. It seemed like a long time; it probably was. "Try again."

Her voice, and again I turned the knob, this time unthinkingly right-handed; it gave with a blow, almost toppling me. "Bad move," said the mask, a petulant sound as the cold hall air slipped over me and I gazed up, my first look outside, and saw instead of my own the video face, and its eyes opened very wide and it showed fat impossible teeth: "Boo!" and I cried out, fell back, Vanese stepping quick and scared inside.

Silence, for a moment, and then "It smells in here," she said. Staring at me.

"I know," embarrassed. "I'm sorry, I must be pretty ripe by now."

Still staring, shaking her head, slow back and forth of those same earrings. "I didn't mean that. It just smells—weird. Like blood or something." And then, slow sad carpet of words as she came forward, "Oh, Nicholas, *look* at you," with all the deep regret I did not merit, a loss magnified, dignified, by the caliber of her pity. She held out her arms to me, and as I moved to enter them, the magic circle of her touch where all would not, could never be, cured but for a moment I might feel as if it was, the skull bounded up like a manic ball and struck her, hard, in the back, I felt the impact in the soles of my feet, saw it in her sudden stagger, and up it came again and weak, still I threw myself with all my strength before it, into its rising way. Direct hit, my cheekbone not cracking but almost, as if it had somehow pulled its punch in the instant before landing, and now in vicious rebound it scuttled snapping after her as she fled for the door, and me after it, clumsy barefoot kicks, almost connecting but instead losing my balance and falling serendipitous and flat atop it.

Vanese in the hall, the door safely .slammed and it bit my nipple, punishing petulance, before pushing free of my weight, then rolled in sullen circles a moment or two, growing revolutions till it reached the darker corners of the room, I couldn't see it but I knew it was there.

"Nicholas?" Breathless, as if she had just run a mile instead of a few yards. "You okay?"

"I'm fine," I said slowly, rubbing my chest. "Vanese," more slowly still, "don't come here anymore. I know I asked you to, but don't. Even if someone tells you I asked you to again. Because I won't. Okay?"

Silence.

"Okay?"

"Yeah. Okay."

"Things are just going to get worse."

"Yeah." Sure, and sad in the certainty. "Will you just promise one thing?"

"I'll try."

"If it gets too bad, will you get out?"

Quiet metallic rattle in the darkness behind me, a sound like knives in a drawer. "No," I said. "You know I can't."

"Can't what?" Cruelly abrupt, Nakota's voice, and then Vanese in a tone I had never heard: "Can't not save your worthless ass," and a whack, something hit hard against the door and Nakota's snarl, Vanese's high-pitched curses and a sound at my feet, looking down in anxious impatience, now what, to see the skull spinning in happy little circles. A brief impotent kick, of course I missed in the echo of Nakota's damaged howl, and Randy's voice saying, "What the *hell* is going on here?" and then a bunch of voices, and I sat down and shut my eyes.

When I opened them the skull was lying placidly close, staring up at me with its stupid sockets, one of which closed in an impossible wink and without thinking a second I reached blind behind me, came up with a glass bottle of something and, right-handed, smashed it down with all my painful weakness, all my tired rage, and incredibly the skull splintered, chunks of steel and splits of glass, orange juice in my face and I cried out, pawing and blinking, and when I looked again the pieces of the skull were scuttling to the darkness, joining as they went.

I sat in the darkness and thought about Vanese, arms held to embrace the sorry mess of me, the look in her eyes as open wide. I never saw her again.

TEN

Later, through the murmur of her goons clustered around the door like cancerous cells: "Not funny, Nicholas."

"Shut up, Nakota. Okay? Just shut up." Sometimes, I thought, it would be worth it to die, just to stop hearing that voice. Like an ache in the ear, like a bad tooth audibly rotting. Like a cancer that talks. My one and only.

Malcolm, a cheap indignance that somehow sat well on him: "That bitch could've broken her *jaw*."

The mask spoke before I could: "You shut up too. I wouldn't mind killing *you*."

Nakota's sudden cackle, it was her kind of joke, mostly because it wasn't. Then, but seriously folks, her eternal one-note tune, "Nicholas, you have got to realize we're going to get in. At least one of us," crude transparent threat, I covered my closed eyes with my fingertips, gently patted the tiny cuts left there by the skull-splitting glass. The mask kept talking, its comments directed to none of us, the principals, ha-ha, instead to the widening circle of usual geeks; it used my voice but I couldn't understand the words. Big deal. Bad enough I could still understand Nakota. "It would be so much easier if you—"

"You never used to be boring," I said.

"We're taking the door off," Malcolm said. "Today."

"I don't give a shit what you do." So tired, inside, that it was almost true. "I don't care what happens, I don't care if you chew your way in, if you use yourself as a battering ram, whatever. Do what you want. But I'm not helping." They kept talking, arguing with me (when had it ever mattered if I was listening or not?) and each other, and the muttering others who milled close and far, the tempo of their voices drifting like scum on an incoming tide.

I did my best to ignore them all, sat finishing my meal: a warm ginger ale, chewy antique saltines, and raisins, a little red box of raisins and my eyes filled with quick and stupid tears: I remembered eating them in my lunch at school, saving the box to prop on my desk and pretend the Sun Maid was winking at me. As I thought this the little face on the box came alive, melted like living wax to become Nakota's, complete with her customary impatient sneer, the basket she held filled not with grapes but tiny skulls. Sickened by this cheap cruel grotesquerie—was it really necessary to fuck with *everything*, did it all have to twist into the same gleefully ugly shape?—I flung the box away, heard the minute dusty sound of its landing, the immediate and larger sound of its retrieval, fetched back to me with the box turned so I could see the face again, the Sun Maid again, her little eyes rolled backward in terror as the crooked teeth of the skull bisected her.

"Oh you motherfucker," I said, and a calm, the stilling sensation of absolute rage descended on me like the slowly settling mantle of a saint and I grabbed the skull, ignoring its snapping mouth, moved not toward the Funhole—my first impulse, but none of that Brer Rabbit shit today, nice try but I'm not buying—but toward the door to open it, who gives a shit, who really cares anymore because I am TIRED, I am TIRED to DEATH and I yelled something, yelled as I pushed the skull at the door

and my hands went right through it, skull and all.

Malcolm shrieked. I heard the skull hit the floor of the hallway, felt something, Nakota's slippery clutch most likely, as I pulled my own hands back through the seamless door. To stare at them, rocked back on heels and haunches, gaping like a monkey with a nuclear device. To stare particularly at the hole of my right hand and note, with a kind of dreamy detached nausea, the living leakage crawling up my fingers, painlessly chewing the flesh as it went.

Eating me alive.

And the more I watched, the less I feared. Because it really couldn't get any weirder, now could it? Weirder or any worse, no. Just more of the same, world without end, Funhole forever.

Skin and bone, dissolving. Matter over mind.

Nakota pounding on the door, Malcolm yelling something about the skull. Other voices. I hoped Randy was there, it might make him happy to see his skull-thing capering around, baby's first step and in front of company, too. I heard my own voice once removed, the mask issuing some kind of proclamation, hear ye hear ye, that guy in there just lost it for good.

Which was for once the truth.

Close by the Funhole, back curled C-shape and aching, red eyes so sleepless they rubbed against my lids like dry rubber, I sat watching the relentless creep of the fluid on my body, as if given free run it was going for broke: up, now, past the mountains of my knuckles, leaving a transparent reddish coating that was somehow not strictly devouring but dissolving the flesh beneath to form something—new.

All of which for some reason made me remember Nakota, the clot I had once caused to form on her sleeping shoulder; childish pique, the way you might deliberately spill some coffee in the house of someone you don't like; just a little meanness. Maybe I had done a greater wrong than I knew. Not from her point of view—she would love it, probably had and just hadn't bothered to tell me—but from my own. but it was kind of late in the day to worry about morals, or fairness, especially as regards Nakota, who considered the concept of fair play as quaint as that of true love.

Outside, the mask's jabbering sermon droned on and on, swill unworthy of a TV preacher, twice as insulting because it was using my voice. Stabbed in the back by a broadcasting mask giving off bullshit the way garbage gives off a stink, attracting the same kind of shiteaters, all of whom were ten times scarier than me. On a good day. I wanted to tell them all to go home, that unwashed gaggle of the crouching faithful, imagining them slack-jawed in their bulky coats, grinning as they bit their nails, but they were too busy listening to Radio Free Funhole and besides, I had my own concerns. Selfish? Yeah, but then again I hadn't been myself for some time. Ho-*ho.*

Up the hand. Watch it crawl. Blinking my burning eyes and I thought, Do you really want to do this? Do you even have a choice? Of course I had, we always do, isn't that what free will is all about? Freedom of choice. Just like a beer commercial.

And all the while behind me the holy smoke rose, pervasive and praline-sweet, approval's incense because apparently, finally, I was doing it right. Whatever the plan was, I was falling in with it. Maybe literally, someday? No, that's too big a leap, too much faith for me because I had none, only the certainty, dry as my eyes, that things would continue just the way they were.

You would think, I thought, it would hurt more, *feel* more, something. But no. Just the march of fluid and the trickle of smoke, the drone outside and the mumble of the worshipers, stupider bastards there never were unless you count me, lying like a fetus beside the mother of all holes, watching myself be painlessly eaten alive, a living chrysalis. And proud of it, too, which was maybe the funniest part of all. Or the sickest. But it's so *nice* to feel wanted, isn't it.

I fell asleep, I must have, numb and dumb in the darkness with my tickled nose drunk on smoke and woke to Randy's voice, saying my name with the insistence of a ringing phone. I still had no real sense of the passage of time, day or night: it was just lighter or darker or variations thereof. Now it was darker, definitely, and there were definitely more people outside. Lots more people, some of them loud, most of them clustered around the door; shit around an asshole, one might say if one were Nakota. They were talking to me, or more accurately the mask, which of course to them was the same thing, Nicholas Nicholas blah blah blah, mumble blurt and giggle and still Randy's voice, harsher now: "*Nicholas,* man, are you okay? Nicholas!"

"Yeah," and raising my hand I saw it coated to the wrist now, the congealing fluid a salmon color that was very beautiful if you could ignore its amazing textural mimicry of tinted chicken fat. It didn't gross me out but then again by this point I was no man for the niceties anyway.

Wondering if he'd heard me, I said it again and louder, into a quiet, so quick it seemed artificial, was the joke on me again? Embarrassed, "I'm fine," I said. "What's going on out there?"

Commotion, sudden and vast for such a small space, war of voices saying my name and Randy's bellow and somebody's cry, elbow work, yeah, Randy's fuse was getting shorter as the days went by, and so was mine. Manifesting in my case as extreme passivity. It really does take all kinds.

"Shut the fuck *up!*"

"Randy," my mouth right by the door, "Randy?" and Randy's shouted answer, "Tell them to shut *up*, man!" and so I said it, in my own voice.

And they listened. And obeyed.

Which made me feel nothing. I should have felt frightened, shouldn't I? But I didn't. Not nervous at the implications of control, not guilty, not even sneaky-pleased; the usual rules did not seem to apply. Maybe when you give yourself over to an anomaly it automatically negates all the rules? Certainly Nakota thought so, that was why she was so hot to be where I was now. One of the reasons anyway. Besides the fact that she had always considered herself the uncrowned queen of the bizarre.

But what she failed to notice, or maybe had and didn't care, was that no rules also translates into, and past, no safety, to the chilly land where no one's in charge and that most specifically means you. Or in this case, me. Maybe she'd thought about that, too, and just didn't give a queenly shit. I did; not enough to stop, obviously, but enough to wonder, what would it be like to pass at once and finally into that daunting atmosphere, that place where the rug stays permanently pulled out from under you, where the murderous tilt is the lay of the land? How would it *feel?*

Still silent outside, except for Randy's tired breathing, even a horse gets tired. I opened my mouth to talk to him and realized I was shaking. Little fatty drops of fluid trembled off my arm, dropped onto my knee and lay atop the rank material of my jeans like fastidious oil on water. The sense of people listening.

Randy spoke again, something about did I have enough to eat and drink and what was goin' on in there anyway, man, what's happening with you? Are you all right? "Been hearing some noises," he said.

"Me too," though I had no idea what he was talking about. "What's going on out there?"

"Well for starts we got the usual shitload of assholes out here, *Shrike's* friends, and they're hanging on every word this fuckin' mask has to say—"

"It's not the mask talking!" A girl's voice, nasally indignant, a seconding chorus and this time I said it louder: "Shut up!"

"Like I said, it's a real *crew* out here," and in each word I read Randy's lessening control, scaring me because Randy was the one, now that Vanese was gone, the only one I could trust or depend on, "and plus which they keep watchin' the fucking *video* when they're not out here listening to this stupid-ass mask."

The video, wonderful. "Randy, where's the skull? Your steel skull?"

"Around the doorknob. I mean its mouth is. Kind of clamped around the knob." A ghost of creator's pride, I didn't mention how glad I was to have it gone, or at least away from me.

Randy kept talking, I was glad he couldn't see my yawn. Just so tired. Of talking, of listening. Tired of this smelly room, my smelly self, of the father of stinks there on the floor. Call me Nakota: What would it be like to go down there? Charnel house? Garden of unearthly delights? And why don't you find out, you chickenshit? And tired, of course, of that, too. Speculation becomes meaningless when it never blossoms.

What will happen?

Because *anything* could happen. I could wake up and my hands could be alligators, I could roll over and find my internal organs turned to shrill and individual mouths, find myself turned to livid garbage, corroding on the bone like the slick pulp of rotten fruit, something that decency if not kindness commends to instant burial in a Hefty bag. Or worse. It was like falling in a bottomless pit, literally endless, exponential dissolution in as many ways. No end in sight. You might say.

As I lay, sunk and drifting, past hearing (if there was anything left to hear; the hall had gone silent some time ago), the odor of the Funhole changed, blending to a warmer reek, harsher, iron, stink like pain and what you do to get there. Hot smell.

And in the heated silence: giggling, slow and sly glissando, deliberate as the sensual strop of the knife, and I smiled too, scared smile, lips like rictus and the heels of my cold hands pressing into my eyes so hard I saw the familiar miniature constellation that upped my fear because it meant that some of my responses would, still, be normal, that even I wasn't fucked up enough for what might happen, what this new malicious giggling might portend. What exactly would a process find funny, anyway? And no one could help me. And I couldn't get away.

love you

And the cold rising burn of my erection.

And the sink of bile in the back of my throat.

It was hard to tell, then, if I was asleep or awake. Mostly awake, I think, because parts of me hurt, in various stages, feet, back, legs, neck. The hole that was my hand kept up an incessant mocking throb, just to remind me of the bad old days, you thought things were twisted then, huh? Huh.

From the hallway I heard nothing: not Nakota, not Randy or Malcolm, the Church of the Transcursing Dumbshits or the mask they worshiped, of course I was in a very poor position to call anyone dumb. All alone. In the dark. Serves me right, but would it have served me righter if I was smarter, or is this the real price you pay for not thinking things through? Driftwood, punished by a whirlpool.

As I lay adrift in that continuous night, I heard sounds that kept my eyes sealed, flutter and burn behind the thin shield of my lids, consciously abetting the lash crust of mucus.

Just in case.

"—*cops*, man! He could be dead in there for all we know!"

Nakota, calm and superior: "He's not dead."

"How the hell do you know?"

"How do you know he *is*?" Malcolm, the closest voice to the door. "It hasn't been that—"

"It's *been* three—"

A voice I didn't recognize, it sounded drunk. "Guy been in there three days and *counting*."

"Who're you," a sneer from Malcolm, "Mission Control?" and just to shut him up I spoke.

"I'm not dead," I said, my eyes gently struggling to open, the lashes gluey with dried crumbly mucus. "Just blind."

Not true: vision sharp but somehow still distorted, as if looking through heat shimmer or faintly bubbling water, the dirt and angles of the room newly crooked and vast; and with dry reluctance turning my sight to myself. And saw at once beneath the surface of my coated skin— and oh shit so *much* was coated now, both arms covered, shoulders, chest and back, so much had happened while I'd been away, While You Were Out—and what I saw was not my physiology, the humdrum process of blood and bones but what those blood and bones were becoming.

Had already become, in some spots.

Motes swarmed, slow dazzle, great glittering gouts of surges tiny as electric sparks, and where their waves touched became no shore at all, no blood and bone but part of the new, the latticing of some vast personal underpinning, I had been right to speculate on the worst.

I was becoming a process.

All bodies are, in some sense; engines driven by the health or disease of their owners, jackets of flesh that are the physical sum of their wearers. But to become your disease? To become the consumption itself?

You're really fucked now, I told myself, too shocked to be frightened (but was I really? Tell the truth for once in your life), looking at all of me: see there, at the tips of my fingers, see those whorling specks? And there, in the bend of my elbows—flexing, staring—some bright new pockets as neat as the holes a gardener digs, ready and waiting to be filled; with what?

What am I, I thought, right now?

They were talking to me: "Nicholas." Randy, too exhausted to be relieved, maybe he would rather I was dead, I imagined a lot of people might feel that way, and now let's hear from their spokesperson: Nakota, peremptory, instructing me to say something, *talk* to them Nicholas, right, talk to the nice people as they talked at me, asked questions, but I held my hands up to the weak skittering light and watched their creature motions, especially around what had been the palm of my right hand, nexus for the change: see what happens when you let the devil in?

I started to cry.

Randy, yelling something but not to me.

Nakota's harsh answer, all her answers were. Turning onto my back, tiny hardened clumps on my lashes and my tears rolled, shiny little balls, across the floor to the Funhole, jumped in like cartoon swimmers into heaven's Olympic-sized pool. I felt a cool convulsive movement in my bowels and I shit, once, a handful of little hard cubes against the seat of my crusty jeans, rolling as I moved, cute and painless down my pant legs, mute zircon shine on the dusty floor, tender by-products from the recently human.

Nakota. Her voice.

"Nicholas? Will you talk to me?"

No I won't. Even though you're the only one who wouldn't back away screaming. The only one who'd like me better this way.

The mask spoke.

Like a tape jammed to ON, instant loud oration about flux, change, capital *C*, we must surrender to the Change, like telling Nazis we must corner the market in six-pointed stars, telling them—it seemed to me, though at this point I would win no points for accuracy—that what they least imagined, the points too far to see, they would reach, they would become. Not all, of course—what good is a religion, even a backdoor one like this one, if just anybody can go to heaven? What good's a club if you can't keep some people out? But most, all of whom greeted this screed with fervent revival moans, hungry bullshit eaters and their daily bread and I was on my knees, fists clenched and mouth wide, Get out of here get the fuck out of here but nobody heard me because I wasn't making a whole lot of sound, I tried to scream but only hoarseness, maybe my vocal cords had spontaneously mutated to rubber bands or angry eels or something even less imaginable, and still I :wept and still the mask talked and through it, the only one, Nakota:

"Nicholas," with all the precious tenderness I could not believe, a depth of the love she had never felt or cared to, feelings like organs undeveloped, unmissed by her and unsuited, too warm for the cold world through which she moved, "Nicholas, let me in. Please. You need me now."

And I wanted to.

I wanted to so bad I almost did. Because I was *tired*, you see, tired of being alone, of rolling through the darkness of my own change; of standing between herself and a consummation she had maybe been born for, far more so than me because I was just Joe Nothing, just Mr. Ordinary Asshole who by tripping had fallen in much too far, grappling in endless sloppy circles until I was so tired I almost went for the door and maybe even tried but tripped again, isn't that just like me, fell on my face and my forehead hit the floor, it hurt, just like a regular person I had hurt myself. And I recalled, triggered sting of memory, an ice-pitted sidewalk outside somebody's party and Nakota, fierce pratfall onto her ass, on her back, I heard the bony smack as she fell to lie mouth open, making a silent sound, and me, anxious scramble over to her, are you okay? And she reached up to my succoring hand and yanked me down, hard, I fell onto my knees and then I saw the silent noise was laughter.

And that was just like this.

But things were different, now; things had *Changed*.

No *way*. No fucking way.

Hands and knees and on my feet, braced as I rose, I was shaking from the inside out and I put my mouth against the door, lips mashed and moving against the wood, and I said, with the clear diction of absolute truth, "If you all don't get your asses away from this door and out of this hallway I'm going to come out there and *do* things and I'm going to start with *you*, Malcolm," and without thinking I reached out my hands

through the door

and grabbed hold of someone, I felt a headful of hair in my grip
and I banged that head, boom, against the door, once again for good
measure because I knew just by the feel that it was Malcolm's, knew
it before his squeal and bucking jerk to escape and I released him,
grinning to myself and glad to have hurt him, heard Nakota's happy
gasp and felt, yeah, her touch on mine, felt the strong greasy heat of
her greed and "I'll break your fucking hands," I said, and squeezed,
brutally hard, kept squeezing, increasing the pressure until she finally
screamed, till I felt her body, independent of her will, try to get away.
And I let her go. With regret. Because no matter what it still felt good
to touch her.

"Everybody but Randy," I said, "get the fuck away from this door."

A pause, then a timid voice saying, "Randy ain't here."

"Then go *get* him, asshole."

A longer pause, unsteady shuffling, they wanted to stay but they were
scared. The head cleared its throat and I reached up, pounded as high
as I could, where I thought the chin might be.

"You shut up too," I said, and it did.

"Nicholas?" Randy's voice, shaking. He hadn't gone far. Maybe he'd
been hanging around to watch me rip off Malcolm's head, a pleasant
thought but more effort, etcetera. Had to save my strength, after all.
Because it *wasn't* after all, not yet, stay tuned.

I was shaking too, I had to sit down, I was sitting down without
trying, slipping bonelessly to the floor. I tried to peek under the door
since I was down there anyway, but all I could see was the toes of some
oily biker boots.

"Nicholas? It's me. Randy." A pause. "Shrike said you broke her finger."

"Good. Next time it'll be her neck. Are all those assholes gone?"

"Pretty much." Cautious. Like talking to a tiger. "What happened?"

"I'm tired," I said. "I lost my temper." My hands lay clasped like
prayer, dovetailed by my tired face and I looked at them, the maggoty
dance of the shine inside and with a snarl of exhausted disgust ripped
them apart, one from the other and a gluey sucking sound and one of
the fingers of my right hand appeared to adhere to my left and Randy
was saying something, I didn't hear him, I started to laugh from the

perfect depths of my revulsion as the motes beneath my skin roiled and dribbled into a living tattoo: NAKOTA.

"Eat shit," I said.

"What?"

"Nothing. Randy, can you board up the door or something?"

"I'll be doing good if I can keep the fucking cops away, man. You don't know what it's like out here, people are just acting crazy, you know? Just crazy. The neighbors, Shrike's fucking friends, everybody. I can't do anything about it, I can only kick so many asses." His voice still trembled, the vibration of depleted anger, weariness, even tears. The idea of Randy crying was strangely pitiful, maybe because tears were nothing I thought of in conjunction with Randy.

"It's that goddamned Malcolm," he said. "He's worse than she is, you know? Shrike, she's just out there, you know, like a cat or something, you know how a cat will do when it wants out? Just keeps hanging around the door and scratching and crying till you get tired of its bullshit and just let it out."

Or in.

"But him, he keeps stirring them up, you know, showing them the fucking video and talking about how the head's some kind of hotline to the Funhole and he's the man with the clue. And then he was getting into this shit that you're dead, you know, since you're in the picture now, and—"

"What?"

"The video—I saw it too. You're in it now."

Dull fear, what was left to be afraid of, now? Faint embarrassment. "What am I doing?"

"Changing, kind of. Getting—lighter. Like you can see through you, you know? What's the word, transparent, yeah. You're transparent."

"Do I say anything?"

"No. You really don't see much of you," oh boy, a joke? No. "Just enough to know it's really you. Shrike freaked, at first. Malcolm was pissed, but now he's got it all turned around that only he knows what the hell's going on." He took a deep, deep breath, like trying to put out a fire from within.

I didn't want to talk about the video; instead I asked him, "What does Vanese say about all this?"

"Vanese." Another breath. "She won't talk to me. I call, she hangs up, or her mother says, Don't call her no more, she's upset. I *know* she's upset, man! Last time I saw her, she said, Don't come by me anymore until all that shit's over with. She said, I don't need that shit."

I sat back, silent, at my usual loss, no advice from me, the perpetual fuck-up and wasn't most of it my fault, anyway? Wasn't it? Self-pity is a potent luxury but I didn't have time, maybe I didn't have enough self left to feel sorry for. Maybe I never had.

I said, "I'm sorry about that," and I meant it. And the selfish part of me muttered, If only the positions were reversed, if only it was Nakota who would have nothing to do with all of this. Which was of course ludicrous, if she had wanted that she wouldn't have been Nakota. My love, insatiably drawn to all that was lowest, cruelest, most dreadfully inverted. Like me.

Randy was still talking.

"—*outside*, right? And Malcolm, you think he'd go along with it just for the crowd control, right? But he won't. Like he's a fucking priest or something."

"Malcolm," I said, "tempts me."

"Yeah, I saw the tail end of that, what you did. Wish you'd've pulled him all the way in, man." And then what I had known was coming: "I don't know how much longer I can put up with him. Or any of this. It's not, I just want to have some kind of—it's just too weird, Nicholas. I mean I thought I wanted things to be weird, but not like this." Half a laugh, so tired. "I mean, it's been like three days since I even went to work. I'm gonna get fired, if I'm not already."

"And Vanese," I said.

"Yeah. Vanese."

Flexing my palmless hand, head bent and contemplating the fresh jelly of my bush-league stigmata. My roving finger appeared to have reattached itself when I wasn't looking. Fingers do the darnedest things.

"Randy, maybe it's—"

"I know," cutting me off, "I know what you're gonna say. But you don't understand, you don't know what it's like out here. I mean, Shrike's pretty weird now, I don't even know if she's been paying the rent or what. Maybe the manager'll try to evict her. The neighbors are getting pretty fucking tense, maybe somebody'll call the cops. You don't want the cops, Nicholas, you don't know what they'll do to you. They'll, maybe they'll, *put* you somewhere, you know?"

"Somewhere like a hospital ward?"

"Maybe somewhere worse."

Like a body bag? If I had enough body left to bag, ho-ho and who gives a shit, you're probably talking to the only one left who does. Except Nakota. Who would cheerfully and in an instant climb over my struggling body to get to the Funhole, or if that was denied her, then vivisect me if they'd only let her make the first cut.

"Randy, who cares about all that shit. Just go."

"*I* care!"

Think Malcolm, I thought, think shitty. Better yet, think Nakota. "You can't do anything about anything anymore," in my coldest tone. "I'm in charge now."

"Oh nice try," I could almost see him shaking his head. "But I'm not that stupid."

"Then don't *be* stupid. Go home."

"How do I even know if it's you talking anymore? How do I know anything?"

And he cried, I could hear it in his voice, and something in me wriggled and cracked, bleeding like broken skin, tears leeched from me and falling to lie in minute and glossy circles on the floor by my face. "Randy," I said when I could talk, "go and get a mirror. A little mirror. Okay? Okay, Randy?"

No answer but I heard him walk away. In the silence, wondering if he would come back, the miserable wriggle of my billboard skin spelling things I refused to read, words or bullshit runes or whatever nasty jokes could scrawl and spin in glyphs I could not help but understand if I looked. If I looked.

So I didn't, sat instead eyes closed and waiting, and finally Randy's voice. Maybe it really was as long as it seemed.

"I got the mirror," he said.

"Okay. Lay it down, under the door—right, like that, a little more. Now," positioning myself, careful now, "look at me."

Silence, then, with hesitation: "'S too dark, man. I can't see anything. Turn the light on, if it still works."

It did.

Randy's wordless sound. And it hurt, oh it hurt to hear that sound and know what I really looked like, what I *was* like now, so far beyond any kind of fringe that even someone like Randy, neck-deep from nearly the beginning, could still flinch, could still turn away like a gawker who'd suddenly seen more than he'd bargained for: I mean don't mind a good wreck but did you see that guy with half a head, I mean *shit*.

Did you see that guy who'd turned into a walking hole?

"Nicholas," shakily, a little farther back from the door now and I doubted he knew he'd done that, stepped away, it was a visceral move. "Are you okay?"

"No."

"Does it hurt?"

"Does what hurt?"

"That—*stuff*. All over you."

"No."

He was quiet. My skin prickled, itched as more fluid gurgled down my legs, could feel its jaunty ooze. I waited, riding the silence between us, the pause before good-bye, thinking of so many things to say.

Finally, "Well," I said. "Tell Vanese I said hi."

"I will."

"Don't tell them you're taking off, okay?"

"No, *hell* no."

And no more farewell than that—what exactly did you expect, I asked myself, mocking my own letdown: a manly exchange of fluids, a glorious speech at death's door? "I will always remember you, brave Nicholas"? *Shit*. Gone. Back to Vanese, and work, his art and his beer and watching TV at night and driving his tow truck too fast. Back to the real world, the one place I wanted, now and belatedly, most to go, the norm and the safe thing denied me and as I mourned in silent envy I was glad he had. In any good disaster there are always at least a few survivors, and now the both of them could tell that story, back and forth in all its gaudy bleakness, and be certain of at least one other's sure belief.

And me, alone now. With Nakota, her ruthless single-mindedness, idiot Malcolm and their hair-trigger delusionist cadre. And the talking mask, one face for them and its secret one for me. And the skull on the doorknob and the bubbling fluid eating me more than alive, turning me into the world's ugliest ambulatory chrysalis, far less than human but still feeling like one.

And the Funhole, never forget it, wellspring of all situations and the pivoting center around which this dark circus revolved, drunken orbit of ferocity, fear and hunger, simple stupidity and desire.

But I'm so tired, I thought.

Time, going by, and sounds. In the hall. And I closed my eyes and thought I smelled meat, roasting. Burning.

And as if on cue, Malcolm's triumphant voice, so loud that I twitched, weak nervous startle: "We're takin' the door off now, Nick," excited, grinning no doubt that special dipshit Malcolm grin, staying prudently out of reach. And Nakota, cold in the background and directing somebody, a bunch of somebodies, the brains behind the motion which was no big surprise, crazy or not she was still the only one out there who had any brains at all.

Talking, mumbling, voices as confused and bumbling as their owners, Nakota's commands and Malcolm's dumb forever override, do this do this no don't do that. Get another board. Put that thing down. Everybody listen to me!

"Nakota," I said, from the depths of my exhaustion. "Leave it alone, okay?"

Malcolm, yelling back: "Shut up, asshole! We're comin' in!"

And I was *tired* of Malcolm, you know? That excuses nothing, I realize that, but I was just so tired of the endless yammer that was Malcolm, a voice with legs, and I put one arm, right arm, through the door and caught at something, someone, wriggling and squeaking and I turned it loose again, hunting, the way you feel around without looking into a bag or a drawer, you'll know when you have what you're after.

And I did.

And I *squeezed*.

Screaming.

"Let him go, Nicholas!" Nakota's voice above the yelling, babble and confusion and something sweet between my fingers, "Nicholas! Let him *go!*" but I didn't. No. Scaling up more octaves than you'd think the human voice could handle. Jerking and bumping up against the door, less screaming now, just a kind of low-pitched gagging sound that went on and on, annoying as a running toilet in the middle of the night, gurgle and burble and finally it stopped.

Silence. My head hurt, and I felt awake, suddenly, and as suddenly ashamed, another stupid temper tantrum. And then Nakota, enraged: "Oh good work, dickhead, I think you just broke the asshole's neck."

Oh, God.

Deep fundamental nausea as I snatched back my hand, heard through the door the hurricane sibilance of her curses, the thump and stutter of her drag-away disposal, letting my own body droop in closed-eyes shock as behind me not a sound but a blossom as fragrant as a good solid belch.

And on the wall above the door, a confusing swivel of light and the mask turned inward now, purpose served perhaps and free now to follow another agenda: looking down, facing me with the face from the video, full-blown and absolute, all nothing, all mine.

Well, his neck wasn't broken. But he was plenty pissed off, and scared, which made him more pissed off , and it didn't help when Nakota laughed through the door to me, "Hey Nicholas, you know what? He shit his pants! His expensive leather pants," giggling her dry endless giggle, even I felt sorry for him. Though I snickered too, which didn't help and so on.

But shaken or not, pissed or not, he still had theories, he still had words; even death couldn't take words from Malcolm, I was convinced of that. Not that I had a second engagement in mind, oh no, I had promised myself I would never touch Malcolm again. Or anyone else if there was any way, *any* way, I could help it. The way I had felt, the terrible sick shame, was deterrent enough; I never wanted to feel that way again. Even though, as Nakota said later, even if I had killed him it was "just Malcolm."

Just Malcolm had, during an accelerated daylong nurse of his throttled windpipe, developed a new theory concerning me and my walk-on role in the video. "It's a portent," he told me through the door; as he spoke I had the impression that he stood on the balls of his feet, poised and fleetly nervous; maybe our brief choke festival was just what the doctor ordered; still I was out of the doctoring business for good. Let someone else improve his character.

"A portent," again, and portentously, just to make sure I got it. "You're fading, Nick, no pun intended."

"I really don't want to talk about this, Malcolm," I said, in my new, polite way, distractedly eyeing the monochromatic fireworks going off in my left knee as the mask sneered down at me like a mocking mirror. "I really don't have anything to say."

"I wish you would both shut the fuck up," said Nakota, not even brusque, "especially you, Malcolm. Nicholas, I'm only going to say this once." Silence from the gathering of idiots, ringing her like scum. "We all know it's me who should be in there. You ever say it yourself, in the video. I'm a perfect candidate for a change. A becoming."

"This," I said, suddenly aware of my own anger, not hot but warm and chafing, an itch in my mind, "is like every stupid philosophy book I ever read in college, only worse. Next you'll be saying it's a big existential garbage can," and I turned my back on the door, on the mask. "Why don't you people go home?" I said. "And speaking of home, Nakota, when's the last time you paid the fucking rent?"

"The rent?" Honestly perplexed. "Who cares about the rent?"

"I do."

"If you care so much, why don't you come out of there and do something about it?"

Not by the hair on my chinny-chin-chin, and you're not as smart as you think you are, either. "You can sleep in the streets if you want, but won't that impede your access, a little? Cramp your style?"

She ignored that, ignored me, began to talk again, rapid-fire histrionics and an offhand direction to somebody else, not Malcolm, do this or get this, just another in her unlimited supply of demands and I just stopped listening, I turned my face away and shut her off in my head. I'd rather remember you the way you were, Nakota, back when I could still stand you.

Leaning back, my changing body so much weaker now, bumping gently into an empty Ritz cracker box, the filmy plastic skin of a package of cheese, had I eaten those things? When? Was I still eating? Maybe the Funhole was feeding me, like a raven in the desert, maybe I was eating myself. Consuming myself, to feed the change? That would make sense, wouldn't it.

So much sense, in fact, that the whole idea made me feel like puking, I didn't want to think about it anymore. Lying flatter, in the dirt and sticky dust, my ear nudged by something pointy and soft and I saw the bear pad, and I smiled.

Empty pages. Better that way. I had had some ideas, hadn't I, of writing more poems, sharp and deliberate prod to the reanimate corpse of my zombie talent, had I imagined a topical application of the bizarre might succeed where sheer bent-browed struggle had failed, who was I kidding? Not even me. So why deface the simplicity of a little bear pad with my bargain-basement angst, why try to describe the indescribable when I had completely failed to explicate even the known? Known, shit, even the *boring.*

I reached for the cover, to close it decently and for good, but my right hand stuck to the page, tugging at it and "Shit," and instead of ripping it came away whole, and wet, big juicy Rorschach of red and on an impulse (*oh really?*) I pushed the torn page underneath the door.

"Here," I said. "Make a speech about this."

The quality of the silence that followed told me that this was an extremely bad move. Nakota's "Hey," and gleeful? Oh yeah. You bet it was a bad idea, you asshole, why do you persist in giving her ammunition when she can already blow your ass to hell with the stuff she's got?

"Hey," again, to them, "look at *this*," and their delight in hers, probably none of them had brains enough to understand whatever it was she thought she saw there, the only symbolism they recognized was the meaning of the golden arches. But they chattered back and forth, one to the other and all to Nakota, who seemed to be ignoring everyone or at least spoke to no one, not even Malcolm, whom I heard struggling for airspace: "But I think what it means—wait a minute, you guys, listen to me—I think—*listen*—"

And Nakota, feverish, implacable, all of her

one tense tremble that I could feel, earthquake weather, in the surface of my skin, in the violin quiver of my loosening bones: "It's the insects. Nicholas! It's the *insects*, the same stuff that was on their wings. Runes, remember?"

Runes my ass, that's what I'd said, and now when I did believe I had even less inclination to believe, more reason to, but in the end it was—it *was*—just more shit I didn't want to know about, because why shouldn't it be true? Exact minute replication, transmitted from my rotting hand, of the phantom scribbles on the backs of ruined bugs' wings, surely that was a tiny piece of strangeness in this huge sprawl, I can do the White Queen one better, I can believe ten impossible things before breakfast and nine before my hand falls off completely. Trump *that*, Queenie.

"And Nicholas—" her fist on the door, here's another queen. "I *know* how." Queen of heat and brutal desire, of everything crooked and twisted and wrong, something very wrong about her voice, now, something ominous and ominously exultant. "It's like a key," as intimate as if she spoke into my heart, and I thought, She's been right all along. She's the one who should be in here.

Then why not let her in?

Oh no, maybe I said it out loud, "Oh no," laughing the way you do when you refuse completely. I moved, slow because it was difficult, as far away from the door as my exhausted muscles would take me—was it harder to move today than it had been yesterday, was that some kind of portent or just faulty memory and when was yesterday, anyway?

Back against the door, looking up once to see the nothing face above looking down at me, and I closed my eyes and started walking, not backward, but through my memory as if it were a house with many rooms, some small, some locked, some doorless, some with tenants so aggressive and powerful I crept past them in silence and hoped for their clemency. So many rooms, and Nakota in most of them, or all the ones that mattered, anyway.

Especially, of course, the rooms in the Funhole wing. Watch your step, please.

Her passion had always exceeded mine, her impatience; all the ideas hers, really, all the way back to the bugs in the pickle jar, through the video, and Randy, even Malcolm (though in the final analysis he was my mistake), all the plans and notions hers and me the straight man, stumbling after, and how not to fathom her ridden, enraged, by her own jealous want and that want turned foul as an old infection, as crusty as a sour boil as she watched me, always ahead of her, the chosen one who kept saying, "Who, me?" Me, the empty vessel; not you, dear, cold caldron of desire. Was that why it *was* me, after all? The perfect stooge and puppet, incapable at last not only of guiding but even holding the reins that had inexplicably been placed in my hand—but when had any of this shit been explicable? The real question wasn't who but why me? But how do you get an answer from a process? And how delude yourself to trust it, if you got one?

I remembered her refrain, not plaintive but as wistful as she ever got, "What would it be like to go down there?" What would it look like? Alice's rabbithole, we had called it in the very beginning, before we knew better, before she started to hate me. Still with all her poisonous excess, I could never have had a better, a more suitable companion, never someone else.

Another memory, did this really happen or did I only want it to: fucking her against the walls of the Funhole, telling the beads of her sweat like some strange rosary, her head hunched down and eyes closed like fists, her hips hard against me like a beating heart. Hair flying in my face, I always loved her hair, I always loved her. I always will. I always will.

So much of our time—not *wasted*, but spent, transformed, transfigured, what was her new word? Transcursion. Yes. A long transcursion, and maybe it was a waste, after all, but if it wasn't for the Funhole, for all the grand compelling horror of its presence in our lives, would we have had any time together at all, would she have continued to bother with me, be my lover—however brief and ugly—again?

Let her in.

No. She's mine.

"She loves you," the mask said, sweet duplicitous reproach, but even I was too smart to fall for that bullshit. Love me, never, and we could never have been normal, greeting-card lovers, no walks in the park for us, she was definitely the midnight-shamble-through-the-graveyard type and very likely would not have permitted me to shamble with her unless it was at a decent two paces behind. I couldn't mourn what would never in all the world have happened, but I felt the sadness, as if I could.

So much, missed, the time instead spent sitting in the dark and waiting for something to happen.

Something's going to happen here.

Yelling outside and Nakota's howl, nothing I wanted to hear so I put my hands, my slick and dripping hands against my ears, stuck them closed, stubborn and prim, gluey like blood and kept thinking, remembering, the times spent staring down into this blackness that had finally not only run my life but run it over, killed in effect not only the things that were my pleasures but the body that hosted those pleasures. And in return, gave me what?

Fear.

The most potent of the gifts.

And exhaustion, the grayest.

"Nicholas," her cold insinuating voice, but vibrating, prickling with a triumph that instead of frightening me confirmed in sorrow my blank new visions, my scary old thoughts, "Nicholas, I can *read* these runes. And I was *right*."

Maybe she was.

Now there's no one left, out there, to impede her with arguments or threats; now there's only her tools and flunkies surrounding her.

Irresistible force and immovable object, yes sir, that is my baby. In the end I never could, never had been able to stop her; I could barely slow her down. So why stick around for the main show? Why not just get it over with, once and for all and for good?

love you

better

Rising, my legs weak, all of me all a-twitter because I was (was I?) really going to do it this time, no more bullshit fuck-around, headfirst into the maelstrom. I couldn't finally, stand—irony is everywhere—leg muscles in open rebellion, crawled instead past my old shiny pile of shit, crawling to the darkness, white as a maggot creeping onto the lip of a fabulous wound.

"Look out," I said to no one.

Shaking, yeah, my arms unable to hold my weight, moving now on sheer willpower, humping boneless as a worm through the dust on the floor, the faint barefoot marks obliterated now by the labored smear of my passage. See, I can be determined too, I can work for what I want. Sweat on my nose, running slow and exquisite, cool and itchy and into my mouth and it didn't taste salty, no, it didn't taste like sweat at all.

Empty bottle of something rolling gently into my leg and my head so close, almost dangling over the open blackness, shivering, shivering, feeling a metallic cold against my skin and in my open mouth, impossible to breathe in that negative air.

But I don't need to breathe, I thought, where I'm going.

And Nakota's yell and her banshee laugh, too loud, *much* too loud and again that echo from the Funhole, twin to her voice, and I turned to see the door bowing inward, *bending*, like hot rubber and steam in my eyes, scrabbling to make the last few feet push that body, push that motherfucker to the limit, come *on*, and the mask crying out, "Come in! Come in!" and she there, coming at me, bending with a diver's grace to insert herself, finally, into that big black hole, fuck it with her thin arrow of a body and her greedy smile and her dissatisfied grinning soul. Prey and predator, all in one; eat, and be eaten.

"Look out," she said, my last words but with an inflection I could never match, wide ferocious rapture and stepping onto me, it was deliberate, I know it was because it was *her*, all of her defined in that gesture and I grabbed her ankles right above her sneakers, sunk my hands, my strong new rotten hands into her flesh and squeezed, crying out as she did not, squeezing all the way to the bone. Feeling the pivot and gash of her tendons, the slippery juice of her blood, crippling her backward as the bones warped and. splintered and, finally, her shriek, as wet a cry as I had ever feared hearing, and I saw the bright betrayal in her eyes, more monstrous even than the pain, the certain hatred that I was as she was and always had been, had been hiding my evil under the thinnest, strongest veil: of weakness. Nicholas Wiener. Cutting her off, literally, at the ankles.

"You cocksucking son of a bitch," in the cold dull voice of profound shock but there wasn't room in her, now, for much more talk, sodden fall onto her back, whack like that night on the sidewalk and I lay panting and sluglike beside her, I'm sorry I'm sorry I'm sorry and I realized that whiny wrong-speed voice was me, I'm sorry about that too and "If you're so *sorry*," from her mouth but not her voice, oh no, not at all, "then *why* did you *do* it?"

"Why didn't you just wait." I whispered. My voice made tiny puffs of grayish pink in the air above the Funhole. "You wouldn't have had to wait long."

Which was true. Which was why there was no answer.

She was bleeding to death, I knew that, lying beside her in her blood and I tried to touch her, my red hands on her stumps, and with difficulty she opened her eyes, drunk voice (but her own), raised brows and all, "It said you were the key. It said you were what made it work."

"I'm sorry." I'm sorry, dear, that I cut your feet off, there really wasn't a better way. "I never ever wanted to hurt you."

"Then you fucked up."

Her feet were still there, strange in shoes on the lip of the Funhole and I saw something, dark, not so much arm or tendril as suggestion of both come slipping out, quick and steady

oh no you don't oh no you *don't* you greedy fuck, you don't get any of her and I *grabbed* those feet, how fast I moved for someone recently paralyzed; you should have held on to me longer, asshole, it was you slowed me down to give her time to get in, time to use the key you finally gave her. Some tricks can backfire can't they, can't they? *"Can't they!"* hugging the feet to me, cooling relics and she groaned, a sound almost theatrical in its volume, and I heard, from the hallway, the noise of someone throwing up, big irregular bursts of sloppy sound.

I put her feet down (a safe distance, I may add) and took her, held her, like a cold baby against my oozing chest, rocking her, back and forth and her eyes closing, go to sleep baby, go to sleep honey, her mouth opening, pulling down in a grotesque arc like a stroke victim's; pulse wild and arrhythmic, eyes opening so so slowly and in a cracking voice she said, "You *hurt* me, Nicholas," as if in the end she could believe every evil but that, and I cried onto her face and saw my tears, little and last brutality, become as they fell small Funholes, dark and tiny pits in the landscape of her skin.

Crying, and I kept rocking her, rocked her until I realized that she was dead. Her mouth stayed ugly, but when I closed her eyes, the lids obeyed, stayed shut. I kissed her face. It was so cold.

For a long time I held her. I knew it wasn't really Nakota, not anymore, but even just her empty body gave me the last comfort I would ever have, and while I held her I could still make believe I didn't know what to do next.

"Do you remember?" I asked her. Close to me, finally, whispering into her ear, I always held closer than she did, I always needed her more. "The rat, no, the mouse? I was pretty mad that day. And that *hand*, shit. You sure like to scare me, don't you."

Dead head lolling as I shifted position. Her tongue tried to get out of her mouth but I poked it gently back in.

"I wish we'd never made that video," I said, stroking lightly at her hair, brushing through it with slow fingers: it was dirty, I realized with sad surprise, greasy. She was dirty, too. Some kind of crust in the corners of her mouth, dirt under her nails. It made me angry, thinking of her, so consumed by the Funhole that she forgot, or didn't bother, to wash, to take care of herself in even the most rudimentary ways; who knows when she'd eaten, or slept. Little bag of bones, crazybones, she felt very light there in my arms. I kissed the hollow socket beneath her throat, cool pebbled skin under my mouth, pressed her head to my chest again.

"I wish we were somewhere else," I told her. Her flesh began to smoke, very gently, an odor like burned cotton candy, smoldered, but was not consumed. Cold burn, and from the Funhole my name, repeated sweetly, the refrain of an old, old jingle, a ditty, a dance.

I'll take my time, thanks, I thought. I'll come when I'm ready or not at all.

When I looked up I saw the rectangle of pale light, the open doorway, it seemed strange to see it after so long. And in it, dark in its light, Malcolm's face, peering in at us.

Very yellow face, sick face. Maybe it was him I heard puking. Staring as if his eyes were pails scooping sights, water in the dry land of his life. He was a tedious son of a bitch and I was tired of him. I wasn't going to hurt him, but I felt he deserved a little something.

"Come here, Malcolm," I said.

He didn't want to, of course. But he did. He was stupid, Malcolm, stupid like me but in a different way, more selfish, meaner. He would never have tried to stop Nakota, never understood that for her there would be no transformations, no ultimate transcursion to fulfillment: she was just another insect, just another fucking bug, there were no signs and wonders to be given to her. I knew those things. I loved her.

"Here," I said. "I want to show you something."

The mask smiled, showing teeth so crooked and bloody that even he should have been warned. But he didn't look up, he didn't see, instead stopped, stooping, to stare at Nakota, at me, the pestilential gallop of the fluid across my body. He stood awhile, looking, then, "You killed her," he told me, as if I didn't realize that.

"Yeah, I killed her . . . I said come *here*," and I grabbed him, he never expected me to be so fast, I grabbed his ankle and pulled him flat as a tablecloth, flat like a magic trick and dragged him, one slewing swoop, to the lip of the Funhole and I said, "Take a good look," and shoved his head in, held it down like drowning, but I knew he wasn't drowning. I knew he wasn't going to die.

Finally I let him up.

Noises, coming from him, dry and gagging. Flailing his arms, reaching up to touch his face. His face—well, part of it was still normal, the eyes, but no transcursion for Malcolm. No nose either. He had a new mouth, though, something like a viperfish. You know what a viperfish looks like? Lots of teeth.

"You got your wish," I said. "Now get the fuck out of here."

He tried to say something back but it was going to take a long, long time for him to learn to talk with a mouth like that. I think he was crying. I didn't see when he left.

Later, lots of noises in the hall. The door had shut itself, world's fastest scar tissue, but I could still hear them, screams, arguing. Apparently Malcolm's appearance had caused quite a stir. Some guy kept insisting on the police. "They can break down the door," he said, over and over. "They can just break down the fucking door."

So can you, I thought, but I didn't say it. I was done talking to people.

Maybe the police are coming, or the manager, or whoever owns this building. I don't know for sure, I think they are, but then again I haven't exactly been paying attention. I've been busy.

After I got Nakota arranged the way I wanted her, safe there in the corner with hands at her sides, I just stopped thinking about anything. Or worrying. Things for me are very simple now, reduced to two ideas, or maybe the double sides of one.

I can never come out.

So I guess I'm going in.

Not right away, though. This fluid is moving so fast, now, my own personal tidal wave and I want to wait until I'm covered, till I'm coated like a bloody blade of glass, before I go. I'm not absolutely sure, of course I have my theories even if I'm not Malcolm, but I don't think it can hurt, anyway. And if somebody, police or whatever, gets here before then, so what. By the time they figure out how to handle me, the icky-sticky man, I'll be gone.

Don't wish me luck. All I want is a smooth ride.

There's still one thing I don't know, though, and with Nakota gone there's no one left to help me speculate: all along she called me the catalyst, said it wouldn't work without me; she said I was the key. But what happens when you put that key in the door? Does it lock, safe and snug? Does it close like water, rushing absolute and smooth to heal the gap, sealing over as if the empty spot had never been? What pretensions I have are something less than grand; I'm not much and I know it, so there's no question of hubris when I say that I'm what it wants, even what it, maybe, came for—the why, of course, is beyond me, always will be and I don't care. All that's left for me to do is put the key in the lock, and close this door for good.

Although Nakota, if she were here enough to talk, might propose something different, might suggest that the same key that locks a door can open it, finally and wide.

But worst of all, the darkest part of me suspects a truth so black it turns my nebulous fears of a Funhole somehow empowered and unleashed by my addition to the laughable specter of an underbed bogeyman: what if it *is* me? What if somehow I'm crawling blind and headfirst into my own sick heart, the void made manifest and disguised as hellhole, to roil in the aching stink of my own emptiness forever? Oh Jesus. Oh God that can't be true.

Because then I'd never stop thinking.

I don't want to hurt anyone, but I'd rather it be *anything* but that.

Love is a hole in the heart.
—Ben Hecht

AFTERWORD

Maryse Meijer

Growing up, nothing scared me. I scoured the shelves of my local video stores and bookshops for the goriest films and the most twisted fiction I could find, but while I was occasionally moved or amused or surprised, I was never truly afraid of the monsters at the heart of traditional horror narratives; they didn't feel real. I knew that truth could be found in fiction, but I couldn't seem to find it where I most longed for it—in horror stories. So I kept searching. And when, at thirteen, I discovered a copy of *The Cipher* tucked deep in the bowels of my local Tower Records, I realized that what I had been looking for all along wasn't a chainsaw wielding maniac or a tortured vampire or a severely haunted house, but something more existentially threatening: what I needed was a Funhole.

The Funhole is not a villain, not a creature, not even a thing, per se, but it *is* terrifying: perfectly round, absolutely dark, and infinitely deep, anything that goes inside it—or merely *near* it—is changed: insects grow extra heads, dead flesh comes alive, steel melts and dances and burns. It's capable of offering pain and a breed of pleasure beyond the limits of reason; but to receive its gifts one must surrender to the unknown, a journey that doesn't just offer transformation, but demands it. We know, more or less, what the Funhole *does*, but not *why* it does it: the Funhole does not ascribe meaning to itself. That is a job left to Nakota and the Dingbats and Malcolm and the rest, who scramble to make grand interpretations, all of which are, to varying degrees, bullshit. When the Funhole itself speaks, through Nicholas's death mask, it lies; perhaps its only honest moment is when it whispers: *want you*, desire offered as provocation and justification both. But nobody in the novel gets what they want, not even the Funhole, as Nicholas is only fleetingly, never lastingly, a willing lover; he remains merely the beloved, as Nakota is beloved by him, as the Funhole is beloved by Nakota. Love, in *The Cipher*, is never requited; and this is one of the novels many horrors, a portrait of desires that are almost always selfish and frustrated, bottomless pits into which each individual pours her darkest wishes for transcendence.

Unlike many horror stories, in which protagonists stumble on some terrible thing while on their way somewhere—or are stumbled upon— the Funhole is always-already *there*; there are no arrivals, no departures, no exotic locations or moonlit graveyards or abandoned houses or clocks striking midnight. There is just . . . life, without glamour or artifice or fantastical set-dressing, and those who face it are certainly no heroes. Nicholas himself is, if not empty, certainly not nearly full enough to elevate survival to the level of actual living. His shitty apartment complex is set in an equally shitty town described as perpetually cold and gray, its dismal atmosphere mitigated only fleetingly by cheap beer, emotionally unsatisfying sex, and free wine offered by pretentious galleries trying to sell bad art. As in all horror stories, Bad Things happen in *The Cipher*: but there is no clear *why*. There is no origin story for the Funhole; there is no backstory to explain Nicholas's inertia, Nakota's nastiness, Malcolm's insufferable idiocy. However troubling the existence of the Funhole may be, the actions of Koja's characters are even more troubling, because they resemble our own, and the unsettling effect of this recognition—of ourselves in the mirror of the Funhole—is the source of both the book's brilliance and its lasting power, which has more in common with the abject absurdism of Samuel Beckett and Flannery O'Connor than the baroque fantasies of Edgar Allen Poe.

Through *The Cipher* I found a way to articulate what I was *really* afraid of: not monsters, but the darker aspects of life itself, in all its casual cruelty, its mundane disconnections, its failures of love, desire, creation. And the form of this revelation still reads as freshly terrifying and apt today as it did in 1991, the Funhole as ageless and urgent as Koja's scalpel-sharp prose; it is a "process," as Nakota says, rather than merely a symbol, something both of its time and place and infinitely beyond both.

It's no surprise that *The Cipher* became a classic of the genre at the same time it transgressed, completely, the boundaries of genre; it fed the desire of a readership that longed for philosophically complex, stylistically sophisticated novels that also happened to be scary. *The Cipher* won the Bram Stoker and Locus awards, a boon for Dell's *Abyss* line, which went on to publish three more novels by Koja, work that is still unparalleled in originality of vision and voice, grounding a gritty urban realism within brilliant stream-of-conscious pyrotechnics. Post-*Cipher* Koja has written books variously categorized as YA, historical, and speculative fiction, but they are as beholden to these categories as her early novels were to horror—that is to say, not at all. The trail she blazed, starting with *The Cipher,* allowed writers like Carmen Machado and Samanta Schweblin and myself to write stories that would, in *The Cipher's* time, have been classified as "merely" horror; those of us in her debt are legion.

What unifies Koja's diverse body of work is its emphasis on creation—what it means to make and experience art, and what happens when those who can't create feed off those who do. The question of inspiration and creation is at the heart of *The Cipher,* with its cast of artists and wannabees and sycophants, and it asks the reader to consider the ways creation and consumption play out in both mundane and extraordinary contexts. Nicholas *can* write poems, but most often doesn't, or else he does so while drunk and destroys what he creates before he's even had time to consider it soberly; Nakota uses her own body as her project, subjecting her flesh and her sanity to the effects of the Funhole; Randy and Malcolm are both working artists whose practices flourish in very different milieus. But all of them, through their interactions with the Funhole, are engaging with the questions of inspiration: how does creation make and unmake us? And at what cost? What boundaries must be transgressed in order to create? Who draws the lines, and where, and what is gained—or destroyed—by crossing them? What happens when we are afraid to create, or afraid of our inability to do so?

"Fear is the greatest gift," Nicholas says, and many of us, who look for the real world in horror narratives, might agree; fear exposes our own boundaries to us, then forces us to consider whether or not we will breech those boundaries. *The Cipher* takes up the notion of the boundary that exists in all scary stories and personifies it, without making a villain or a hero of any of those who gather at its edge; by placing a hole not only at the center of the plot, but in the flesh of her protagonist, Koja gave horror, as an abstract concept, its own body, indistinguishable, in the end, from the fabric of the narrative itself, forever devouring that which gives it meaning.

Koja taught me how to be afraid in fiction, by saying *here*, not *there*, is your monster; in the house next door, in the room downstairs, in your best friend, in your beloved, and, most inescapably, within yourself.

Twenty-three years and at least a dozen re-reads on, I'm still absorbing *The Cipher's* lessons, looking for the Funholes in my own work, my own world. We never find out what lies on the other side of Nicholas's descent into the cipher; the novel brings us to the limit of his journey, which is the limit of Logos, and leaves the rest for us to imagine. But we *do* know that whatever approaches the Funhole *does* change, as do we when we encounter any great work of art; and it is with enormous pleasure that I think of a new generation of readers embarking on the ferociously intimate, transfiguring experience that is *The Cipher*, an encounter that takes darkness itself and turns it, in the shape of a book, to light.

—Maryse Meijer, author of *Heartbreaker, Rag* and *The Seventh Mansion*

ABOUT THE AUTHOR

Kathe Koja writes novels and short fiction, and creates and produces immersive fiction performances, both solo and with a rotating ensemble of artists. Her work crosses and combines genres, and her books have won awards, been multiply translated, and optioned for film and performance. She is based in Detroit and thinks globally. She can be found at kathekoja.com.

Did you enjoy this book?

If so, word-of-mouth recommendations and online reviews are critical to the success of any book, so we hope you'll tell your friends about it and consider leaving a review at your favorite bookseller's or library's website.

Visit us at www.meerkatpress.com for our full catalog.

Meerkat Press
Atlanta